THE CHAMBER OF TRUTH

EDEN CHRONICLES III

JAMES ERITH

COPYRIGHT

THE CHAMBER OF TRUTH
First Published in 2017

Jerico Press

Cover: Tom Moore (tom@beatmedia.co.uk)

THE CHAMBER OF TRUTH is written in UK English.

ISBN-13: 978-1-910134-11-5

www.JamesErith.com

For Orlando

It started out as a story for my Godchildren:
Isabella, Daisy, Archie, Iso and Ernest

Special thanks:
Tom and Marsha Moore, Nicola Traynor, Neil Forbes, Charles, Edward, Philip, Sara and Robert.

CONTENTS

FOREWORD

Author's note:
For those of you who have just arrived at the Eden Chronicles, a warm welcome! Starting at book one - THE POWER AND THE FURY - and reading through SPIDER WEB POWDER sequentially, will give you a better overall experience.
If you don't wish to do that, here's a brief outline of what has happened so far...

Book One - The Power and The Fury

A series of terrifying dreams have been given to Archie, Daisy and Isabella de Lowe. These dreams were made of dream dusts, sprinkled into their mouths by invisible creatures known as dreamspinners. They have also been given special physical gifts, the Gifts of Eden, of which they are unaware.

Unsure with how to cope with these nightmares, the children ignore them. But when the images intensify, scientifically-minded Isabella builds a 'storm glass' in order to try and make sense of what is slowly enveloping her. Daisy concentrates on the school soccer final while Archie hides behind his confusion until he is visited by an old ghost by the name of Cain.

Cain, a once powerful ruler and now a spirit, has escaped from the planet of Havilah via the electrical midriff or maghole, of a dreamspinner. Cain asks Archie to join with him and offers the boy great power and strength.

Sensing that the only way to get rid of the spook is to agree to its demands, Archie affirms that he'll meet with him in eight hours time - in the middle of the soccer final in which he's playing.

The following morning, a befuddled Archie confides in the school bully, his friend Kemp, that he might have been visited by a ghost. Kemp listens intrigued. Archie tells him it must be true as he has the ghost's coat to prove it.

Kemp can't quite believe it, but there's something oddly reassuring about this family's collective madness. As Archie heads to the game, Kemp takes the coat and wanders up to Archie's supposed meeting place.

Meanwhile, the huge black cloud above them continues to grow. Isabella, determined to do something rushes to see the headmaster, Solomon. Her pleas fall on deaf ears. Solomon lies that he's spoken to the weather bureau and tells her nothing untoward is going happen.

Sue, Isabella's great friend, has also received the dreams but wrote them down moments after waking. She realises that she has to tell Isabella everything she knows: if the storm breaks they must survive until sundown. Furthermore, there are three clues somewhere in Eden Cottage, their home, which will lead to three ancient tablets.

The game commences. Daisy is outstanding and scores two goals. After half time, the storm rumbles louder and louder. Kemp's friends on the opposition team target her with kicks and fouls. Archie notices a figure heading to his rendezvous point. Is it Kemp? The ball trickles past him into the goal.

Soon, the crowd bays as the opposition try and kick Daisy out of the game. Suddenly Archie is there in a huge free-for-all on the pitch. Archie is sent off and goes to find Kemp at the suspected rendezvous point with the spirit.

Meanwhile Kemp stumbles upon the ghost, thinking it is his enemy Gus Williams.

The ghost is delighted that Archie has turned up on time and tells Kemp about the prophecy: how the three de Lowes are the Heirs of Eden and how they cannot succeed. Furthermore, everyone will die if they do not make it through the storm.

Archie, hiding behind a bin, hears this too. Both are shocked and Kemp is terrified. But they realise that the ghost cannot see and therefore does not know that Kemp is not Archie.

Isabella marches on to the pitch to stop the fighting. At the same time, Sue yells that the de Lowe's must survive until sundown. She also mentions the tablets in the house before running off. Isabella is dragged from the pitch by the soccer coach.

Free kick for Daisy. It's her last chance to win the game.

Archie and Kemp prepare to run but the ghost has other plans. Cain realises there are two of them. He can only take one. Kemp, figures that the ghost can't see and pretends he is Archie. He tells Kemp (Archie) to run for it.

Daisy strikes the ball as a huge lightning bolt flashes out of the sky directly onto an on-rushing Archie.

Kemp, thinking Archie is dead, decides that the only way he can save himself is to give himself willingly give himself over to the ghost. He puts on the spirit's overcoat to enable a gelling of their bodies.

Inside this new being, Kemp burns.

The storm breaks. Lightning bolts target Archie, Daisy and Isabella. Luckily, Daisy has discovered a gift and can hear the bolts moments before they spit out of the dark sky.

As the girls rush to cross the bridge towards the safety of their home, Eden Cottage, dragging Archie with them, the heavens open.

Inside Eden Cottage the old man who looks after them, Old Man Wood, is beside himself with worry. He's been plagued by terrible dreams. He visits his cattle on the ruin and looks out over the cliff-edge towards the village in the distance.

Three lightning bolts rip out of the sky. His heart convulses. By the time he's inside, the rain has started and it's like nothing he's ever witnessed before.

Sue finds Gus. She hurriedly explains what she thinks is

about to happen. They loot a shop and run off to the boathouse. Gus builds a canopy over the old rowing boat. The rain begins. Gus — to Sue's astonishment — is enjoying himself.

For the next few hours rain beats down relentlessly. The three de Lowes are split up. Isabella, sucked into the floodwaters, swims towards the bank. Pausing for a minute, she senses a lightning bolt coming at her and instinctively pushes her hands out to protect herself. She repels the bolt but the event leaves circular holes in the centre of her palms.

Archie and Daisy attempt to navigate up the flooded lane. They are swept away. Archie realises his twin is on her last reserves. He carries her as Daisy signals that another bolt is coming. With no other option, Archie leaps into unknown waters.

Old Man Wood kicks a panel on his carved old bed. The panels reveal, like TV monitors, where the children are. Euphoric at his stroke of luck, the old man remembers a strange old medicine and gathers his climbing things. He heads out into the storm leaving their housekeeper, Mrs. Pye, all alone.

Old Man Wood finds Isabella and, as the rain stops, rolls over what they think is a dead body. It is Daisy. Isabella screams and points her hands at her, telling her she can't die. A pulse energy flashes out of them. Life flickers in Daisy's cheeks.

Archie is struck on the head. He reels. Thinking he's near his end, he calls out for Cain to come and save him.

Old Man Wood finds Archie, positive that for a minute he's sure it is Archie's friend, Kemp. And why was he crying out the word 'Cain'?

The old man places them in a pit in a cave, the entrance of which was opened by a lightning strike. Under the moonlight, he stares across miles of flooding in disbelief at the flooding and carnage. He nods off.

Waking, Old Man Wood finds that water is rushing into the cave. He panics. But inside, he discovers that the children are bathing in a hot tub of strange minerals which, to his utter astonishment, has cured their numerous cuts and ailments.

Only now, Archie has strange spiky hair, Isabella has two strange holes in her hands and Daisy's pupils have turned red.

Book Two - Spider Web Powder

Following a dramatic and bloody escape from the cave, Isabella, Archie and Daisy upend the farmhouse in their search for clues to the riddles to find three sacred tablets. With the children nearing their wits end, their housekeeper, Mrs. Pye, discovers five filthy small rugs, which she cleans.

The writing on each has the riddles containing the secrets to unlocking the Garden of Eden.

Orchestrating the flood/disaster relief-effort is Commissioner Stone. But a deadly virus has emerged and it is like no pathogen ever seen before. It is quickly labelled "Ebora" and is spreading fast. After a meeting with COBRA the Prime Minister addresses the nation. The whole country is preparing for shutdown.

Meanwhile, Cain, the ghost, disgusted by his own lack of compassion following his brief takeover of Kemp's body, returns the sick boy to Upsall. He leaves him dangling up a tree in the midst of the enormous flooding. Dramatic TV pictures are beamed from a helicopter right around the world as Kemp is saved and hospitalised.

At Eden Cottage, Daisy watches the rescue and, although Kemp's appearance is almost unrecognisable, she's sure it is Archie's friend. She rushes out to look for her brother who is secretly throwing his knives in the shed. But Daisy stumbles upon a portal into another world. She arrives in a huge, dusty chamber—the Atrium of Eden. Terrified, she hears a snap and a piercing scream. Running blindly she finally notices a door that figured in her dreams. She walks through it thinking solely of home.

Isabella, confused by the strange events, seeks out Old Man Wood in order to quiz him and to try and make sense of what is going on. Sitting on his bed, she discovers the curious monitor-like panels with each of the children on separate screens. She watches in horror as Daisy disappears, her screen going blank. She rushes out to find her, sprinting at breakneck speed around the ruin. But while she pokes around the old castle, she's haunted by a creature in the shadows.

With Kemp recovering, Commissioner Stone questions him. The doctors point out that his injuries are inconsistent with the other flood victims. Stone's intuition about who is to blame for the disaster is confirmed. Kemp tells him that if he wants answers he needs to speak with Archie de Lowe.

On the planet of Havilah, Cain has concocted a plan to speed up the spread of the deadly virus. He's added particles of the pathogen to dream powders of his own making. Delighted by his brilliance, Cain's joy is dampened by not having the physical presence that the boy gave him. He thinks of a way to get him back.

All the while, the dreamspinners start using Cain's dream powders. Plague, thought to be contained in the UK, now sweeps the planet as people sleep.

Sue, Isabella's best friend, and her heroic boyfriend, Gus, having been sucked out to sea in a tiny rowing boat, are rescued. While Gus recovers in hospital, Stone, needs a "good-news" media story. He puts Sue in front of the camera.

Isabella's refusal to believe that their strange circumstances are anything more than a scientific anomaly is shattered when Sue, in a coded message while being interviewed on TV, implores them to hurry. They had seven days at the outset of the storm. Already, they are nearly halfway through.

Isabella finally admits she's been holding them up.

Cain goes to Kemp's bedside and offers him the one thing he has never known. A mother. In Kemp's absence Cain discovered that she is still alive and not dead. Cain promises to reunite them and takes Kemp to his palace in which he has now installed a kitchen to feed Kemp's earthly needs.

Trying to make sense of the curious poems, Archie gives Old Man Wood a cup of tea laced with rum and a heap of sugar to soothe the old man's nerves.

But the sugar has been contaminated with Havilarian Toadstool Powder slipped in by the ghost, Cain. This powder all but kills those who originated from Eden.

Delirious and tipsy Old Man Wood belts out a strange-sounding song. When Archie, Daisy and finally Isabella join in, the first stone tablet emerges from the flames.

The experience has left the old man in a collapsed state on the sofa. We join our heroes as they nervously look over the deathly-looking body of Old Man Wood...

The Riddles

'The first you hid in the heart of the house
'That warms you night and day
'Get it out by poking me,
'And singing your favourite song along the way!

'For the second one you have to find
'You burp it from the family belly.
'To do this, you have to eat
'Blabisterberry jelly!

'The third you search for is underneath your nose.
'It's clear, pure and cold.
'In order to draw it out
'You need to send a rose.

'Put them all together,
'Then get out of the way
'What you find will prove a guide
'For all the other worlds.

'You have but seven days and seven nights
'As Earth moves in its cycle
'From first lightning strike and thunderclap
'The world awaits your arrival.'

1 DEAD, OR ALIVE

From all the paper and card and canvasses and various other artworks that had been stripped from their frames and scattered about the floor, it looked as if a tornado had swept through the sitting room.

In front of them, lying on the sofa opposite the fire, Old Man Wood was as still and as white as a stone sculpture. The gentle embers from the fire glowed red and orange, lighting the hearth and accentuating the old man's pale, drawn features.

The children peered over him in shock, their lips trembling.

Tears rolled freely down Archie's cheeks. 'I killed him,' he said. 'The only person who had a hope in hell of figuring out what's going on, and I murdered him.' His lip wobbled. 'It was only tea with sugar and a shot of rum...'

Daisy shook her head. 'He's not dead, Winkle.'

'Of course he is! He hasn't moved or breathed or groaned for ages—'

'Didn't you listen to a word he said? *He can't die*. That's what he told us. He said that he was our great, great you-know, loads of great Grandfathers or whatever it was. So he can't be dead, can he?'

Archie looked at her, confused. 'He's not breathing.'

Isabella reached in and placed two fingers on his neck. 'There is a pulse, Archie. It's weak but it's definitely there. Have a feel.'

Archie replaced her fingers with his, scrunched his face but shook his head. 'I can't feel anything.'

For some time there was an awkward silence.

Finally, Daisy couldn't bear it any longer. 'What do you think we should do?' she said. 'Let him sleep it off?'

'He's got to wake up,' Archie replied, 'to help us find the other tablets.' He sat down on the arm of the armchair and gently slapped the old man's face trying to rouse him. Then he pinched his cheek.

'Come on, wakey-wakey,' he said gently. 'Please, Old Man Wood, you've got to wake up—'

'Water!' Daisy said. 'Let's shock him with a bucket of ice-cold water. That's what they do in films—or we could give him a shot of whisky.'

'NOT alcohol,' Archie said. 'He's had far, far too much of that—'

Without listening, Daisy whizzed off and returned with a bucket half-full of cold water. She thrust it in Archie's direction. 'You killed him, so you do it.'

Archie took the bucket but stood still, utterly appalled. 'I only did it because Isabella told me to. It was her idea, so she should do it.'

They turned to their elder sister.

'Absolutely no way,' Isabella said firmly. 'If you think water shock is the best idea, then I suggest you both do it.'

The twins looked at one another.

'What if he wakes up and properly freaks out?' Archie said.

'Old Man Wood would never do such a thing—'

'Daisy, didn't you notice what happened before? He totally lost the plot. What if he's now permanently unhinged?'

'Unhinged?'

'Well, yeah, damaged beyond repair. You know, like a crazed lunatic psychopath—or worse.'

'Archie, if you haven't cottoned on by now, the whole world has gone crazy, and we're caught in the middle of it.' Daisy said. 'Here, give it to me.'

In one movement, Daisy grabbed the bucket and emptied

the contents in a long stream directly over Old Man Wood's head, the water flowing over his nose and down the deep lines of his face and onto his chest.

Instinctively, the twins took a step or two backwards, in case Old Man Wood suddenly stood up and flailed his thick arms.

But Old Man Wood's deathly face-mask didn't budge.

The twins turned to each other, laughing nervously, slightly in awe at the volume of water soaking the sofa and carpet.

Daisy's eyes were wide open. 'Still nothing?'

'I told you he was dead,' Archie said.

Daisy shook her head. 'But why would Old Man Wood lie about death like that? He would *never* do such a thing—it doesn't add up.'

'Look, you morons,' Isabella said, standing up impatiently, 'we can do one simple test to find out. It'll prove his mortality beyond doubt.' She hared upstairs and returned moments later holding a small compact mirror, which she placed just under his nose.

'This is a classic check used by paramedics globally,' she continued. 'If he's alive, the mirror will fog up due to condensation.'

A roll of thunder boomed around the cottage, shaking the foundations of the building and heightening the seriousness of the situation. Isabella held her hand steady.

'Look, just there.' Daisy said, staring at it deeply, 'a tiny coating.'

Isabella frowned. 'There's nothing.'

'Yes, there is! He's definitely alive.'

Isabella shook her head. But how could she query Daisy when her sister could see extraordinary detail and she couldn't?

'Are you sure?'

'Absolutely,' Daisy said, and she stepped forward and prodded one of his arms. 'He's probably in some sort of coma and needs to sleep it off. Let's get him to bed.'

'But he weighs a ton,' Archie complained.

'Dur! And you're the strongest boy in the world, or had you forgotten?'

Archie shook his head and turned red.

'For crying out loud, Archie, you pulled that tree out and carried me miles, and pushed an enormous ten-ton boulder out of a cave.' She rolled her eyes. 'Come on, get with the programme.'

Archie groaned. 'But I can't do it *all* the time, Daisy. I'm not super-strong now. It's only when I'm angry or really need it.'

'Then I'm going to make you angry, Winkle,' she said his nickname very slowly and deliberately. Very, very angry indeed.'

'Don't, I'm not in the mood.'

Daisy ignored him. 'Winkle, Winkle, Winkle—'

'Stop it!'

Daisy grinned maliciously. 'Where's Isabella? She's usually pretty good at helping me with this kind of thing.'

Isabella yawned and stood up. 'Here, watching you both.' She kicked at a bundle of debris on the floor. 'I hate to be the bearer of obvious news, but if Mrs. Pye walks in here, she is going to have a heart attack.'

'Big deal,' Daisy said. 'She could help us move Old Man Wood if superman-boy here refuses to co-operate.'

Isabella laughed. '"Superman-boy"? That has to be the worst hero-label of all time,' she crowed. 'Logically, shouldn't it be "Super-boy".'

'Oh, Bells. Really?' Daisy said. 'That is so, so... lame.' She studied her watch. 'Anyway, Mrs. Pye won't be over until supper. So either we go to her now and explain what's been going on and how Old Man Wood ended up dead or comatose—or we have an hour to get Old Man Wood into his bed and back to normal.'

The children looked at one another.

'Well, come on brain box,' Daisy said to Isabella. 'Stop thinking and give us a hand.'

Isabella grabbed some matches and lit several candles en-route to Old Man Wood's bedroom.

Then, with a terrible struggle, the children managed, huffing and puffing, to drag the huge figure of Old Man Wood to the foot of the stairs.

'Archie, it is incredibly inconsiderate of you not to find your strength when we could really do with it,' Isabella stormed.

'Yeah, isn't it just,' Archie said, struggling under the dead-weight of the old man's shoulders. 'Can you please grab him—I can't hold him here forever.'

'No.'

Archie summoned his strength. 'Look, guys, I don't know how my muscle thing works, OK?'

Daisy marched up to him and slapped him hard around the face, the noise cracking like a whip.

'Bloody hell! What was that for?'

'Because you need to focus and start controlling this gift of yours—'

'But there's no need to hit me.'

'Yes, of course there is! Get a grip.'

Archie reddened and his mace-like hair visibly tightened. 'Daisy, I'll get you back for this.' He took a deep breath. 'You two hold a leg each.'

Archie lifted and, almost as if he wasn't trying, he started up the stairs bearing almost the entire weight of Old Man Wood.

In no time, Old Man Wood lay in his bed. The flicker of light from a lone candle emphasised the deep wooden carvings on his bed, and the soft glow of the panels at the foot of his bed highlighted the lines on his face.

'I hope he'll be all right,' Isabella said as she pulled the duvet up over his body. 'It can't be good for a man his age to be ill like this.' She laid a hand on his forehead.

'What if he's been poisoned? That's what *he* thought it was—he definitely said something about poison,' she said, as if thinking her thoughts out loud. 'But where would it have come from? And why aren't we all infected?'

'Maybe he caught the virus we heard about on the telly?' Daisy said, as she also rested a hand on Old Man Wood's brow. 'What if he caught it from visiting those trees he told us about—you know the ones, Archie.'

'You're right,' he said. 'He went right underwater—whereas I didn't.'

'But *I* did,' Daisy said.

'Did what?'

'Got drenched when I fell in the ditch on the way to that weird atrium place. And I'm all right, I think.' She randomly sniffed her armpit as if that was an indicator of health.

Isabella squeezed her shoulder. 'I'm afraid there's not much we can do about it—but pray,' she said softly. 'He needs to rest, that's all—there's nothing more we can do to help.' She moved a pillow out of the way so that the old man's head lay flat.

'Archie,' Daisy asked, cocking her head, 'what did you put in his tea?'

He raised an eyebrow. 'Two measures of rum and a spoonful of sugar. I dipped my finger in it and licked it—utterly disgusting.'

'But there was also something really random about it,' Daisy said. 'Like toadstools and squealing.'

Archie shook his head. 'Daisy, you do come up with some rubbish.'

'No, I don't.'

'Well, it did the trick; we found the first tablet, didn't we?' he said.

'All I'm saying is that I definitely thought there was something in it.'

'Uh-oh, here we go—your magic eyes again, eh?' Isabella quipped. 'Well, I won't be having any tea from you, Archie. Poor, dear Old Man Wood.'

'If you ask me, that tea had magic mushrooms in it,' Daisy said. 'Don't they kill you?'

Isabella shrugged. 'I don't know. What gets me is this: we only found the tablet because of the song which came from the clues on the five ancient rugs, so does this mean Old Man Wood has been around for as long as he claimed? You know, since the beginning...'

'But the beginning of what?' Daisy added.

'I don't know,' she said. 'But how would he know about the song and the storm and everything else if he wasn't telling the truth?'

Archie nodded. 'And remember his despair that *he* was somehow to blame—'

'And, of course, there's this weird bed with its wooden telly panels,' Daisy added.

'And spying on us too,' Archie said, taking off his beanie and stroking his foremost hair spike.

'The one thing we do know is that we have to solve the riddles—so we might as well try and figure out where the next tablet is as fast as possible. Something about jelly—'

'Blab—' Archie tried. 'Or blisters—'

'Heck,' Isabella blurted out.

'What is it?'

'Oh, nothing,' Isabella said, but her face told a different story. 'Really, it's nothing,' she said.

'You sure?' Daisy said, sensing her discomfort.

Isabella groaned. 'I forgot to tell Old Man Wood about his cattle.'

Archie and Daisy looked confused. 'What about them?' Daisy said.

'When I ran off to find you, I went up to the corral in the ruin and counted the cows and the sheep—two were missing. I was going to say something but we got caught up in all... this.'

'He'll be gutted if it's true,' Archie said. 'Especially his cows. But they can't exactly go anywhere—'

'Unless they're stuck in the mud,' Daisy said.

'Or they've been struck by lightning and gone A.W.O.L.'

'Or washed away in a mudslide.'

'We'd better check—it's the least we can do.'

'You two go,' Isabella said, a little too quickly, 'while I look after Old Man Wood.'

'Why?' Daisy snapped back. 'Are you afraid of the dark?'

'No, of course not,' she said. 'It's just that I've already been, and you haven't.' But Isabella wasn't telling the half of it. She'd been scared out of her wits by a strong sensation that invisible eyes had bored into her and somehow talked to her brain.

Archie grabbed her arm and pulled her up. 'Come on. We

could do with some fresh air, and that includes you, Bells,' he said. 'We won't be long and besides, he needs quiet and rest.'

Old Man Wood's chest moved slightly and the briefest sigh passed his lips. The children looked at one another and smiled.

Archie studied Old Man Wood's unmoving face. 'By the looks of things, he'll be out for hours. With any luck, in the morning he'll be able to help us with the next riddle. And anyway,' he said, as another thought struck him, 'if any of the animals are stuck it'll take all three of us to pull them free,' and he smiled at his sisters, 'Superman-boy or not.'

Above them, a large moon emerged low in the young night sky, chasing away the remnants of the storm. It cast a thin light over the sodden ground, the starlit sky mirrored in large, overflowing puddles. The children picked their way carefully up the hill towards the cattle, avoiding fallen trees and deeper pools, using torch and moonlight to guide them.

By the edge of the ruin they stopped and sat down on a low stone wall—part of the old escarpment—and looked out across the valley at the immense, grey, moving mass of water reflecting the crisp moonlight.

The whirl of helicopter blades in the distance cut across the silent night.

'I hope the Talbots are OK. Their house has probably been submerged,' Isabella said, brushing away a strand of hair with her gloved hand.

'What about old Granny Baker?' Daisy added. 'She's not moved in years. I wonder if anyone managed to get her onto a rooftop.'

'What, in her wheelchair?' Isabella scoffed. 'Poor thing, she's probably floating towards York with all the rest of them.'

'You are unbelievable sometimes,' Daisy remonstrated. 'There's suffering down there in the valley on a scale we simply can't appreciate. People are hurting, their loved ones are missing and, just because we survived and Sue and Gus survived, it doesn't make it OK. Think of those messages on your phone, Bells! Houses ruined, possessions gone. Death, everywhere. Don't you get it?'

'Of course I do,' she fired back.

They looked forlornly over the mass of water until Archie broke the silence. 'They're looking for us, you know. We're wanted like... like murderers, like escaped convicts. Maybe we should turn ourselves in and tell the authorities everything we know—

'Seriously?' Daisy said, appalled.

'Yeah?! Why not?'

'Because they simply won't believe us, that's why.'

Isabella nodded. 'The mere fact that Sue was telling us to get on with finding these tablets and went so far as to stand in front of TV cameras and come up with an appalling anagram means that she has to be deadly serious. If she thought it was a better idea for us to come in, she'd have probably turned to the camera and said, simply, "Come on in, de Lowes, you have nothing to fear". The fact that she didn't, and then had to shroud it behind some dodgy word-play, means, in my humble opinion, that we have *everything* to fear.'

Isabella grabbed hold of Archie's hand and looked into his eyes, as though in reassurance. 'Archie, whatever Kemp may have told them, it's more than likely that we are presumed dead. I mean, just look at the destruction out there and the list of lost and missing people on the texts on my phone.' She swept her hand over the wreck of the Vale of York in front of them. 'Sue won't have told them anything. Solomon might have, but there's every chance he's been struck down with this disease. After all, he was bang in the middle of it. So the mere fact that they had to put out a wanted notice on national telly after a monumental announcement means that they're grasping at thin air.'

Archie wasn't so sure. 'Do you think they'll come after us?'

'I'm afraid I don't know what to think, bro,' Isabella replied. 'But don't you think they'll have other things to worry about? There must be over a million people displaced, or dead—and that alone is going to keep them pretty preoccupied.'

'Yeah, of course,' Archie agreed. 'But what if they've figured it out?'

They fell silent again, none of them volunteering a response.

Archie thought it might be the right time to bring up the extraordinary revelations of Old Man Wood. 'Where do you think Old Man Wood comes from? He... he's... he's... do you think he's an alien?'

'Alien!' Daisy said. 'What deranged alien planet would have an old bodger like him? Planet "Apple"?'

Archie chuckled. 'So you think he's human; human-ish, like us?'

'Yeah, of course he is,' Daisy said. 'He's just a bit of a stir-fry, slightly bonkers, kinda random, super-old, wizardy-person.'

Archie and Isabella exchanged sideways looks.

'Then how do you explain how he fits in?' he said.

'Some deep, ancient magic he knows about—or it's a bloody good illusion,' Daisy replied. 'He's probably been practising since he was a little boy—'

Isabella guffawed. 'The only thing Old Man Wood practises is making apple juice and growing weird-shaped carrots,' she said. 'Of course he's an alien,' she said. 'As everybody knows, producing apple juice from sixteen varieties of apple tree is a well-known alien trait.' She smiled at her sarcasm. 'Seriously, if his bed and the rugs are not of this Earth, what other conclusion can there be?'

Daisy took off her pink glasses and rubbed her eyes. 'What if,' she started, 'an alien took over Old Man Wood's form—?'

Isabella spluttered.

'No, really. I mean, how else can we explain his weird songs and strange rugs with moving poems? He might be part of an advanced alien race from space—'

'Advanced?'

'OK, maybe not so advanced—'

'Daisy,' Isabella said, 'if you were an alien, would you really choose Old Man Wood as your representative on Earth over five billion other possible candidates?'

Daisy looked offended. 'Why not?' she said. 'He's the kindest, sweetest man in the universe and he wouldn't harm a fly. If you were an alien wouldn't you go for the kindest, nicest person?'

'I don't know,' she said, frowning. 'Probably not—'

'Well, I would. It's stereotypical nonsense stirred up by Hollywood that aliens are always bad, apart from, of course, ET.'

Isabella shook her head. 'There's a perfectly logical reason for this though: bad people are generally manipulative and don't care about anyone or anything aside from their own circle. Therefore, they crush good people and win—'

'No, they don't. Good people have a habit of coming out on top. That's why the human race has been so successful—'

'Nonsense,' Isabella said. 'Humans are only winners because their brains are more advanced than anything else's. We can think things through—unlike someone sitting pretty close to me. It doesn't make a spot of difference if people are nice or decent or—'

'Stop it, Bells,' Archie interjected. 'Daisy was only offering a theory on the back of inexplicable evidence. Have you got a better explanation?'

Isabella poked at the see-through hole in her hand, her hair over her face like a veil, and held her silence.

Archie rubbed a hair spike through the cloth of his beanie. 'What if he's actually telling the truth?' he said. 'What if he really has been around for all this time and he simply forgot everything—like he said?'

Isabella guffawed again.

'I mean, they used to live to a great age in the Bible didn't they—so maybe he's from Old Testament times and got stuck in a time-warp ...?'

'Oh, shut up, Archie,' the two girls said in unison.

'No, no,' he countered, refusing to give in. 'I'm betting Old Man Wood was the exact same person he is today when Dad was a little boy. And I bet you he's the same person in all those oil paintings we collected from around the house.'

'Thank you, Winkle—'

'I just don't believe he's capable of making up such a tall story.'

Archie paused, allowing the girls a moment to respond. They didn't. 'So, maybe he's a wizard. We've seen the moving bed panels, so we know he's full of magic tricks, and he's full of pain about forgetting his "life mission" which, as far as I can tell, involves saving this place called the Garden of Eden. And we all know Eden existed in biblical times, either as a real place or as part of the creation story.

'Maybe,' he continued, 'it's not only an allegory for early man, but a story about an entirely different planet? Maybe the whole story at the beginning of Genesis is a kind of code, a cleverly plotted fable full of clues, before it delves into the history of the early Israelites?'

Isabella flicked the hair off her face, her eyes glowing with wonder. 'I'm quite amazed,' she said, 'that you were actually paying attention to my lecture.'

Archie grinned. 'Yes, of course I was. The thing is, there are too many oddities. He talks to trees and grows star shaped carrots and is fixated by apples. And the tablet only came out after we all sang his weird song which blew the house apart and in so doing proves that the riddles on the rugs are true.'

The girls nodded in agreement.

'More importantly, he featured vividly in our dreams as a great, old, wise, mystical man who may well be part of time eternal and who is actually trying to help us.'

They sat silently on the cold stone. A chill grey wind blew gently across them, smelling of damp, matching the girls' mood. What he'd said rang true; they just didn't want to believe it.

'OK, Mr. Know-it-all,' Isabella said. 'Explain why it happens to be us and not anyone else.'

Archie shrugged. 'Perhaps it's because we just happen to be the poor sods who live in Eden Cottage, who he looks after,' he said. 'Think about it. The cottage is full of curiosities, like the rugs and your atrium-y place, Daisy—'

'But why can't he remember anything?' Isabella said bluntly. 'He's no help whatsoever. Every time we want to know something, he dithers, or goes off on one of his walks, or gets giddy, or drunk or... or he dies.'

'Isabella!'

She put her hands in the air. 'What I'm trying to say is that he hasn't actually helped us with anything—'

'Don't you think there's a reason for that?' Archie said.

'What do you mean?'

'The reason he can't tell us is because he doesn't know. He sort of knew it once but doesn't anymore.' Archie removed his beanie and scratched first one, and then another hair spike. 'Anyway, if he is as old as he says he is, no wonder he's forgotten everything.'

'What are you talking about?'

Archie shook his head. 'Seriously, can you remember things from when you were three or four years old?'

Both girls shook their heads.

'Exactly! You can't. If Old Man Wood's as old as he says he is, it's going to be a pretty big struggle to get him to recall detail from hundreds, if not thousands, of years ago. When the tablet came out of the fire, he knew about it in a vague, roundabout way—like with the song—and he needed us to prompt him and vice versa—'

'Problem is, Winkle,' Daisy said, 'we still have to solve the riddles.'

Isabella nodded.

'And we're running out of time.'

Isabella looked sheepish. 'I know, and it's my fault,' she said quietly.

'That's irrelevant now,' Archie said, warmly. 'Deep down, Old Man Wood knows everything—we need to coax it out of him, show us how to do it.'

'Certainly won't be easy if he's dead,' Daisy added.

'Even if he's alive,' Isabella added, 'he's going to slow us down.'

Spitting rain now fell. They screwed up their faces as larger drops began to fall. The children stood up ready to move.

'Tomorrow we have to find the remaining tablets,' Archie continued, adjusting his beanie. 'They hold the key to finding this 'Eden' world—whatever it is—even if we don't know why it involves us.'

Daisy draped her arms around Isabella and Archie's shoulders. 'Don't get me wrong, guys, but let's be honest. Without Old Man Wood, I don't think we've got a chance of finding anything.'

2 PRESSURE MOUNTS

Commissioner Stone yawned. He stared at himself in the mirror, noting dark purple bags under his eyes—even darker than the last time he'd looked. As he dragged a razor across his face, even his stubble felt harder than usual.

Another fitful sleep—four hours tops. He needed twice that.

'Good morning, sir,' came a muffled cry from outside the hotel suite door. 'We have the deputy PM and the Head of the European Commission waiting for you.'

Stone nicked his narrow, bony chin and a bubble of blood dropped into the basin. He swore. 'Tell them I'll call back—give me ten minutes.' He cupped his hands and splashed cold water on his face, the shock running through his body. Exactly what he needed.

He towelled his face, hoping the cut would start to congeal, and applied a generous splash of cologne. The liquid stung. *But it was nothing*, he thought, *to what lay ahead.*

He opened the bathroom door, his dressing gown fastened around his midriff, to find his room packed with people. On seeing him, they all spoke simultaneously.

Stone stared open-mouthed.

'Sir, you need to see this,' said a large lady with short red hair, thrusting a file at him. He brushed it aside.

'We need to speak, urgently,' a small, squat, dark haired man with a bushy beard demanded.

Stone ignored all of them and made his way through the throng to the bed. 'What the hell is going on?' he yelled as he spotted Dickinson remonstrating with a man in a white coat. 'Dickinson,' he roared. 'What is the meaning of all this?'

The officer extracted himself. 'Bedlam, sir,' Dickinson said, calmly. 'I've kept them at bay for the last half an hour but couldn't keep them out. We've got trouble from just about every department in this country. Actually, more like the world.' He cocked his head. 'Best if we head back to the bathroom.'

Stone grabbed his trousers and looked around at faces he'd previously noted from the newspapers or television.

'Why in hell are they here?'

'All the Government facilities are overwhelmed, sir, or unobtainable. The PM has vanished.' He locked the door. A strange silence filled the cubicle.

Commissioner Stone dressed, then closed the lid and sat down on the toilet. Dickinson settled on the edge of the bath.

'The Ebora virus has spread overnight, massively,' Dickinson began. 'Apparently, you're the only person with any real authority—that's what they're saying—and this is according to the PM's office. Most of that lot arrived in the last hour—it's like a helicopter park out there. One hundred and five at the last count. Amazing no one's been killed if I'm honest.'

Stone swore under his breath. 'Right, here's the plan. Set up three secretaries with desks in the hall and we'll process this lot like a post office queue. While they're doing this, I want you to go and find Doctor Muller and my cousin, the headmaster, Solomon. Bring them in straightaway.'

Dickinson unlocked the door, fought his way across the room and stood up on the bed. 'Your attention!' he shouted. The noise level abated. 'Commissioner Stone will come out and address you if you give him some room. So please, let's have a little decency and order in here.'

He slipped off the bed and wormed his way out of the room.

Stone made his way over, clambered onto the bed and addressed the room.

'Thank you for barging your way in,' he said, his Yorkshire accent heavy with sarcasm. 'Having woken up barely fifteen minutes ago, I must inform you that I am not as yet up to speed with developments. As you can see, I am not even fully dressed.'

He smiled and scoured the room, reading their faces. *They're on edge, scared witless,* he thought, *the whole damn lot.* Time to be friendly, reassuring. If they want leadership, they're going to have to wait for it, not swamp me.

Dickinson poked his head around the door and nodded.

Stone cleared his throat. 'Now, please. In order that we can deal which each one of you, I would like you all to give your details to my secretaries who are waiting in the main hall. I will then be able to get round to seeing you as soon as I can, in an orderly, civilised manner.' He sounded like a customer relations officer.

'And if your query cannot be met by me, then you will be referred to the correct department—'

'But this is urgent, it cannot wait—' a suited gentleman with a foreign accent shouted.

Stone's pale blue eyes bored into him. 'I don't care who the hell you are, sir. Understand? We do this my way or I'll toss you back out into the flooding. Get it?'

The tall man's dark eyes met Stone's, before turning away.

Stone grabbed his jacket and made his way into the bathroom while the melee departed.

In just five hours, the world has gone mad, he thought. *And I'm the one expected to supply the answers.* He swore.

Stone adjusted his tie and studied his reflection in the mirror. *I don't even know the bleeding questions,* he thought, *let alone the answers.*

Dr. Muller moved his jaw from side to side and nestled his spectacles on the arch of his nose. 'We have a pandemic, as I suspected.'

'You're suggesting the disease is out of control?'

'I'm not suggesting, sir—'

Stone swallowed. 'Has anyone reported in—the geneticists, the scientific fraternity—has Dr. Harries called?'

The doctor shook his head. 'There's been too little time. The spread is unprecedented—'

'What of the boy? Has he been found?'

Dickinson stared at the floor. 'We've searched everywhere. Not a trace, I'm afraid, aside from the ash we found in the toilet.'

'Have forensics tested it, carbon tested or whatever they do?'

'It is just ash, sir.'

Stone thumped the desk. 'I don't care if it's shit! Is there any good news? What the hell are we going to tell everyone? They're clamouring for information. What do you suggest? Tell them we don't know a bloody thing? Tell them that our one hope—our one pinprick of light—has simply vanished into thin air? How's that going to sound?'

The others shifted nervously.

'Does the Prime Minister know?'

The doctor took a deep breath. 'Half of the cabinet have Ebora. The rest are involved with the containment process with the military chiefs and others.'

Stone gathered himself. 'Doctor, what other cheery news?' he began sarcastically. 'Has it spread out of the containment zone? Out of Yorkshire? Don't tell me it's reached Manchester and Leeds?'

The silence said it all.

'Oh, Christ,' Stone said. 'It has, hasn't it?'

Dr. Muller's face remained impassive. 'I'm not sure how to tell you this, but reports are coming in from across the pond. As people are waking up, they're reporting the same signs. And we know how fast it incubates—'

Stone eyed him curiously. 'The pond? What—the English Channel? It's reached Europe?!'

'Plenty of cases in Europe have also been reported, Commissioner. But I meant America. Across *that* pond—the Atlantic.'

Stone's eyes nearly popped out of his head. '*America*! *America... are you bleedin' sure?!*'

Dickinson marched in. 'The US Secretary of State would like to speak to you.'

Stone uncurled his fingers, pulled out a handkerchief and dabbed his brow. 'Can't he speak to the PM—one of the Cabinet?'

'Here's the problem. The PM is indisposed—'

'Indisposed?'

'Yes, unavailable, sir—'

'Yes, I know what indisposed means.'

Dickinson whispered in his ear. 'According to the Prime Minister's wife, he has Ebora symptoms.'

'Christ alive!' roared Stone, kneading his temples. 'What next?'

'Well I was coming to it, but the Home Secretary instructed me to let you know that as of 07:00 hours this morning, you have been granted full powers to do whatever is necessary and with any means known to humankind to get to the bottom of this, sir. She's waiting for your call.' Dickinson raised his eyebrows. 'May I suggest you call her before you talk to our American cousins?'

Solomon bustled in, shutting the door firmly. He exhaled. 'Who on earth are all those people in the hall?'

Stone lifted his eyes at the sound of Solomon's voice and removed his glasses. 'A spokesman for the President of the European Union, the Secretaries of State for four of our near neighbours, the First Minister of Scotland, the head of OPEC, a couple of major global industrialists, a supermarket chief executive or two, the supreme commander of European forces, Field

Marshall Allen and the Chairman of the London Stock Exchange. And that's just for starters. Even Lord "bleedin'" Sugar and Sir Richard "blast-off" Branson are apparently en-route. And then there's Bono on the phone every fifteen minutes. Anything else you want to know?'

Solomon wiped his brow. 'Good Lord. I'm sorry, cousin, I had no idea— '

Stone leaned back in his chair and clenched his hands. 'What did you discover at Upsall, headmaster?'

Solomon knew this wasn't an informal chat.

'Plenty—I'd like to think—though a little more time would be beneficial—if at all possible.'

Deep down, Solomon knew a lot more time was needed. He'd looked upon the stained glass windows in a totally new light and in it he'd recognised the de Lowe children, the flooding, the pestilence and he'd touched on something—a message maybe, that he felt the de Lowe's knew.

The question was, how much should he tell Stone on the basis that this "feeling" was entirely conjecture?

Stone raised his eyebrows and smiled back, but his eyes were hard. He'd recorded Solomon's movements on a hidden camera. He knew Solomon's every move. 'Tell me,' he said, 'what you discovered.'

Taking a deep breath, the Headmaster began. 'As you know there is an extensive library in the tower at Upsall. I tried to find some connection to this plague and, given the shortness of time and the large selection of tomes therein, I struggled to come up with anything of note. However, I was drawn to the stained glass that fronts the chapel. You know of it?'

Stone flicked his eyes at Dickinson. *So far, so good. Exactly right.* 'Yes, a murky thing—'

'It is a triptych,' he continued. 'Three stained glass paintings as one that show the Father, Son and Holy Ghost. On them are references to water, pestilence and one other curious-looking event. The first two are, of course, relevant to the situation we have at present.

Solomon wiped his lips. 'Before you jump to any conclusions

this is standard imagery commonly found in medieval artworks. However, if you're searching for an easy connection, a soft target if you like, it's right there on the glass.'

'What about the de Lowes? Is the stained glass related to their ancestry in any way?'

Solomon nudged his glasses and moistened his lips. 'Almost certainly,' he began. 'I believe the family would have been involved in the building of the monastery and, thereafter, in the formation of the window. Records I unearthed tell of a family here under the name of "De L'eau" at Domesday. Then, I discovered one even earlier name.'

He paused and looked at his cousin. '"Aquataine".'

Solomon smiled in his head-masterly way as he noted the confused look on Stone's face. 'The link? Well, clearly it's in the commonality of the word for water: De l'eau is the French for "water" and, the Latin for "water" is Aqua—as in this name of, Aquataine—'

'Shouldn't it be Aquitaine,' Stone said, 'you know, with an "I"?'

'My thoughts exactly,' Solomon said. 'But I've seen the name spelt this way on several parchments, so I don't think so. Perhaps it is trying to tell us that there is some connection between the water of the surnames and the water that surrounds us.'

The Commissioner rubbed his face, touching the shaving cut on his chin. This was exactly what he'd hoped for, just the sort of information he needed. 'So, we have a flood that begins in Upsall. And we have a pandemic that begins in Upsall. We have a girl who predicts the flooding whose ancient family name means "water", and we have an eccentric old man — a hermit — who lives with them, who is of unknown origin. We have a stained glass window in Upsall with three figures surrounded by flood and disease. *Uncanny, isn't it?*' he said, cocking his head to the side. 'So what, or perhaps, *who* connects these things?'

Solomon smiled back his most practiced teacherly-smile. 'Am I getting a sniff, Charlie, that you're attempting to link the de Lowe family to the disaster?' He raised his eyebrows. 'If you are, then my question is this: what could those three possibly know? They're school children, how can they possibly be involved?'

Stone smirked. 'There! The conundrum, in a nutshell. You tell me?' he said, throwing the question back. 'What dirty little secrets might an old family like the de Lowes harbour, huh?'

The headmaster shrugged. *Whatever happens, don't rise to his taunts*, he told himself. 'I'm not sure I quite understand.'

Stone's manner changed. For a brief moment he trailed a finger over some papers and then looked up. 'By the way, I thought you might like to know that we've found two more of your pupils.'

'Goodness me, who?'

'A girl by the name of...' Stone looked over at Dickinson.

'Sue Lowden,' Dickinson added, reading a clipboard. 'And, a chap by the name of Gus Williams. He's in hospital.'

Solomon peered over his glasses. 'That's terrific news! Yes, they're mine alright. Lovely kids,' he said, enthusiastically. 'So much anguish and darkness and now two survivors. Amazing isn't it?'

Stone cocked his head. 'She was interviewed on the telly. Said she owed it all to Williams—saved her life by making a canopy over a small rowing boat. A right hero.'

'She's a fine student and he's a decent lad.'

Stone drummed his fingers on the desk. 'The thing is, when my man interviewed her she mentioned she was a very close friend of Isabella de Lowe,' he said, his voice barely above a whisper and soaked with irony. 'Now, isn't that a surprise?'

Solomon didn't like the way this was going. 'Not at all,' he said, trying hard not to show any feelings. 'Those two were almost inseparable.'

'Is that so?' Stone said, glaring at the headmaster. 'Apparently, Isabella de Lowe gave her the idea to find the boat. Now that's pretty sharp thinking, don't you reckon?'

'Yes, as I said, they're smart kids.'

'So smart that she even managed to tell her about it before the storm struck.'

Solomon's face dropped. 'She's no fool, Charlie. She's a brilliant student—'

'As you keep telling me. Let's go again. This is the same student who went out of her way to ask you to call off the match and your celebrations, because she knew that vast storm was heading your way? The same girl who made a "storm glass" to prove it.'

Solomon didn't know what to say. 'I've told you all I know,' he said examining his watch. 'I take it you're getting Sue and Gus transferred back here.'

'Yes, of course,' Stone said, rubbing his hands. 'For some proper interrogation.'

Solomon's eyes hardened. 'You'll do no such thing.'

Stone slammed his palms on the table. 'I'll do whatever it takes. And I don't care if it's the Pope, the President or Her Majesty, the Queen. My job is to find out what the hell is going on here—'

'But torture, Charlie? She's a child—'

'*I need her to talk,*' Stone said coldly, his eyes boring into Solomon. 'And I'm running out of time.'

'I will not let you do that with my pupils,' Solomon said standing up.

Stone grinned. '*Especially* with your pupils, it seems.'

'You always were hard, Charlie, and I don't begrudge you your situation, but these children are in my care. You'll interrogate her over my dead body—'

'That can easily be arranged,' Stone said. 'Sit down old man.' He nodded at Dickinson who pushed the Headmaster down. 'Count yourself lucky you're not going to feel a few volts up your arse as well. And one more thing, before I discuss our progress with the Deputy Prime Minister and the US Secretary of State. That boy, you know, the one found up a tree, burnt like he'd been sprayed by some flammable liquid. We found out his name. A bit of a tip off.'

Solomon tensed. 'Who was it?'

'Kemp. The boy's name was Kemp.'

'Kemp? My goodness—'

'Yeah. Ring any bells?'

'Yes, golly-gosh. Indeed. Well, well. How remarkable.'

'Isn't it? Funny how your pupils keep popping up from the dead in the most unexpected places.'

Solomon shook his head. *It was impossible. Kemp's coat had been found.* Besides, Kemp was renowned for being a poor swimmer.

'Do you want to know who Kemp called for?' Stone said. 'The one and only person he named—the person who he implied might have the tiniest inkling about what's going on out there?'

Stone stood up and moved in close to his older, portlier cousin and whispered in his ear. '*Archie de Lowe.*'

Solomon's jaw dropped.

Stone walked round to his chair behind the desk, sat down and leaned in. 'I thought you were here to help me headmaster, not get in my way. So, do you now understand why I need to know what these kids know? *Comprenez-vous?*'

'Yes, of course. Very well,' Solomon croaked. 'But let me do it, Charlie. All you'll do is scare them. They trust me, I promise you.' Solomon raised his eyebrows, his heart thumping wildly as he mopped his brow. 'Let *me* ask the questions, my way. I know how these children work. I'll get the results you need.'

Stone eyed him for a while. 'Fine,' he said. 'A helicopter with thermal imaging is on its way to their cottage as we speak. If any of the kids are there, we're going to pick them up. So, believe me, headmaster, if you don't get everything I need—full co-operation—I'm going to be hot on their heels and no-one's going to like it. I can absolutely assure you of that.'

3 AT THE RUIN

The courtyard by the ruin was surrounded by the last few remains of a wall which had, over time, disappeared under mud and moss and bushes and the odd straggly tree. As they approached, a thick silence filled the air, broken only by an occasional grunt or gloop of feet swilling about in the mud near the old corrugated iron-roofed corral.

On hearing footsteps, the livestock groaned and mooed and baaed before tentatively emerging from the tin shelter. For several minutes Isabella, Archie and Daisy counted and then recounted the animals while speaking in soothing, calming voices.

Archie shook his head. 'Three out of nine cattle and one sheep missing. Bella, is that right? Have you guys checked right at the back?'

The children walked slowly into the body of the metal-roofed shelter, their boots sticking in the ankle-high sludge, slurping at every movement, making sure each step counted so they wouldn't slip or slide, occasionally leaning on animals that refused to budge.

Suddenly, a terrible whirring noise rattled overhead, making the structure rumble. The children automatically folded their torches in their tummies and held their breath, and Daisy plugged her ears too. In no time, the helicopter had passed.

'Let's go!' Isabella cried, turning. 'We can be saved!'

Archie grabbed her arm. '*From what, Bells? Saved from what, exactly?* It's just like Sue said. They're onto us—best if we stay hidden until we've found these tablets.'

Whirring sounds filled the night sky as the helicopter appeared to linger over the cottage before flying off.

By the time they'd waded out of the corral the helicopter was a distant speck in the night sky.

'Do you think they knew we were in there?' Daisy said rather breathlessly.

Archie shook his head. 'It shot up from under the cliff face, so I doubt it. Anyone find the missing animals?'

'No, and I counted twice,' Daisy said, her voice muffled as she held her nose.

Isabella groaned. 'That means that two more have gone since I was last here—although I could have been wrong with the sheep. They looked terrified enough at the time. Did you notice how their eyes are glazed over. Three look sick, diseased, even.'

The thought that somehow the disease had spread to the animals was not welcome.

'Let's go home,' said Daisy, shivering.

'Right away,' Isabella agreed, but almost immediately, a strange, slithering noise could be heard from nearby. She looked around, her eyes bulging, her face as white as snow.

Out on the grassed area of the old ruin they shone their torches over the rocks and bushes and, as they did, a cold chill crawled over the three children—as if they were being watched.

Daisy's teeth began to chatter. 'We need to get out of here,' she said, flinching. 'There's some weird thing hanging about 'round here.'

'What is it?' Archie asked.

'I dunno,' she whispered.

With their senses now on high alert, the children started through the rock-dotted courtyard towards the track, hairs erect on the backs of their necks. A low rumble rolled out through the evening sky. Collectively, their pace quickened.

Soon they were running.

Without knowing how it had happened, Isabella found

herself sprinting, skimming over fallen trees and dashing past piles of rock, hurdling huge puddles and suddenly she was at the end of the field near the cottage.

She turned to check on the other two, but saw nothing except the night gloom. *Perhaps,* she thought, *they'd gone another way.* But where? They weren't that stupid. She smiled. *It's these feet again, making me run like the wind. They'll be back soon enough*, she thought, and she let herself in, conscious that she was barely out of breath.

Daisy and Archie watched Isabella accelerate away from them into the murky darkness. They stopped to catch their breath and looked at each other quizzically.

'When did Bells learn to run like that?' Daisy panted.

Archie shrugged. 'Don't know. But that was utterly ludicrous,' he said, leaning on a smooth, grey boulder. 'Actually, if you think about it, she tore around the property in about twenty minutes yesterday—'

'And she must have bounded up the two hundred and twenty-two stairs to escape the collapsing cave like some kind of super-leopard,' Daisy said.

'Did you notice another thing?' Archie said, as he rubbed his chin. 'She hates it up here. She was shaking like a jelly.'

'Yup. I noticed that too. Sweating too, and as white as a sheet.'

Archie peered into the gloom. 'Daisy, I think we owe it to Old Man Wood to find the other animals. What do you think?'

'We can try.'

'Cool. Let's check if there's anyone or anything about who shouldn't be.'

Daisy moved her head from side to side as though examining the area. 'Something's hanging about. I can't tell what it is though. Sounds a bit like a... do you think it might be a bloke stealing them? Making creepy noises to scare us off?'

'I don't know,' he said quietly. 'But it isn't right. I think we should find out.'

'What if it's a lunatic, with a gun?'

Archie frowned. 'Then we should find out.'

'Can't we wait till morning?'

'We won't have time. Come on.'

Daisy eyed him curiously. 'Very well, brave brother—ye with the spiky hair. Lead on.'

Archie smiled. 'Do you want to go first?'

'Oh, get a move on,' she said, taking the lead and marching back the way they'd come. 'Let's see what's lurking yonder, huh?'

In silence, the only noise being the squelching and squishing of their boots in the mud, they doubled back to their original position and then headed further in towards the fallen-down castle keep, strewn with boulders.

'To be honest with you, Archie,' Daisy said as she went, 'I could hear something moving about after we'd counted the animals. But the thing is, it wasn't a sound I've ever heard before.'

Daisy picked her way through the old walls and slabs of stone of the ruin with ease, despite the thick cloud that obscured the moonbeams. The harder she concentrated the easier it became.

Soon she was manoeuvring as if it were light, skipping over rocks and jumping across gullies as though it were daytime, her senses on high alert.

Carefully, she crept up to a shaft of rock and leaned into it, remaining quite still, listening. There—again, the exact same noise as before; a curious mix of heavy, syrupy breathing, like large, wheezy bellows. 'You must be able to hear it now?' she whispered.

There was no response.

'Winkle?' she whispered into the cold night air. She turned. 'Archie! Where are you?'

It hadn't even registered that Archie wasn't right behind her. She retraced her steps, weaving back through the low ruins, her eyes following her footprints.

Without warning, her legs disappeared from under her and a

heavy, hard object struck her sharply on the back of her head. Disorientated she fell forward, her arms pulled hard behind her back. She tried to wriggle free.

'REVEAL YOURSELF,' said a familiar voice.

'Let go of me!'

'Who are you?!' he hissed.

Daisy couldn't believe it. 'Your sister, you bloody numpty!'

'Whoever you are, YOU are not my sister.'

'Unfortunately, I am, Archie, you stupid, spiky, knob-end.'

There was a pause while Archie, baffled by the response, wondered what to do next.

'OK! What's my nickname?'

'Winkle. I alone call you Winkle. I don't know why, but it just suited you when you were little and it stuck because it really, really irritated the hell out of you.'

Archie loosened his grip. "Winkle" was her private name for him. Slowly he turned her round to face him, not loosening his grip on her too much.

'What the hell was that all about—?'

'Your... your eyes, Daise!' he said, 'what's happened to your eyes? Are you... all right?'

Daisy pushed him away. 'What *are* you talking about, there's nothing wrong with my eyes,' she said crossly, 'apart from being red, like traffic lights on stop.'

She rubbed her skull, more concerned with the blow to the back of her head. 'That really hurt, Archie—what's up with you?'

'No seriously, Daisy. You're lucky I didn't smack you harder. Look, are you sure you're alright? I mean... look, I don't know how to tell you this but they're glowing, like dishes. It's like you're an alien! Your eyes are burning like torches. I thought YOU were the monster.'

A chilly wind blew over them. They shivered.

'I'm really sorry, Daisy. I didn't realise—'

Daisy hoped Archie couldn't see her tears. 'I don't know what's happening to me, Arch,' she whispered. 'I've got these weirdo eyes which kind of go into overdrive when I concentrate. You won't believe what I can see—things in incredible detail—

like individual particles in the storm glass—or objects miles away, or seeing stuff in the dark. And every time I use them, it gets stronger and I discover more. It's like a game, going up levels all the time.'

She wiped her cheek and continued. 'Remember when we came up here and looked out over the flooding? I got a bit caught up wondering if I could actually see people sitting on their rooftops waiting for help. Well, I could! I really could see water flowing through the streets. And running up here tonight—it was as clear as it would be on a sunny day, apart from... well, it wasn't, was it?'

Archie couldn't think of anything to say.

'Archie, it's not the only thing; I can hear amazing stuff, too. When the rain stopped at home, all you lot could hear was the sudden quiet but I heard drips of water splashing directly under the house.'

'So, what do you think it is?'

Daisy rubbed her eyes. 'If I'm right, I think it's got something to do with the water in the third poem. The "clear" and "pure" bit.'

Archie repeated as much as he could remember.

> 'The third you search is under your nose.
> 'It's clear, pure and warm (I think).
> 'In order to ... something or other
> 'You need to send... hmm, can't quite remember.'

'At first I thought it was to do with bogeys—you know, being underneath your nose. You think there's a stream under the house?'

Archie looked at her with renewed wonder and, instinctively, even though Daisy's eyes were still glowing, but not as brightly, he moved in and hugged her.

'Does it hurt?' he asked, his voice hushed.

'What? My head?'

'No, you daft cow. Your eyes.'

Daisy shook her head. 'No. Just goes a bit tingly, that's all.'

They both sat quietly. 'Can I ask,' Archie said cautiously, 'what was it *really* like in this atrium place you went to? Did you use your mega-eyes in there? Did you hear anything else apart from a great blood-curdling scream? And did you really get out just by looking at a door—?'

'Simmer down, Winkle,' she whispered. 'The atrium was terrifying... it's hard to remember anything in detail. I was lucky—'

Suddenly, a snorting sound, like a wave blasting through a blow-hole, burst out from the other side of the rock.

Archie crouched down.

Hooves clattered on the flattened rocks nearby and pounded the wet ground. Cattle and sheep ran quickly. A crisp bark, cracked the air, slicing through the silence followed by a low, hissing sound.

'What the—'

Daisy pushed a finger over his lips. She could hear his heart thumping.

'What is it?' Archie whispered, as they slipped down the cold slab of rock.

'Sshh. Let me listen.'

Shortly, another strange bark was followed by a hiss, this time much closer.

'It isn't a fox, or any kind of dog,' Daisy said, under her breath, her brow furrowed in concentration. 'It definitely isn't a bird call, or a ferret and it's not a cow, or a goat, or anything from the deer family. I don't think it's a cat—you know, like a lion or leopard or panther. It's certainly not a chicken, or a sheep, or any of the rodent family. It's not a hyena because they laugh... and I doubt it's a crocodile, because I've never heard one, and they go "snap", but it could be a bison or rhino from Africa, so —'

'Daisy!' Archie hissed, 'stop! You don't have to go through the entire animal kingdom.'

'Oh. Sorry,' she said.

'So, what is it?'

'I don't know! But it's definitely not an elephant or a bear or a llama ...'

Archie glared at her.

For a few moments they sat stone-still behind the large, weathered slab of rock. Smeared across the dark sky ran the wavy form of a rain cloud.

'What are we going to do?' Daisy whispered, trying not to appear too cowardly. 'We can't stay here shivering all night only to get eaten.'

Archie nodded. 'Any ideas?'

'How should I know? What do *you* think we should do?'

'*I don't know*.'

'Well, it was your idea!'

'Sshhhhh,' Archie squealed, 'it's really close!'

The slither of something snake-like moved just out of eye-shot. The twins hugged the rock. Then it grunted loudly, and barked.

Daisy squirmed and her ears filled with pain. Tears flowed down her cheeks. She smothered her ears.

'Daisy!' Archie said. 'What is it?'

'A noise! Incredibly high-pitched. It's killing me.'

For some strange reason he couldn't quite understand, Archie stood up, ricked his neck from side to side and jumped out onto the grass to the side of the rock ready to face whatever it was head on.

'... NO!' Daisy cried.

But almost immediately the farm bell rang, its toll echoing eerily up the hillside.

In a flash and with a slither, whatever had been there, vanished.

Daisy shook her head and stepped out to join Archie. The painful shrilling noise had evaporated, like the strange beast.

Holding their breath, the twins moved around to the other side of the rock. Nothing. Just the same, curious, track-marks.

They listened and waited, exchanging looks, wondering if it was safe to run for their lives. With Daisy's eyes on full beam, they simultaneously sprang off and sprinted through the mud and over branches and rocks towards the track.

As they stopped to catch their breath by the old rutted path, a voice came out of the dark below.

Instinctively they crouched down.

'Yoo-hoo!'

'Who... who's there?' Daisy called out.

'Only me!'

Archie and Daisy exhaled audibly and smiled.

'What are you doing up here, Mrs P, scaring us to death?'

'Well, little ones, I came to find you. And I thought I might see a helidoctor, rescuing all them poor folk and that. But I might ask you the same; what you doing, you two, out here in the dark at this time?'

Archie caught Daisy's now back-to-normal eyes. 'We were looking for, er, for... for Blabisterberry Jelly,' he said, at which they both burst out laughing.

'For, eh... what?!' Mrs. Pye shrieked, her voice sounding a little more shrill than normal. 'Jelly? At this time of night?'

'No, Mrs P—it's a kind of joke,' Archie said. 'It's something we've got to find—apparently. But don't worry—it's not important right now.

'Did you find any "helidoctors"?' Daisy asked.

'I didn't, no. Got a little waylaid I'm afraid to say. But I heard one right bang overhead while I was lying in me bath. Stayed there some time, too, till me water went all chilly and I ended up with granny-fingers.'

For the rest of the walk they moved in silence, their boots squelching in the mud. When they arrived near the cottage, Mrs. Pye coughed, very lightly, but just enough to send a shiver down their spines.

Mrs. Pye, aware that she was being looked at, started coughing more until Archie felt compelled to give her a pat on her back.

Could Mrs. Pye's cough be linked with the bark they'd heard at the ruin? No, not Mrs. Pye.

Perhaps all the strange events of the past day had simply stretched his mind so that now he was over-alert to every squeak, splutter and cough.

4 CAIN AND KEMP

For Kemp, the euphoria of being alive, and not in hospital, remained. No interrogations by that dreadful man, Stone; no being stuffed full of tubes and wires; no nurses covered in protective clothing padding and prodding him and filling him with disgusting medicines or sharp needles. No worries about anything.

Much to his astonishment, Cain had delivered on all his promises—food coming out of his ears, a palace to run about in, servants at his disposal, and jewels and treasure everywhere. The place was smothered in riches and Kemp was dazzled by it all.

Cain's demands on him were minimal. Schmerger, the strange, bearded, unsmiling servant, had given him a salve for his burns which healed in record time and Kemp soon felt better than he had for an awfully long time.

For the moment at least, Cain's mood bordered on delirious. He sang and laughed and showed Kemp around the palace, telling stories—all of which sounded ludicrous—and repeatedly told Kemp that it was all his. Not only that, but it was his to do with as he wished.

His to enjoy, his to destroy—if he so wished.

Overshadowing this, Kemp wondered whether Cain would deliver his mother as he had sworn he would.

Festering at the back of his mind, he wondered if Cain had

fabricated the truth about his mother. After all, evidence suggested that she had died a long time ago.

It didn't help that he didn't entirely trust Cain. Cain was dangerous, he sensed, and Kemp couldn't help asking himself why Cain wanted him so badly? *What, exactly, was the ghost's grand plan?* he thought.

Cain hadn't avoided the subject, since Kemp hadn't asked, but Cain's demeanour compelled him to require some answers.

That time came at supper.

Kemp grabbed a spoon and helped himself to a bowl of beef stew. He couldn't remember eating anything quite so tasty in years. Cain's overcoat floated across and parked up next to him.

'Why?' Kemp asked.

'Why, *what*, boy?'

'Why do you need me?' Kemp asked bluntly. 'What's this Prophecy of Eden thing-a-me-jig you told me and Arch about? What's it got to do with you?'

'I wondered when you'd ask,' the gap between Cain's hat and collar said. 'The universe is exceedingly old, boy. Every now and then there's a shift, a repositioning in how it aligns itself.' He appeared to sniff the air. 'It is doing so right at this precise moment and your friends the de Lowes, by way of a long, ancient and rather tedious selection process, have received dreams in which they have been given instructions on how to open the Garden of Eden. If you must, it is the ultimate test for your entire species. If they fail, then mankind will be seen to have failed and life on Earth will be erased. Earth will begin afresh, with different, new beings.'

Kemp looked incredulous. 'Archie has to save the world. Ha-ha, that is bloody hilarious.'

He grabbed a chicken leg and licked it before biting deep into the flesh. 'Fat chance he's got. In any case,' he said with his mouth full again, 'it doesn't make sense. Humans are doing all right, aren't they? We're civilised and all that—we've got TV and the internet, satellites, fast-food, nuclear stuff and massive football stadiums. What's not to have?'

The ghost sighed. 'Running a planet is far more than those

things, my dear fellow. I know it'll be difficult, but you're going to have to stop thinking like a ridiculous Earth human. There's really no use for it here. You see, the energy of the universe is made by zillions of things and, when something happens in one area of the universe, it almost certainly has a knock-on effect elsewhere. Humans were given a time in charge but, in all honesty, they haven't really cared for the others particularly well, have they? I've heard that it's gone a little lop-sided.'

'Others? Lop-sided? *What others?*'

Cain coughed gently. 'The other animals, plants, soils and living things that they were meant to care for. All organisms have a purpose and neglecting one puts tremendous pressure on the others. The knock-on effect, if you will.'

Kemp sneered, but nodded almost knowingly.

Cain interpreted this as a green light to continue. 'If your friends succeed then there is hope for the planet that the present incumbents might turn it around, though it is highly unlikely. If not, then new inhabitants will be made in the Garden of Eden and filtered in to what will essentially be a brand new Earth. With any luck, we should be able to control that filter.'

Kemp crammed a parcel of cheese wrapped in bacon into his mouth and chewed it thoughtfully. 'So what you're saying is that humans have massively screwed it up, right?'

'The long and the short of it is this: if mankind hasn't evolved and matured enough to survive a few simple tasks, then it simply doesn't deserve stewardship of the blue planet—Earth. Your type of mankind will come to an end. Another will begin. It's happened before and it will happen again.'

'Blimey. And everything you've just said,' Kemp said in between wiping his mouth on his sleeve, 'was given in dreams to those de Lowes.'

'Indeed. This shift in the universe sparked a series of dreams sent out by the dreamspinners. That's the name for the ugly spidery things we travel through.'

'I wondered how they fitted in.'

'They are the most ancient of all creatures that belong to the universe—if they are creatures.'

'Those things with the electricity-filled abdomens belong to the universe?'

'Absolutely.'

Kemp cupped the back of his head in his hands and leaned back. 'You know what, Cain, I think that is the biggest loads of bollocks I've ever heard.'

Cain eyed him curiously. 'I don't understand.'

'What I mean,' Kemp said, 'is that it doesn't make any sense.'

'It makes perfect sense,' Cain said. 'Nothing could be clearer.'

Kemp scrunched his face up. 'You're saying that Archie, Isabella and Daisy have been chosen to survive some massive challenges and if they don't, several billions of humans and everything else on the planet will get trashed.'

Cain sounded undeterred. 'Some trees will probably survive and much of the sea-life made it through last time. But yes, everything else will be destroyed.'

Kemp helped himself to a large slice of chocolate cake. 'It's not very fair, is it?' he said. 'I mean, what kind of universe comes up with stupid stuff like that? For school kids?' A drizzle of chocolate slipped out from between his large, plump lips. 'Anyway, you don't reckon they'll do it, do you?'

'That, my boy, is why I wanted to save you. The challenges were designed for strong, wise men, versed in nature and in magic and in war. You're right, they were never designed for children.'

'But, you didn't want me, you wanted Archie,' Kemp said, his voice hardening.

'Of course. But Archie's folly is your opportunity,' Cain replied, his deep voice smooth and syrupy. 'Archie is an Heir of Eden who has been given a strong ancient gift—why shouldn't I have desired a union with him?'

Kemp felt slighted, but it was true. 'What are these gift things that make them so important, then?'

'Physical attributes mainly,' Cain said, 'extended uses of the senses; heightened vision, hearing, smell and increased strength—that sort of thing. Nothing too dramatic.'

'Wow. Cool,' Kemp said thickly. 'And this Garden of Eden—

what's that all about? Why does it have to be opened? Why doesn't everything stay the same?'

'You really are full of questions. Perhaps it is all this food.' Cain smiled. 'The answer, my boy, is many-fold. You see, the Garden of Eden is where new species were created and developed. If a species proved successful it was placed upon a planet to develop and evolve and primarily have some sort of useful function.'

Cain paused and wondered how much he should tell. 'For a long while, the Garden was closed. You see, there was a... how should I put it... a disagreement about how it functioned, about the legitimacy of what was being created.'

'Sounds like a right load of tosh.'

'Indeed,' Cain said, 'whatever tosh means. But it was certainly complicated.'

Kemp bit into an apple. 'But if the Garden of Eden is miraculously opened, won't everyone survive?'

Cain chuckled throatily. 'The chances of Eden opening is so utterly remote that it is almost not worth considering, but I have in place my own safety net of sorts, just in case.

'You see, after the flooding, comes pestilence, which is out there causing bedlam. All the clues are written down at the beginning of those old historical books you Earth humans seem to get so much pleasure from. Anyway, I thought I might speed the process up.'

'Don't tell me,' Kemp said, 'you've given the disease to the de Lowes?'

Cain suddenly realised the boy was smarter than he looked. 'Not a bad idea, but unfortunately, the Heirs are protected. Now, here's a clue. Those ugly dreamspinners came to me with the news that there are no more dream powders remaining from their main stores. So, in return for a bit of help from them, I have allowed them to create some dream powders here, subject to a few modifications. Do you understand?'

Kemp rubbed his greasy chin thoughtfully. 'Yeah, I think so.'

'Very well. Try again.'

'OK,' Kemp grinned and rubbed his chin. 'How about you've

given the disease to all the world leaders through your dream-spinner mates, and as they get ill, each country blames it on the other and then they blow the shit out of each other.'

'Bravo. Another fine suggestion, but no, I'll tell you. All I've done, my friend, is slip a little of the disease into my brand new store of dream powders.'

Kemp smiled. 'And these dreamspinners dish out dreams every night—around the world?'

'Precisely.'

Kemp wiped his mouth with his sleeve. 'You're spreading this disease as people sleep. That, my ghostly buddy, is blooming genius.'

Cain was delighted. 'You see, I'm not just a pretty face.'

Kemp banged the table as he laughed. 'They won't know what's hit them. And so fast and un-warned and utterly brilliant—they'll never work it out because no one really knows how dreams work, right?'

'Absolutely. My thoughts too,' Cain said. 'Superb little plan, isn't it?'

However, a thought struck Kemp and his face darkened. 'You promised to bring my mother here, didn't you? That was our deal.'

'And I will,' the ghost said, purring. 'I'm glad you mentioned this because I wanted to talk to you about your mother. It's important that our relationship is based on the truth. Don't you think?'

'Truth?' Kemp said, nervously. 'What is it—is she dead? She is, isn't she?'

Cain remained silent.

'Or... she's in a mad-house or something?' Kemp's voice creaked.

Closer than you think, Cain thought. 'Do you know how your parents died?'

Kemp nodded. 'Car crash, in the hills.'

'Correct. Before I returned you to Earth, I met up with your father's ghost.'

Kemp looked astonished. 'You can do that?'

'Why, of course. After all, I too am a kind of spirit, though I have considerably more substance than the truly dead. Spirits are easy to find if you know how, but frightfully airy and irritable. Your father told me about your mother, about the accident when you were just a babe. He told me many things.' His voice dropped. 'But the most fascinating thing is that your mother never died. She was found. She survived.'

Kemp's brain slowed to a halt as he computed Cain's story. The apple in his hand dropped to the floor.

'She lives, truly. Your mother is as alive as the next person.'

Kemp swallowed. 'You're having me on,' he said very quietly.

The ghost made a sound as if it were sucking in a mouthful of air. 'No, boy.' The ghost removed the hat and placed it on the table.

Kemp shook his head. 'I thought you'd bring her to me as, you know, as a ghost, a spirit or something.'

'My thoughts exactly. I too am most surprised by this turn of events—'

Kemp eyed the top of the coat curiously. 'You're sure this isn't a joke, right?'

'I swear, on my death, that I am telling you the truth. However, the news isn't as good as you might wish. You must be prepared that, if I bring her to you, she will reject you. There is a strong chance that she will not want to know you.'

Kemp looked confused. 'That's not true, Cain. Of course she would. I'm her son.'

'I understand how you feel,' Cain said, sighing. 'However, she remembers nothing of you. She suffered damage to the brain—'

'Brain damage?' Kemp looked wounded. 'But mothers always, always know their children,' Kemp said defensively, 'no matter what. She'd know me, I'm sure of it. What's her name?'

Cain's overcoat stood up so that he was standing in front of the boy. 'I didn't think you'd believe me, but I do not lie. And the terrible part of this is that there is a strong likelihood that you too will reject the woman.'

'As if I would do such a thing,' Kemp stormed. 'Never! Who is she?'

'Very well,' Cain said. 'But don't tell me I didn't warn you.'

Kemp levelled with the ghost. 'Tell me who she is.'

'Your mother,' Cain said slowly, 'is the exact same woman who looks after the de Lowe children—'

Kemp's eyes hardened as he worked out exactly who the ghost was talking about. Then he burst out laughing. 'You're having me on, aren't you? Mrs. Pye... Mrs. bleeding Pye? Is that the best you can do? Mrs. Pye, that big, ugly, old hag.' Kemp slapped his thighs and bent over double, great guffaws spilling out of him. After a while, he straightened and then sat down. Only now, his eyes watered.

The overcoat sat down beside him. 'I told you this wouldn't be easy. Often, young man, things are best left exactly as they are.'

Kemp's mood changed fast. In no time his face raged with anger. 'Listen here, Cain,' he roared, 'I'm telling you, Mrs. Pye is NOT and *cannot be* my mother. Do you understand?' Kemp stood up, tears flowing. 'She can't be. It's impossible.'

Cain hovered next to him and whispered in his ear, 'Thing is, boy, it is the truth. She really is.'

5 HAVILARIAN TOADSTOOL POWDER

Isabella let herself in, stripped off her waterproofs and entered the kitchen. She added a couple of logs to the belly of the stove, grabbed a clean tea towel and dried herself off.

She popped the kettle on the range and, while she waited for it to boil, she shook as she remembered the sensation that had entered her mind and filled her with dread. *Those eyes,* she thought, *and that noise,* which had washed through her head like a mass of incomprehensible, jumbled words and sentences.

She poured the boiling water. A cup of tea for herself and an apple tea for Old Man Wood, in case he was feeling better.

On the table were two candles and she searched around for a match. She looked in all the obvious places but either they'd run out or they'd been taken next door. She felt heat building in the tips of her fingers and, thinking of a flame, she clicked the end of her thumb and forefinger. To her amazement, a tiny spark flew out. She laughed, nervously, and inspected the end of her thumb and her digit. *Static?*

She tried again and this time another spark fizzed out, fading in the air. *But it doesn't make sense.* Something had to make it spark. She clicked her fingers again and this time a tiny flame shot out of the end of her thumb. Isabella didn't know whether to jump for joy or scream in terror.

But the strange thing was that it didn't hurt and, if anything, felt entirely natural. She sat down and studied her fingers in more detail, a surge of euphoria rushing through her. She placed a flame below her fingers, but they didn't discolour or burn or singe. It was as if her hands had become impervious to heat and pain.

Isabella lit the candles, knocked on Old Man Wood's door and entered, placing the candles on the tables. Then, she went back for the tea, which she set beside the still outline of the old man lying in his bed.

'We heard noises at the ruin!' she said softly as she busied herself about the room. 'I left Daisy and Archie out there,' she said, leaning briefly over him, his face obscured by the dim light and the folds of a blanket. 'I'm afraid there's bad news with the cattle: three cows missing and one sheep. Too dark to tell which ones though.'

She lit another candle on his table then returned and jumped up onto the bed, which wobbled and creaked a little. Then she lay back on the soft downy pillows at the side of the old man.

Old Man Wood lay perfectly still and she very carefully reached over and read his pulse. She squinted. Faint, but definitely something. She propped herself up and turned her gaze towards the wooden panels at the foot of the bed.

'You'd have seen us, if you'd watched the panels,' she said.

No response at all.

Isabella sighed, 'There's some tea for you—apple tea, to make you strong,' she said, remembering his tea-mantra.

As she sipped hers, she turned her attention to the images on the wooden panels.

There was Archie, crouching down as if waiting for something. In Daisy's panel she could make out a running human figure, similar to her sister, but with glowing eyes, like car headlamps.

Why was Daisy's panel doing strange things?

A strange slurping sound emanated from Old Man Wood. 'I think her panel's gone a bit funny, Old Man Wood,' she said, nudging his arm. 'There's tea on your bedside table,' she repeated, 'if you'd like it.'

Suddenly Archie attacked the figure with the bright eyes and threw it violently to the ground.

Isabella sat bolt upright. 'Archie's beating it up! He's pinning it down!' she cried, leaning towards the panels. 'Go Archie! No one messes with Superman-boy!'

She chuckled at the thought, and stared at Daisy's panel. 'Oh! Hang on!'

Archie's beating Daisy up? she thought. *Are they messing about?* 'Hey, Old Man Wood, did you see what led up to this?'

For a moment she wondered if she should dash up there and sort them out but, as she viewed, they seemed to slump down behind a rock, chatting.

She checked her watch. Typically, delicious smells would drift out of the kitchen at this time, at which point Old Man Wood would nearly always comment on what it might be and rub his tummy in anticipation. But there were no fabulous smells and still he didn't stir a muscle. 'I wonder where Mrs. Pye is?' she said. 'I'm starving.'

Isabella leant over to his side of the bed and called out, sweetly, 'Old Man Wood?'

No reaction.

'Can I get you anything?'

His face, in the dim candlelight, looked milky-white and a terrible fear swept through her that he might have passed away while she was talking to him.

She slid off, grabbed a candle and walked around the large bed to the other side and set it down on the bedside table. Old Man Wood's face was mostly hidden by the folds of a thick pillow and his body was covered by a duvet. She perched on the edge of the bed and gently levered the pillow out of the way.

Isabella's heart began to race. Something about him didn't look right.

'Come on, Old Man Wood, wakey-wakey,' she teased. Nothing, again. A terrible panic began building in her mind. 'Please. Wake up. Please.'

She moved in to inspect his face, lifting the candle up to offer more light.

She cupped a hand over her mouth as her stomach lurched. 'OH-MY-GOD!' she said standing up quickly but with the presence of mind to put the candle down first.

Old Man Wood lay motionless, his eyes shut, his skin as white as snow. Dotted over his face in tiny clusters were tiny white toadstools which she traced all the way down his neck.

She folded back the duvet and unbuttoned the top three of his shirt buttons. As she folded back the lapels, she stepped back from the bed stunned.

Before she could help herself, she retched.

WHAT ARE THEY?

In the candlelight tiny, pulsing, toadstools poked out of his chest like minute pins holding weenie umbrellas.

Instinctively, Isabella reached for his wrist and held it, counting. A murmur, the faintest, faintest dimmest of beats, that's all.

Get an ambulance. No, it won't get here—the air ambulance—they're rescuing people from the flooding. What about phoning the hospital, they'd know what to do?

She clenched her fist. With no power, they had nothing. No phone, no communication.

In any case, she thought, *the hospital probably didn't even exist anymore.*

COME ON. Think! THINK!

She slapped her forehead as if it might trigger an idea; there must be some way of making him better! Resplendix Mix! Old Man Wood's potion he'd used on them. *But where was it?*

She tore round the room searching for the strange bottle without a lid.

She rummaged through his coat and trouser pockets, through his chest of drawers and then ran downstairs and scoured the sitting room.

She returned up the stairs, entered Old Man Wood's room and leaned against the wall. Reality was hitting her hard. *We're lost if he doesn't survive*, she thought.

Then, without knowing why, she moved towards him and placed a hand on his brow. Pinpricks of heat, like mini, red-hot needles emanated from the toadstools. She kept her hand there, her palms crossed on his forehead.

Now the temperature built. Her hands were tingling, sucking out heat. The longer she did it the more disgusted and furious she became until a rage began to bubble up inside. And the angrier she became, the hotter the heat pouring into her hands. Soon the heat was almost too much to bear.

She removed her hands and quickly turned down the duvet covering his body. Suddenly a large, vile green toadstool the size of a hammer sprouted out of his belly and sliced through his shirt. Isabella squealed.

She rocked backwards, holding her mouth. '*NO!*' she cried. '*NO!*'

Now that his shirt had slipped off his chest, she could see hundreds of multi-coloured fungi littering his body, like bits of confetti, *eating* him.

Old Man Wood's last words, she realised, weren't about the poison *in the water*—they were concerning the poison *he'd taken.*

Isabella backed away towards the door. *Someone, give me the strength to do something. Anything.*

She stared and the longer she did the more frustrated and cross she became. Fury filled her growing like a furnace.

Another large, green and red toadstool sliced out of his chest, the noise like tearing metal foil.

Without warning, her whole body burned as though on fire. The surge consumed her, the heat inside her body roaring until her blood boiled and her temples throbbed as if her arteries might burst.

Her eyes blazed as if they were made of lava. She clenched her teeth, but the intensity deepened, hotter, faster—until her entire body was set to explode.

She extended her hands and pointed them at the two main, menacing toadstools, thriving, it seemed, with each flashing pulse, growing taller and fatter.

A strand of hair blew over her face as a wind picked up around her. From her hands an orangey-pink mist radiated, wrapping Old Man Wood in a wispy pink cocoon. Soon, it looked as though he was surrounded by fire.

Isabella let out a long piercing cry of anger and pain.

A second later, the body of Old Man Wood rose above the bed, the pink glow encircling and rotating like candy floss.

A high-pitched whirring noise built up and up until the intensity was almost unbearable, the cocoon swirling faster and faster.

The toadstools on the old man's body began to quiver, like birthday candles on a bowl of jelly.

All of a sudden a toadstool exploded off Old Man Wood's body, smashing into the ceiling. Then another—shattering the mirror—and another through the windows.

Toadstools from every part of his body rapidly discharged, peppering the walls, ceiling and bed. The noise was like a gun fight, fires starting on the wooden panelling surrounding the room.

All the while Isabella stood still, her hands extended, her concentration absolute as the swirling glow over Old Man Wood forced the toadstools out.

Soon, her energy wavered and the cocoon around the old man weakened. Only one remained. The large, lime green toadstool on his chest.

Exhausted, her strength gone, her body spent, Isabella had nothing more to give. She dropped her hands. The pink energy fizzling away.

Dizzy, her head as heavy as lead, Isabella stumbled into the wall and fell to her knees.

'I can't,' she cried. 'I'm so, so sorry, Old Man Wood... I'm so terribly sorry.'

And she collapsed on to the floor.

6 THE RING OF BABYLON

Gaia reached out a long, silvery claw. So, Asgard had sided with Cain and the news coming back through the ether painted a bleak picture.

Cain had added the plague to their dream powders to make lethal dreams. The spread was unimagined, unaccountable, swift and devastating. *It was the perfect mass-murder weapon.*

'How many dreamspinners are using Cain's spider web powders?'

'Hundreds,' a smaller dreamspinner vibrated, 'maybe thousands. More go every minute.'

'And each one uses his powder?' She already knew the answer.

I need Genesis, she thought. *She'll know what to do.*

She reached out for the vibration of the old dreamspinner, channelling her energy into the universe. A wavy, strange vibration tickle returned—slight and distant.

In a flash, Gaia inverted through the electric middle of her body, flashing through the universe to the spot where she desperately hoped Genesis would be.

She arrived moments later in a cave. A cave as tall as a mountain and half as wide. Was there such a place on Earth, or Havilah?

Gaia's opaque, silvery legs walked on the air towards the middle as though on an invisible grid.

Genesis would not be invisible here, Gaia thought, and she altered herself so she might also be seen. By doing so, she would see any dreamspinners that had themselves turned visible.

As she suspected, Genesis was waiting for her. 'You have come. Good. At least there is one of the ancient order still in possession of their faculties.'

Gaia had almost forgotten what a large, intimidating dreamspinner Genesis could be. Around her neck, and down the length of her shimmering silvery body, grey hoops gave her a formidable appearance. And far from the broken creature that had departed to die after giving the boy his Gifts, she looked menacing.

Her three black eyes pierced into Gaia. 'You know?'

'I do, mother. Our order, our traditions, are being dismantled, our purpose lost, dreamspinners corrupted. Asgard has aligned with Cain. Disease spreads from powders made from the spider webs in Havilah. As the sun goes down while Earth rotates, he spreads dreams of fear and failure. Death extends across the planet.'

Genesis tilted her head. 'Cain should *never* be trusted. Asgard has showed him our secret and he has grasped it in his ghostly hands. Dreamspinners have been led to believe that the Heirs of Eden cannot open the Garden of Eden, so Asgard makes it his business to determine our future. He sees no hope in the Heirs of Eden.'

Genesis raised herself up. 'But the Heirs have *every* chance. That is why the universe selected them. Furthermore, there are ancient mysticisms that Asgard does not know.'

The great dreamspinner's posture fell a little and her vibrations quietened. 'I should have shared these with you many suns and moons ago, Gaia. And when I do, I will make a calling to stop this madness.'

'A calling, mother?'

'Yes. You will see. I alone know of it. There is a power to recall dreamspinners from every corner of the universe. But first, let me inform you of the ancient ways, for my time is not long now, and you, Gaia, will take my place. One mother of the universe to another.'

Genesis rose up again. 'The prophecy is far from failing. Even now, as the old man suffers from Cain's poison, there is hope. For he is protected by a charm the Heirs possess and which Cain long ago abandoned. It is the magic of love. Besides, these Heirs are not so weak or so frail as Asgard imagines, nor are they so stupid or so slow. It is a clever choice to use children as the Heirs; they are neither too cowardly nor too proud, as Asgard assumes. And they learn fast. And, moreover, it contains the element of surprise. Cain and the Mother Serpent will underestimate them.'

Genesis dipped one long, bony leg after another into the electric blue fire of her maghole, which raged harder than Gaia had seen for some time.

'You helped the old man find his Resplendix Mix, did you not?'

Gaia was astonished. 'Indeed. I wanted balance—'

'Balance. Good.' Genesis hummed. 'Now you will need to go further. The old man once possessed a branchwand. Find it and deliver it before the third tablet is found. Discover the dreams for informing him of its purpose. I will show you how to do this.

'And know this: Cain's twin, Abel, is not so crazed anymore. Time has banished his anger and he seeks his revenge. Like Cain, his shadow grows. And even though Seth, the little brother, will not come out of his place of hiding, he has promised a great gift.'

'But what of us? Is Asgard truthful? Is our time at an end?'

Genesis flicked her legs into her maghole. 'Tell me, Gaia, what do you know of the Prophecy?'

'Three tablets lead the way to the Key of Eden,' Gaia replied. 'The lock must be released to open the Garden and then life will begin anew, the Garden reborn. New species will come unto Earth and Havilah. But one failure will prove mankind's failing, and the Earth will be cleansed.'

'And, tell me, what if the Heirs have the three Tablets but do not find the key? Do you know what happens then?' Genesis asked.

'They die—?'

'No, not necessarily. Opening the Garden requires that a

great power be unleashed. We dreamspinners have the means to create this, when there is no more. These things have been long forgotten.'

'Create? Create what, mother?'

'Here.' Genesis passed over a polished white ring made of a glass-like stone.

'What is it? I know of no such things.'

Genesis' dark eyes sparkled. 'This is the Ring of Babylon, hidden on the walls of the cave and shrouded from common knowledge. But Adam will know, deep in his lost mind.'

Genesis ruffled her body so that she appeared, for a moment, larger, like a huge angel, her silvery, almost see-through body cloaking her strange spidery frame. 'If the Heirs succeed, there is a choice even if they cannot open the lock.'

'I do not know of it, mother.'

'If the children survive, a new world will arrive.'

'If that time happens there is one thing the Heirs must do. Point the ring at the red planet. One of the Heirs must push their breath through it. That is all. But it must be done before the sun goes down on the eighth day.'

'For what purpose?'

'The Garden of Eden is dead. One breath of life through the Ring of Babylon will create holes in space through which will be sucked life-givers.'

'For life-giver, you talk of comets?'

'Yes. When one life-giver collides with Earth and another with Havilah and The Garden of Eden and Assyria and Cush, five new places of habitation will be formed. This will signal the end of the ancient order and the beginning of the new.'

'So, Eve and the old man, Cain, Abel and Seth will die?' Gaia said. 'I had no idea. Then a new time really will begin. A new time for us all, even dreamspinners...' Gaia flickered her legs out. 'Then Cain cannot prevail. He fails.'

Genesis dipped a couple of legs in her maghole. 'After a great sleep, the Heirs of Eden shall be the stewards.'

'The Heirs? But there are only three. How are they to reproduce and populate?"

'There are others, Gaia. More than you realise. When the time is right, the process of populating the worlds will be quick enough. But when they are of an age they will die, as it always should have been. The mistake of endless life will never be repeated. Remember, Gaia, this may only happen if they are alive at the end of the seven days and if they have the tablets.'

'After defeating Gorialla Yingarna, the mother serpent—'

'Yes, and if they overcome Blabisterberry Jelly.'

Gaia shuffled and cleaned two legs in her maghole simultaneously. 'One failure—'

'Is all it takes,' Genesis interrupted.

'I understand.'

'Good. Remember it well. And Gaia.'

'Yes, mother?'

'Cain and Asgard and his band of deserters must never know of the Ring of Babylon. There. You know all that I know. Now I must summon dreamspinners and put a halt to the error of their ways. And while they come to me, they are not spinning dreams filled with poison.'

Genesis produced a thin, shiny stick the size of a small piece of wire, glittering as if it were made of one piece of elasticised diamond. She tapped on it quickly as if it were a drum, creating reverberations that hummed high and low, deep and soft, loud and searching.

'Stand with me, my daughter of the universe, and watch.'

Back in their invisible state, the two dreamspinners waited as the humming continued wailing, its sound at once both harmonious and haunting, singing into the expansive universes.

It didn't take long.

Moments later, as if by magic, dreamspinners started popping out of the sky into the huge cavern in tiny flashes, pinpricks of light, until the huge chamber was packed with thousands of opaque, spidery-looking creatures with fiery, blue middles.

7 SOLOMON'S INTERROGATION

'Headmaster!' Sue rushed up to him and gave him a hug.

The headmaster hadn't anticipated it and only after a moment reciprocated.

'You survived!' she said, 'I can't believe how lucky we are.'

The words filled Solomon with a pang of guilt; *how had he lived, when so many had died?* he thought. 'And you are well?' he asked. 'How is our hero, Gus?'

'Oh, he's doing really well, thanks,' she said, smiling back at the familiar, yet slightly less rotund face of the headmaster. 'In fact, he's bored and itching to get out of his bed. Seems like all he had was a sort of mini-flu.'

'What a great relief,' Solomon said, and he meant it.

Sue looked around. 'Cool place, isn't it? What's it called, Swinton Park? I heard it was once a beautiful hotel.' Another helicopter buzzed overhead and settled down just behind a large cluster of bare trees just out of sight through the windows. 'I've never seen so many helicopters in one place,' Sue said, almost in awe. 'Have you met the Commissioner? He's a bit of a creep if you ask me. I've got a "debriefing" with him in half an hour.'

The headmaster had forgotten what a lively, pretty girl she was—and clearly desperate to talk. 'Sue, I wouldn't mind a brief catch up before you see him. Find out all about your extraordinary adventure. Can you spare a moment—outside? Have you got a coat?'

Sue caught his eye. 'Sure.'

They pushed open the double doors that led from the reception and rounded the thick stone walls heading up the path in the darkness. Solomon continued on around the lake towards the gardens.

'Headmaster, where are we going?'

'Please, call me Solomon, won't you, Sue? We're not at school now so you can leave the airs and graces behind, don't you think?' He smiled his head-masterly smile, his small, tea-stained teeth a little too evident. 'A little bit further, if you don't mind stretching your legs.'

He stopped for a minute and turned to face the vale behind them. 'Such a beautiful place isn't it, perched here on the Dale-side of the Vale? Did you realise that Upsall is almost exactly opposite on the edge of the Moors, right over there?' he said, pointing into the distance. 'And have you seen the lake? It's well worth a visit in the morning. Dug by hand, so I'm told, and now overflowing like a mini Niagara Falls. A most impressive sight.'

Sue thought this commentary was rather odd but, as they walked around a clump of dense yew trees, she spotted a bench lit by an old street light. Solomon beckoned her to sit down.

He pulled out a notepad and a pen.

We're being monitored, he wrote. *You are in terrible danger.*

'Can you hear the geese over there?' he said. 'They're Canadian, you can tell by their distinct call.'

I'm bugged. You are too.

'Er ... Gosh—wow!' she said, the colour draining from her face. She shook her head and felt a hard nodule on her lapel. 'You're very knowledgeable,' she stuttered, her brain fizzing. 'Are they, er, related to Iberian Geese?' she said, racking her brain about birds.

He nodded encouragement.

Why? she wrote.

'Perhaps,' he said peering at the pad. 'You may well be right, I'm no expert. There used to be a famous deer herd here, but I believe all the animals have been put down,' he continued. 'A very ancient breed, by all accounts.'

They're on to the de Lowes.

'Oh! I like deer,' she said, rather thickly.

Crap, she wrote, before scribbling it out.

Solomon was a little taken aback and gave her one of his most knowing looks. 'I can't begin to tell you how thrilled I am to see you again,' he said. 'Tell me, how did you find that old rowing boat? I'm rather astonished it held together. Was that Isabella's idea?'

He scribbled fast. *I have to ask.* He pointed at her lapel again and gave her an encouraging look.

She grabbed the notebook and coughed as she turned the page. 'Well, yes! I suppose it was. Isabella realised the huge storm cloud might blow at any time. It was pretty obvious really. I mean, there was lightning shooting out everywhere, and all they had to do was run up the track home. She probably reckoned I wouldn't get home so, just in case, she suggested the boat. In hindsight, it was totally inspired. Then, luckily, I bumped into Gus.'

Sorry, don't normally swear.

'Sue, can I ask? What made Isabella so infatuated with the storm cloud? I know you both came to see me with a home-made barometer, was it something to do with this—were you just playing "scientists"?'

Sue shot him a curious look, trying to ascertain what sort of reply he was fishing for. 'Yeah, I suppose so. Isabella went a bit crazy on weather forecasting and...'

She stalled and stared at the ground.

'My dear,' Solomon said. 'Is there something you'd like to tell me?'

'Well, yeah, there is one more thing—but it's a bit weird. Actually no, don't worry about it—it's probably irrelevant.'

Solomon pressed her. 'Tell me everything,' he encouraged. 'I'm intrigued that Isabella knew enough to think of getting you a boat, but why didn't you simply head up into the tower—like many of the children and me?'

'We did calculations, sir.'

'Calculations? Whatever for?' Solomon raised his eyebrows in anticipation.

'OK—this will sound ridiculous.' Sue took a deep breath. 'I'd had a dream about a storm. Actually, it was more like a nightmare. Thing is, it felt so clear I thought it might be a premonition, you know, when you see something before it actually happens.'

Solomon nodded.

'Anyway, I told Isabella about it. You see, I always try and write my dreams down the moment I wake up. Amazingly, she believed me.'

'So it's happened before?'

'Yes. A couple of times. Anyway she then got all excited about it—in a scientific, meteorological way, you understand—'

Solomon smiled encouragement and mouthed: '*good*'.

'—and then she started looking at storm data on websites and she got more and more carried away until she made a barometer which kept bottoming out and all the while, much to our astonishment, the cloud kept growing until she came to the conclusion that this one was going to be the biggest of the lot. From her calculations, I don't think she thought the school tower would make it.'

'And all this came from a dream?' Solomon said, almost to himself. 'Fascinating.'

He handed Sue a note, with a finger over his lips.

No more!

Sue smiled back at the headmaster. It was nice to have someone to talk to.

There's more, she wrote, *much more*.

'Getting a bit chilly, isn't it?' Solomon said, rubbing his hands together. 'Let's go back inside shall we?' They linked arms. 'I am so terribly sorry about your losses. I am afraid our whole community has suffered dreadful personal tragedy. We are very much the lucky ones— I doubt if the populace will ever really recover. Life has a habit of bouncing back, though, so let's hope that maybe one day things will return to something near normal.'

Sue looked pensive. 'Why are there so many people rushing around with protective kit on?'

'You mean you don't know?'

Sue shook her head. 'I've heard there's some kind of virus out there. Is it true?'

Solomon pushed his glasses back on. 'My dear, absolutely. The country is in quarantine, everything—and I mean *everything*—has ground to a halt. According to a military chap I sat next to at lunch, half the towns and cities are up in flames. Mass looting—general pandemonium. By a total fluke, Swinton Park is possibly the safest place in the world, right now.

'You look a little pale, Sue, let's sit down by the fire. I thought they might have told you.' They walked inside, took off their coats, nodded at a couple of uniformed men who rushed by and sat down by the fire. 'But I guess there have been other things to worry about.'

Sue's face had gone white. 'Seriously? Is it the truth?'

'Indeed. Never more so. Why do you think Gus is in his little room? I believe it has been named *Ebora*, a rather crude blend of the Roman word for *York*—Ebor, and the *Ebola* outbreak in Africa. The problem is, these scientists have absolutely no idea how to contain it.'

'None at all?'

'Not only does it spread by touch and by bodily fluids, but it appears to fly through the air. And the strange thing is that, quite suddenly, it turned up the length of America, as though it flew west with the night. Maybe it did, who knows?'

'America?' Sue said. 'That's impossible.'

'Yes, both sides of North America and South America too, apparently.' He exhaled loudly and smiled. 'In a way it's a miracle neither of us has caught it. But, since they have no idea how it operates, there's no preventative advice that they can give to those who haven't been affected.'

Sue screwed her eyes shut and clenched her hands as the magnitude of what he was saying sunk in.

Solomon noticed, reached over and patted her arm lightly. 'As you know, it all began right here in Yorkshire. Upsall is the epicentre, they say. On the meteorological charts, the storm mushroomed out of Upsall and covered a good part of the United Kingdom. The animations are most impressive. We're here because we're about the only people known to have survived. Our dear friend, the Commissioner, seems to think that there is something, or someone, in Upsall that can tell us more.'

Sue scribbled on the pad. *There is.*

'Sue,' the headmaster continued, alarm in his face, 'do you know of anything that might somehow link this storm or the Ebora with Upsall School or with any of your friends?'

Sue's eyes met the headmaster's. *Do I trust him? I have to—who else is there?*

She pulled her pen out.

It's the de Lowes, she wrote, allowing him to read the page.

She carried on writing and very calmly said, 'No, not that I'm aware of.'

The headmaster smiled and gave her a very faint wink out of his right eye. 'And does Gus know of anything, anything at all, Sue?'

'I don't think so,' she said handing over the notebook.

He read it.

They have to find three tablets. Then kill an old woman—I think.

'—Murder?' he coughed, before realising his mistake. 'In the village?' he added, too late. He passed the notebook back as he waffled on about a rather curious death claim in the village, hoping to mask his slip-up.

Sue cringed. She scribbled again.

If they fail, we die. They're running out of time

Solomon looked up, his face red from his gaff. 'Exactly as I thought,' he said. 'I never suspected anything else from you other than complete honesty.'

How do you know? he wrote.

She took back the pad. *I dreamt about it. So far, everything true.*

She handed the book back to the headmaster. He smiled at her and tossed it onto the fire. 'Thank you, my dear. Now, I think it's time we'd paid a visit to the dear Commissioner. He's been looking forward to meeting you.'

As they stood up, a crowd of people arguing loudly walked into the room. Solomon leant in very quickly and whispered into her ear. 'Sue, whatever happens, you absolutely *must* trust me.'

Solomon and Sue waited for half an hour in the ante-room outside his office as a stream of people filed in and out. Every so often they caught a few words or exclamations from Stone as the door opened and closed.

Dickinson, smart as usual, his hair neatly combed to one side, ushered them in and remained with them, sitting to the side of the desk, his tablet switched on ready for note-taking.

Stone rubbed his eyes, leaned back in his chair and drew a hand through his thick silver hair. He fixed Sue with a crooked smile. 'So, I'll tell you what we know,' he began, talking directly to her. 'And as I go, why don't you fill in the blanks. And please, don't muck me about, girl. We're fighting a losing battle here and if I don't think you're co-operating, I have the means and the methods to make you talk, understand?'

Sue gulped and nodded.

'Firstly, this storm and Ebora have both got something to do with Upsall.' He lifted his eyes to meet hers. 'Secondly, there's a connection with the de Lowe family.'

Sue gasped. 'How do you know that?'

'So you agree, do you?' Stone shot back.

'No, I... er, I never said that.' She flashed a look at Solomon.

Stone knew he'd struck gold. 'We know—don't we, headmaster—that there's something a bit quirky with this family? You see, your friend Kemp told us.' Stone said, going straight for the jugular.

'Kemp? He's alive?' she stammered before controlling herself. 'What would Kemp know?'

Stone smiled shiftily. 'Oh, he appeared to know all about it.'

'About what?'

'You tell me.'

For a moment there was silence. Stone leaned forward. 'Tell me about your dream, Sue?'

'Dream?'

'Yes, those things you have at night, you know, while you sleep—I'm told you had one all about the de Lowes. A kind of premonition? Am I right?'

Sue nodded.

'Why do you think that was?'

'I don't know. I dream quite a bit and I write them down. I like trying to work out their meanings.'

'How very interesting. I used to write a diary at night when I was your age until my mother found ink smudges all over my pillow.'

Sue smiled. 'Oh, I use a Biro or a pencil so it doesn't make such a mess.'

Stone pressed his intercom. 'Has it arrived yet? Good. Send it up when you're ready.' He turned back to her. 'Excellent. That means your diary won't have deteriorated in the floodwaters too much.'

'You can't do that,' Solomon stormed. 'They're a girl's private thoughts—'

Stone slammed his hand down on the desk. 'Screw her thoughts, Headmaster. I can do what I damn well like.' They glared at one another. 'Where are the de Lowes, Sue? Where are they right now?'

'I have no idea,' Sue stammered. 'We last made contact on the rowing boat a couple of days ago. I think they were at home, although the text didn't say.'

'You're lying again,' Stone said. He turned. 'Dickinson. Was anyone at the property when you flew over?'

'Our thermal-imaging camera found the outline of one female adult. More than likely that of their housekeeper, Mrs. Pye. No others, sir. We circled the remains of the house twice, sir. No other bodies in sight.'

Sue felt sick. 'I don't know. Really I don't.' She fought back her tears.

'First Kemp vanishes, now the entire de Lowe family go absent,' he yelled. 'Dickinson, has anyone found the parents yet?'

'Negative, sir. We have a team scouring their last known locations.'

'Tomorrow, at the crack of dawn, I'm sending in a little expeditionary team to check out their little hovel on top of the hill. You better be certain they're not there, Miss Lowden.'

A knuckle rapped at the door. A man with a protective facial mask entered and handed a plastic bag to Dickinson. 'I've given it a bit of a dry, but it was pretty well protected by the bag,' he said, before exiting.

Sue recognised it immediately. 'That's mine—'

'Actually, I think you'll find it's Government property,' Stone smiled as he opened up the pink hardback diary. 'Tell me, what date did you say you had this epiphany?'

Sue face turned to thunder. 'About two weeks ago.'

Stone flicked through, eyebrow raised. 'Gosh. What drivel, all these feeble girlie thoughts. Ah. Here we are. Entry for Tuesday 28th October.

'Another nightmare,' he read.

Stone looked up, his face puce with anger. 'Is that it?' He flicked through several other pages. '*Another nightmare*? Is that all you wrote? What about all this "recording your bleeding dreams"?'

'I did,' Sue exclaimed. 'It's all there.'

Stone hurled the book at her. 'Find it! NOW!'

Sue nervously flicked through.

Next to her, Solomon burst out laughing, stood up and reached into his pocket.

'What's so damned funny?'

'It's just that, oh dear,' Solomon mopped his eyes with a handkerchief. 'Are you, my dear cousin, trying to ascertain what her dreams were all about?'

'Of course I ruddy well am.'

'Well, why don't you simply ask? Sue told me and I have to say that, when she told me, they were so ludicrous I didn't feel it was worth mentioning.'

Stone puckered his mouth. 'So tell me what she told you, Solomon. I'll be the judge of that.'

Sue shot the headmaster a worried look. *I have to trust him*, she thought.

'Sue's dreams were about the de Lowes finding three tablets that had code or whatever it is on them to save the world.'

Her heart sank.

'Tablets?' the commissioner said. 'What kind of tablets?'

'Computer tablets, I imagine—you know, iPads or the like—such as Dickinson's holding. Isn't that right, Sue?'

Sue's eyes almost popped out of her head. She laughed nervously. 'Er, yeah. I told you it was a bit weird.'

Stone eyed them both. 'Well, why isn't it on the recordings then?'

'Because, my dear old fellow, Sue was so embarrassed about telling me that I asked her if it might be easier to write it all down. So she did, on condition that I burned it afterwards. If you seriously believe there is anything worth following up concerning Sue's dream you'll probably find that the de Lowes have long departed Eden Cottage in search of these electronic devices. They're probably looting the High Street as we speak. Otherwise I think you might have to consider that Sue simply had a premonition about a very great storm. People do, you know.'

Stone swivelled on his chair and clenched his fists. It didn't add up.

'You dreamt about a storm, Sue, and in particular its violent nature. You also dreamt of the de Lowes, correct? So what's to say there isn't some fragment of truth to all of it?'

He stood and paced the room, shaking his head. 'Let's consider what we have. One ancient family who live by a ruin next to an ancient monastery, a biblical storm and a biblical plague, and you think electronic iPad tablet devices are involved?'

'That's what I saw,' Sue lied.

Stone moved right up to her, almost sniffing her. 'We'll find out tomorrow then, won't we?' he whispered quietly into her ear.

'If the de Lowes are home then I'm going to squeeze them until they squeak—for a bloody month if need be. If they're not, then believe me, I'll track them down.'

Stone returned to his seat and took a deliberately deep breath. 'Now, where do you think they would they go for these things? York? Leeds?'

Sue thought quickly. 'Perhaps, if there's any truth in the matter, you might be looking at this the wrong way. In my experience, Commissioner, dreams often highlight things that hint of something else. Dreams detect signals of worry or stress in the brain. So if you look at it like that, the key question isn't *where do you find the tablets*, but, perhaps *what you might use them for*. In which case, sir, there's every likelihood they may already have them.'

Stone stared at her and then the headmaster. 'Do you get this kind of shit all the time, Solomon?'

He turned his gaze to Sue. 'So, what you're suggesting is that they're after some kind of digital... code?'

Sue shrugged. 'I don't know. A code or a sequence or something.'

'Do they own iPads or similar tablets?'

'Not as far as I'm aware.'

Stone nodded and checked his watch. 'Right. Thank you, both. Sue you may go.'

A rush of relief swept over her. 'I'm here to help, sir,' she said. 'Please—if there's anything I can do to assist—'

'Thank you, I'll bear it in mind,' he said, smiling badly. 'Right now, Miss Lowden, I have other business to attend to. I've noted your offer and I'll let you know.'

8 SOLOMON'S THEORY

Stone sat down heavily and yawned. 'Still getting bloody nowhere,' he said to Solomon, irritably.

'I've had everyone screaming at me all day. Do you have the faintest idea what kind of huge turd is hitting this continent-sized fan? Well, I'll tell you. This place should be called Turdistan. No one has a bleedin' clue how this Ebora is getting around. It's a total bloody mystery.'

He rubbed his eyes as a wave of fatigue swept over him. 'And now the scientists say they need at least six weeks before they can crack it. Current estimates tell us we don't have six days, let alone six weeks!'

Solomon frowned as an idea popped into his head. He looked up as he accepted a cup of tea from Dickinson.

'Charlie. Something has struck me. Do you have a world map —even better, do you have a world map where the known outbreaks are marked?'

Dickinson nodded. 'Yes, it's on the global updater, sophisticated software developed in Estonia—I can hook it up to the projector if that's of any help.'

'Yes, it would be. And Dickinson, would you be able to play the recording back of me and Sue? There's something I said which may have a little more truth in it than I realised. About a third of the way through, I'd say.'

He sipped his tea while Dickinson played with his gadgets.

'This better be good, Solomon,' Stone said, eyeing him cautiously.

'It's a ruse, Charlie. And you may well throw it back in my face, but I think we're going to need to search a little more 'out of the box' as those young management fellows say.'

Dickinson pressed play. Their voices came across remarkably clearly.

Solomon perked up. 'A little further along. Not much. Yes—here.' They listened.

'... not only does it spread by touch and by bodily fluids, but it would appear to fly through the air ...

'And the strange thing is that, quite suddenly, it turned up the length of America, as though it flew west with the night. Maybe it did, who knows?'

'America? That's impossible.'

'Yes, both sides of North America and South America too, apparently. In a way it's a miracle neither of us has caught it—'

'Stop,' Solomon said and bit his lip. 'Play it again.'

When the passage finished for the second time, Stone piped-up. 'Headmaster, are you suggesting that this virus can fly?'

'No, not exactly.' He turned to Dickinson again. 'Can you spark your projector into life? Jolly good. Now, is there a kind of electronic gizmo which displays a time-line for when these occurrences took place?'

'By "occurrences",' Dickinson said, 'I take it you mean the approximate recorded times of Ebora infection?'

'Absolutely, I'm keen to see if there's a link to the disease being reported in relation to the time of day.'

'OK,' Dickinson said, 'I think I know what you mean.' Dickinson tapped away for a little while.

Soon, a large map of Yorkshire and the Northern half of England filled the screen covering the white wall. At the top was the date and time.

'Right, with any luck, this graphic should play the sequence from the very first engagement with the disease right up to the current minute.'

Dickinson dimmed the lights. 'The map should zoom out as the virus' spread increases,' he said, as he hit a key and the sequence began.

They stared in silence as the map stayed put while the time-clock flickered through the motions. 'OK, now it's midday on Friday—this is when the storm struck,' Dickinson said. 'Would you like me to super-impose the meteorological map as well?' He tapped away, reversed the time and then pressed play.

On the screen, a huge storm-cloud in purple, yellow and red colouring mushroomed out of Upsall moving at an amazing speed until it covered a circular area reaching from Northumberland to Nottingham to the north and south and Scarborough to Manchester on the east and west axis.

'As you can see,' Dickinson said, 'at about five p.m. the bulk of the storm suddenly dissolves into ordinary rain clouds.'

'Dickinson. Pause it there, if you will,' Solomon said. 'Thank you. Is there any way you can overlay a night and day shadow map on top—'

'Showing the sun's passage around the globe? No problem.'

Solomon shook his head. 'Amazing what these little tablet things can do, isn't it?'

The adjustment took a little longer. 'Right,' Dickinson said. 'By the way, just an observation, but notice how the torrential rain cloud dissipates at the exact moment the sun goes down?' He returned to the current graphic. 'Anyway, let's see how this works.'

The map continued on its time-led journey. As the clock ticked through Saturday, a few specks in red, denoting the virus, began to appear, growing in number but generally spanning out only across the immediate area of the Vale of York.

The map then went darker, showing night.

The red dots began increasing in number though the night and the map zoomed out a little to include reports of infection from London and the South of England. Through Sunday, the red on the map widened a little but mainly intensified in Yorkshire, the north and midlands. As Sunday night came around this pattern was repeated.

On Monday, three days after the event, the general increase continued overnight when suddenly the map zoomed out. As morning extended, a vertical line of red dotted the atlas, spanning an area in the northern hemisphere from Reykjavik in Iceland to Lisbon in Portugal and Marrakesh in Morocco.

Then, quite unexpectedly, the globe spun on its head, showing a less orderly but unmistakable colouring of red dots weaving through the heart of Africa all the way down to South Africa.

Now the globe spun again as day broke across the Eastern shore of America.

All three men stood up.

'Pause it there!' Solomon said, his voice quivering. 'Thank you, Dickinson.' He faced his cousin. 'Now, if my theory is correct and the infection has spread at night, as we sleep,' he said, his brow furrowed, 'the next bit should be rather interesting.'

As the line of darkness gave in to the light of morning, following behind, like a red wave, came thousands of tiny dots. And as they watched, Ebora quietly swept across the Americas, North and South, quite literally as day follows night.

When the animation finished the three men remained in silence for a considerable time.

'So, Ebora comes at night?' Stone said.

'In waves,' Solomon agreed, mopping his brow.

'Maybe it's a biological agent, triggered by the dark?' Dickinson added.

Solomon hummed. 'I see where you're coming from, but does it really add up? Ebora originates from Upsall, spreads around as you'd expect with no particular order to it and then, two days later, it follows a strict pattern. As though something has taken it on—'

'Maybe there's a night particle—?' Dickinson added.

'A night particle?' Stone coughed. 'Come on, lad. Even I know there is no such a thing. More likely, someone's taken a flight from here to New York and it's spread hand to mouth—'

'In a day? It's impossible, Charlie. You know that.' The headmaster said, sitting down. He removed his glasses and dabbed his eyes.

'Now, who would like to hear my theory?' he asked.

'I'm all ears,' Stone replied with a heavy drip of sarcasm.

'You're going to find it hard to believe, Charlie, but hear me out. First of all though, here's a riddle for both of you. *What goes by night, has many forms and is given to all people?*'

'This is no time for riddles, Solomon.'

'Actually, yes, I think it jolly well is.'

'Ghosts, spirits?' Dickinson volunteered.

'No. Nice idea. You're in the right kind of area.'

'This is ridiculous—'

'Rain!' Dickinson said.

'Wrong!... although in one sense you are, I suppose, absolutely spot on. Here's a clue. What does the riddle have in common with Sue?'

'Are all your classes like this?' Stone said, flatly.

'She had a dream about the storm?' Dickinson said.

Solomon clapped his hands. 'Now we're getting somewhere. Yes, she *dreamt* about the storm. The answer to the riddle is, "*Dreams*".'

Stone clapped slowly. 'Bravo. Where the hell is this going, Solomon?'

The headmaster was on a roll. 'We know that Sue had a premonition. And it was so clear and so frightening that it even made her friend scared out of her wits—scared enough to chart weather sequences from around the world. And then, lo and behold, her dream came true. In fact, everything about it came true! So what I'm saying is this: either she has some kind of psychic powers or, perhaps, she was given that dream.'

'Oh, bloody hell,' Stone tutted. 'What—by freaking aliens?'

Solomon shrugged. 'I don't know! But what I do know is that throughout the world, come nightfall, the one common factor irrespective of creed and gender and race and animal type... and anything else that sets us apart from one another, is that we sleep and therefore we... dream.'

Stone took his feet off his desk, stood up and paced around

the room, scratching his chin. 'Am I right in thinking that you're saying little alien bugs are flying about dishing out dreams?'

Solomon shrugged. 'I don't know. It is simply a theory. But we haven't got anything else, have we? And Ebora isn't caused by a lack of hygiene or spread by vermin. It is something else, Charlie. We may have to contemplate running with some distinctly unsettling propositions if we're to get to the bottom of this.'

Stone harrumphed. 'Dickinson, what do you think?'

The young officer had gone a little pale. 'I think it's utterly brilliant, sir.'

Stone rolled his eyes. 'Brilliant? Bollocks to that. Brilliant? So, what do you think I should do? Ring up the President of the United States of America and tell him to order his people not to go to sleep, in case they bloody well dream?'

He stood up. 'I can just imagine the scene at the White House. *The Brits have a plan for the Ebora,* he'll say, *this deadly virus they've unleashed on the world. It's called "Stay Awake". Gee, why didn't we think of that?*'

Stone's cold eyes bore into the headmaster. 'In my humble opinion, Solomon, that has to be the most unhelpful crappy piece of advice I've ever heard.'

Solomon eyed him curiously for a while and pushed his glasses up the bridge of his nose. 'Charlie, you're an excellent police officer with outstanding qualities, but sometimes I do think you really are one of the stupidest people I have ever had the misfortune of stumbling upon.'

Stone glared at him.

Solomon continued. 'You must realise that if what I'm saying is anywhere close to the mark, then what we're witnessing, right now, is some kind of alien or extra-terrestrial threat to us as a race. We may well be being led into extermination.'

Stone chortled. 'Wiped out? Don't be silly. Humans always find a way.'

'Hear me out, Charlie. You just said we haven't got an answer. Face it, our brain functionality does not allow us to think of anything outside of our general programming. If you ask me, my dear chap, something sinister and world threatening was opened up in Upsall. This power—or whatever you want to call it—is not only lethal, but without precedent. And, like it or not, it would appear to me that there are only three people in the world who know anything about it. My guess is that those three just happen to be the de Lowe children.'

Stone shook his head. 'They're bloody kids. Kids causing trouble with something they don't understand. That's my guess.'

'But so what if they're kids, Charlie? It makes perfect sense. Their minds are open and not closed—like yours, mine and most of the human race. Take a look at the boy, Kemp. What happened to him wasn't an accident of the storm: those burns, his malnutrition. They weren't the result of Ebora. And then, quite suddenly, he disappears off the face of the planet, leaving a puff of ash. In my opinion, he's a part of this too, Charlie. And it's something we cannot fathom.'

Solomon paced the room like a lecturer. 'Remember the stained glass windows of Upsall church? They clearly showed that after rain, comes pestilence. And Dickinson neatly pointed out that the terrifying storm cloud evaporated at the exact moment the sun went down. The question is, why didn't it continue on to pulverise the rest of the country? Something made it stop, which is why it moved on to the disease. We are being beaten and battered by something brilliantly clever, Charlie. And, it is utterly ruthless.' Solomon sat down. He needed a drink.

'Have you quite finished?' Stone said, as he chewed a fingernail and spat it out over the floor. 'Thank you for that huge load of complete shite. Let me remind you of a couple of things. Firstly, that I run the show round here, and secondly, I do not need any jumped-up loony theories about aliens and dreams. Do you understand, headmaster? What I need is proper, logical solutions and I need them now.'

The headmaster smiled at him wearily. 'As I said, it is a theory, that's all. Please don't forget that all I am trying to do is help you. I lost most of my students in this disaster and I, too, intend to get to the bottom of this one way or another.'

Stone acknowledged him with a wave of his hand. 'Dickinson, did you get the results of the ash from Kemp's disappearance?'

Dickinson sorted through some emails on his computer. 'Ah, here. Inconclusive, I'm afraid,' he said, looking up. 'The carbon dating machine appears to have broken down.'

Stone swore. 'What does it say?'

Dickinson read on. 'Well, the results that came back said that the ash was over a million years old. That the boy somehow —combusted—'

'Kemp burnt himself to death?' Stone spat. 'Incinerated into a small pile of ash in the toilet?'

Dickinson smiled. 'Hence why they think the machine is faulty.'

Solomon sensed his moment. 'Look, if I can get into that house of theirs, maybe I can find out if there's anything that might match what I found in the church. Surely it's worth a try?'

Stone eyed him curiously. 'Yeah, alright. Take the girl with you. She knows them well enough. But on one condition: you only go if they're not there. I don't want you interfering if and when we find them. Is that clear? Our team will be there shortly after dawn. They'll be back by midday. You'll know by then.'

'Good,' Solomon said. He stood up, thanked Stone and Dickinson, and let himself out.

Outside the door, he exhaled loudly.

If the children were there, as Stone suspected, then there was no way he could get the de Lowe's away from the cottage before the soldiers arrived at dawn. And if his theory had any weight, well, then what?

Dickinson sat down. 'Persuasive—your cousin. I like him. I wish my teachers had had his charisma.'

'But not very useful on a practical level, I'm afraid,' Stone said. 'Bloody lunatic if you ask me.' He scratched his creased brow. 'Play that recording again. There's a bit towards the end that I didn't quite understand—it's been nagging at me. Something he says doesn't add up.'

Two can play at this game, Stone thought.

Dickinson clicked back towards the end. Then back a little.

'Yes. That's probably about right. OK, let it roll.'

The recording came to life, filling the room.

'Sue, do you know of anything that might somehow link this storm or the Ebora with Upsall School or with any of your friends?'

'No, not that I'm aware of.'

'And does Gus know of anything, anything at all, Sue?'

'I don't think so.'

- long pause -

Then, not so loudly:

'Murder?... In the village ...?'

Stone leant in. 'What's going on there, Dickinson? Did she mouth something to him?'

Dickinson ran it back and they listened again. 'It's like they're sort of having another conversation, separately.'

Stone put his hands behind his head and exhaled. 'Is there a chance, Dickinson, that Solomon and Sue are taking us for one BLOODY great big ride? Why do I have a very deep suspicion that underneath this Ebora disaster lies some kind of murky secret?'

'What do you want me to do, sir?'

'Go with the crew at dawn. Watch, listen—find out all you can. And believe you me, when we get those kids I'm going to shove so much electricity up Archie-bleeding-de Lowe's backside that his hair will be standing erect for the rest of his life.'

His COBRA hotline buzzed.

'Mark my words,' he continued. 'Sometime soon they're going to have to come running out of their burrow and when they do, I'll be there.'

Dickinson strode towards the door.

'One more thing, Dickinson: I want you to personally radio me when you get to that cottage at first light, understand? I want you to be my eyes and ears.'

Stone picked up the receiver. 'Stone,' he said. He listened for a minute, cringing at the sharp tones cutting down the phone.

'Secretary of State,' he said, trying not to express his irritation. 'No, I didn't realise you've had the Americans demanding to send in their troops, nor coming here to find the cause of Ebora. Please remind them that the best help they can give us is in areas such as forensics and molecular science—'

He listened to the shrill voice on the other end.

'Then it seems to me,' he said, 'that we could do with them helping to keep the peace, not in threatening to blow the hell out of Yorkshire, or any place else they suspect.'

The Secretary of State spoke at length again.

Stone responded. 'On that matter,' he said, 'I have a lead in regard to Archie de Lowe and his sisters. Nothing certain, but I'll know more in the morning when my team have swept through their cottage. I'll call you at eleven with an update.'

Stone replaced the phone and mopped his brow.

It was out of control. The world was in crisis. The Americans now blamed Middle Eastern terrorist groups for planting Ebora and destroying the west, the Chinese were blaming the Russians and the Europeans were blaming the Americans who were ready to decimate the North of England with a very, very big bomb in order to stop its spread at source.

Stone shook his head. *It was already too late for all that.*

He thumped the table. Everything would be a good deal easier if they could just find Archie de Lowe.

9 ISABELLA'S POWER

The twins were by the track, near to the courtyard, when they heard Isabella screaming.

Daisy and Archie looked at each other, then Mrs. Pye.

'It's Bells,' Daisy said. 'Something has happened.' They rushed inside following the noise up the stairs. As they turned into Old Man Wood's room their eyes met a quite extraordinary sight.

For from the crack in the door they saw Old Man Wood's mushroom-littered body levitating in a cocoon of swirling pink light coming from Isabella's hands.

As they stepped inside, the fungi began to detonate. Daisy and Archie threw themselves behind the door as toadstools thudded into the panels and wall and door like rifle bullets. As the noise died down they poked their heads inside. Isabella, on her last reserves, stumbled and fell against the wall.

Archie rushed to her, holding her up.

Daisy followed. 'What is it?'

Archie glanced at Old Man Wood's chest, where the last remaining toadstool glowed from green to white. 'I think he's dying,' he said.

Suddenly, it grew.

Archie ran forward and attempted to rip it off but only succeeded in burning his hands.

Then, without knowing why, he moved behind his sister, extended his arms around her body and directed her wrists aloft. Daisy instinctively did the same so that Archie was sandwiched in the middle, their arms pushed forwards.

He shut his eyes.

'Be strong, Bells,' he said. 'Reach inside and draw out every sinew and fibre—and then go a little bit further.'

The lagging pink cocoon suddenly fizzled into life.

With one last, deep breath she screamed:

'OUT... **OUT!**'

She thrust her hands at the fungi and slammed everything she had at it. Archie and Daisy shut their eyes.

The toadstool quivered and swayed, but stuck.

'More, everyone,' Archie yelled, 'Together, all of us. Bells, ONCE MORE... on the count of three.

'One, two...

NOW!'

A huge volley of power rocketed out from the children's extended arms, the recoil throwing them against the wall. The toadstool flinched, then swayed and shook, before blasting off Old Man Wood's chest, circling the room twice like an out of control firework and smashing into the bed panels at the foot of his bed, spraying the room with wood and splinters.

As the pink cocoon faded, Old Man Wood's body floated down.

Archie and Daisy untangled themselves and picked themselves up off the floor.

Darkness filled the room save for the crackle of fire on the panelling spreading quickly towards Old Man Wood's bed.

Isabella lay on the floor, motionless.

Archie acted fast. 'Daisy, get Isabella out of here!'

He ran to the bed and, in two deft movements, lifted the torso of the old man and then hoisted him effortlessly over his shoulder, his body swamping him like a bear.

Outside, Archie laid Old Man Wood next to Isabella. He looked over her pale sweaty face, brushed her hair away and gently kissed her forehead. Soft breaths came out over long intervals, her face ashen and her eyes closed but ringed with dark patches, like a panda.

'Hey, Bells,' he whispered. 'You did it. You saved him, I'm sure of it.' He detected the faintest glimmer of a smile. A tear rolled down her cheek. He smiled back and wiped it off. 'Back in a minute.' Without hesitating, Archie rushed back in and, wielding a carpet, smothered the flames.

He ran down the corridor to the bathroom, emptied the contents of the bin on the floor, filled it with water and returned to extinguish the glowing embers. Finally, coughing lightly, he rejoined Daisy, who was dabbing Isabella's brow with a wet cloth.

'What were those things?' Daisy whispered.

'No idea,' he replied. 'What she did was... astonishing, utterly amazing! She's got wicked powers!' Archie said, staring proudly at his big sister. 'Awesome.'

Isabella stirred.

Daisy offered her a cup of water. 'Did you know you could do that, Bells?' she asked.

Isabella smiled.

The twins grinned but a groan moved their attention to Old Man Wood.

Archie felt for the old man's pulse.

'Nothing,' he said. 'It's like it's vanished.'

Archie wiped his nose, holding back his tears. 'We're too late.'

Daisy reached out and took the old man's hand. 'I'm so, so sorry, Old Man Wood.'

For several minutes, Archie and Daisy sat by the old man's still body.

Finally Archie spoke. 'What happens now?' he whispered. 'How do we find the tablets without Old Man Wood?'

Daisy shook her head. 'I don't know. We've had it, haven't we?'

A strange groan came from the floor, like a whiny floorboard. Archie and Daisy looked at one another, then moved their gazes downwards.

'Well, I'm not bloomin' dead yet,' a deep, croaky voice said.

'Old Man Wood!' Daisy cried, giving him a hug.

'Aw, ow! Gently now,' he said, as he opened his eyes.

His accentuated wrinkles formed a smile and his eyes shone like jewels in the candlelight. 'Apple juice,' he said. 'And a little bit of Resplendix Mix, if you don't mind.'

'Yes! Of course,' Archie said. 'Where is it?'

Old Man Wood forced saliva into his mouth. 'Coat,' he said. 'In the bootroom.'

Archie switched on his torch and tore off downstairs, returning with the strange medicine and a bottle of Old Man Wood's apple juice.

'Here,' he said, offering the golden liquid of the Resplendix Mix to Old Man Wood's lips. The moment it touched them, colour began to return to his cheeks. Old Man Wood blinked and sighed and then ooh-ed and ah-ed and grimaced as the healing medicine went to work.

Archie took it over to Isabella and did the same. Just a drop, like Old Man Wood said. The bottle opened for her and, before long, Isabella's eyes were wide open.

Then Old Man Wood smiled, a look of intense happiness on his face. But, as footsteps creaked up the stairs his expression quickly turned to alarm.

The children froze. Then slowly they turned to face whatever was coming up.

A voice rang out from the dark beyond them. 'What, in the Devil's name is going on?' it said. 'I don't know what's got into you lot. Making every effort to totally destroy the house, huh! What a terrible din, the likes of which I can't remember.'

Mrs. Pye peered into the dark. 'Been lighting fires have you? Well I hope there's a good reason for all this queer behaviour.' She shook her head. 'Your tea's on the table, or had you forgotten?'

She trudged slowly back down the stairs, tutting.

The four of them sat on the landing, chuckling like naughty schoolchildren.

Archie was the first to speak. 'What happened? What were those toadstool things?'

The old man sat up and slowly stretched his arms out wide. 'All I can say is that it's not every day you get poisoned with Havilarian Toadstool Powder. It's the most deadly powder known to... well... certain things. If I am in fact alive, which I suppose I must be, then I'm probably one of the few that has ever survived. So how did that happen? Who or what do I have to thank for saving my flesh?'

'You'd better thank Isabella,' Daisy said, clapping her hands. 'She did it and I have to say, it was wicked!'

'Well, I never,' Old Man Wood croaked. 'And how—?'

'Using a cocoon of pink light and energy,' Archie said. 'But your cool wooden TV panels got smashed to bits.'

Old Man Wood seemed unconcerned. 'We needn't worry about that now. What's important is that we're here and I reckon we'll be a good deal stronger for it.'

He shuffled over to Isabella and helped her up into a sitting position, and then wrapped his arms around her. 'Thank you, littlun,' he said into her ear. 'I owe you.' Then he picked himself up off the floor, stood up and ran his arms high above his head. 'Right, as Mrs. Pye said, tea is on the table and I for one am *famished*.'

Old Man Wood's body tingled as though it had been crammed full of electric-tipped feathers and his head fizzed with excitement.

Right now, his secrets, his magic and even his purpose were pouring back to him as though a chain had broken and unlocked the gates of his mind.

The time had arrived, no doubt about it. The opportunity to help the Heirs of Eden plot a return to the Garden of Eden had come at last. Finally, just as he'd quietly suspected, the chance had come to re-ignite the sparks of creation.

The children *had* been given the Great Dream and, it appeared, the legendary Gifts of Eden. Old Man Wood shut his eyes and smiled; that was enough thinking for now.

First, he needed nourishment. Then he would let the memories fill his head.

10 A LESSON FROM THE PAST

'Why did those toadstools make you so nearly die Old Man Wood?' Daisy asked as she scraped her fork around her plate. 'You said something about Havilarian Toadstool Powder but we've never heard of it before. Did you poison yourself?'

Old Man Wood chuckled, his chest heaving up and down. 'It is no mystery, my littluns,' he said, 'and, no I didn't. You see—'

'But what exactly was it?'

'A terrible substance, no doubting it,' he said, studying their blank faces. 'Must be something close by, but *how it got there* is indeed a mystery. In any case, whoever did it must have tried to put us off—to stop you lot making it to the other worlds—'

Archie dropped his fork and it clattered over his plate. 'What other worlds?' he said. 'I didn't know there were other worlds. I thought all we had to do was find three tablets. How many worlds are there?'

'Three,' Old Man Wood replied calmly and without pausing. 'There were five, but two of them blew themselves to pieces. Now, if I remember rightly, those ones were called Cush and Assyria—though I don't reckon there's much there any longer. They got a little too clever for their own good and forgot what Nature was all about.'

He leaned back in his chair and rubbed his chin. 'Without

sounding too miserable, it might be that Earth is heading the same way. But anyway, where was I? Ah, yes. The other two planets are Earth and Havilah. Yes,' he said, thoughtfully, 'those two are the last remaining ones. Of course, there's also the Garden of Eden, but no one knows what's happened there. It's been closed an awful long time, since the great flood—'

'*The Garden of Eden*?' Isabella interrupted, suddenly wide-awake. '*The Garden of Eden,*' she repeated, '*with the flood*? *That* Garden of Eden?' she leaned across the table. 'You're talking about the Biblical place, with Adam and Eve, the serpent, Cain and Abel, Noah... you know, Genesis... animals going in two by two?' She fixed the old man with her hardest stare. 'It isn't a real place, you know. Everyone knows that!'

Old Man Wood frowned. 'Well, er... no. I mean, yes. Oh appley-deary me. In the books, it's not quite the same thing... only a smidgen of it—'

'Look,' Isabella said. 'Those Bible stories succinctly explain life before the records that come after it. If you carry on like this, Old Man Wood, we're going to have to think again about putting you in an old people's home.'

Daisy rolled her eyes. 'Bells, I thought you'd left all that behind?'

'There's no way in the world that Genesis and Creation could have physically happened.'

'It's *worlds*,' Archie corrected her.

Isabella glowered at him. 'Life on this planet *evolved*, everyone knows that.'

'Ah,' Old Man Wood said. 'I was getting to that bit—'

'There's more?' she said.

'Oh yes, littlun. You see, once upon a time, there really was a great flood on the Earth—like the one we've got now I suppose—'

Isabella slumped back in her chair. 'And now, it's a nursery story.'

'Back then,' the old man continued, 'the "Rivers" flooded and remained flooded so nothing could travel from one world to another—'

'Rivers?'

'Oh yes. The Garden of Eden and Havilah are like Earth in a geographical, roundabout kind of way.'

Isabella massaged her temples. 'This is completely and utterly crackers,' she said. 'No known life forms in the universe have ever been found. And, furthermore, you're damning a whole civilisation of believers.'

Old Man Wood laughed, 'Bella, this isn't going to be easy—'

'Easy—?! The Bible and those other religious texts are sacred books, worshipped globally—'

'But the beginning holds the clues to what's going on NOW,' Old Man Wood argued. 'How else were they going to pass on the knowledge, the special secrets—?'

She glared at him. 'Entire cultures begin with this story!'

Old Man Wood shrugged. 'Well, no-one knew it'd be quite such a popular story at the time. And, anyway, it seemed like a good place to start—'

'Oh my God,' Isabella said, slowly. 'This is deeply, deeply flawed,' she said, shaking her head.

'What are *Rivers?*' Archie interrupted. 'I take it these aren't *real* rivers are they? And anyway, isn't Assyria somewhere in Africa? I'm sure Mum and Dad mentioned it last time they were back.'

Mentioning their parents made the children suddenly a little reflective and an uneasy silence hung in the air.

Old Man Wood turned to Archie. 'I haven't explained it properly, have I?' he said, relieved to move away from Isabella's grilling. 'But you're absolutely appley-right about one thing! *Rivers* are the connections between worlds—'

'Like wormholes?' Daisy said, as though a little spark had burst into a flame. 'Portals that transcend space, and all that stuff.'

The old man clapped his big hands together. 'Why, that exactly!' he said. 'Wormholes, portals, *Rivers*—they're one and the same thing. And yes, those places here on earth, Assyria, the Garden of Eden, Cush and Havilah, many others—were named in memory of their own worlds far, far away in other universes a long, long time ago.'

Daisy continued, intrigued. 'So, you said that people stopped travelling from planet to planet through these "Rivers". Why did these worm-holey things close down?'

'Hmm. Now, that's a good question,' Old Man Wood said, his face deeply lined in thought. 'War and a difference of opinion, I suppose. You see, those stories, like that Genesis one, were nearly right,' he said, his face darkening. 'But, oh, what a terrible time, even if it did save Earth and Havilah.'

'I don't understand. How could a massive flood *save* Earth?' Daisy asked, confused. 'Didn't everyone die apart from Noah? And anyway, what happened to this Garden of Eden place?'

Old Man Wood hummed as he thought about his answer. 'As far as I can remember, hordes of bad folk found a way of going back through the *Rivers* and into the Garden of Eden because, up until then, you could only go out of the Garden and not in. As a result, the Garden found itself being poisoned; its structure eroded and destroyed, and then ... war.'

Old Man Wood's eyes filled with tears, his brow deep and furrowed. 'A terrible war. People tried to make a claim on the Garden of Eden, and when the fighting finally stopped, blood covered the worlds, rivers ran red, flames singed the land, bitterness ran through veins, treachery mastered minds. Hatred and anger everywhere. A horrible time.'

Old Man Wood wiped his eyes and pulled himself together a little. 'To put it to an end, there was a moment of extraordinary sacrifice, one moment that alone is worth the Garden of Eden coming back to life.'

For a while, silence reigned as Old Man Wood stared into the distance. The children hardly dared to breathe.

Isabella took a deep breath. 'OK—so if what you're saying has some truth to it, what made this Garden of Eden so special?' she asked quietly. 'Why did it matter?'

Old Man Wood regarded her, his face deadly serious. 'Because, my dear little Bells,' he said, 'it's where everything began. That's why—'

'Everything?'

'Yes, everything. How do you think all these billions of things that make up the world around you actually started?' He studied their puzzled faces. 'Everything—dinosaurs, people, trees, fish, bugs, flowers, bacteria, clouds, particles, atoms, matter, energy—even your dreams—were all started in the Garden of Eden. From there, each creation began to grow and mature or die, or, as you lot say, evolve.'

Isabella shook her head. 'But I thought life began on Earth from a collision involving a meteor or a comet?'

The old man leant back in his chair and roared with laughter. 'Big-bangs, lumps of rock in space colliding with each other,' the old man said. 'Oh, yes, those life-givers did happen, but a long time before the living things came about. And it took an awful lot of knocking and banging them together to make the right kind of place. And who says they won't come again?'

Isabella's face had turned the colour of milk, Archie glumly stroked his foremost hair spike and Daisy massaged her temples.

Old Man Wood clapped his hands. 'But enough of all that. It's complicated—and anyway, weren't we talking about Havilarian Toadstool Powder?'

The children nodded.

'Well, young 'un's,' he continued, 'Havilarian Toadstool Powder is a very rare powder that blends itself to look like anything it's mixed with: liquid or solid—so it's hard to know how I digested it. It's so deadly that it's the only thing that can nearly kill me ...'

'What do you mean?' Isabella queried, her voice barely above a whisper. '*Nearly kill you.* Does that make you... I mean... are you... please, don't tell me you can't... actually... die?'

'I'll die if I return to the Garden of Eden, one day,' Old Man Wood said slowly. 'But if I don't, then I suppose I'll carry on like I have done, indefinitely.'

Isabella coughed and looked as if she were about to vomit all over the floor.

Daisy, on the other hand, shut one eye and ruffled her hair deep in thought. 'You're saying you've been alive... *forever?*'

Old Man Wood smiled back a little warily. 'Yes, littlun.'

'Blimey,' and then she swore, '... sorry, WOW!' Daisy squealed. 'You've really lived... that long? Forever, and ever, amen?'

Old Man Wood shifted, turning pink.

'Then, that makes you... you're... you're immoral?' Daisy squealed.

'It's *immortal*, not immoral, you numpty,' Isabella snapped.

'Yeah, yeah. Whatever,' Daisy said, nodding. 'Pretty awesome.'

Archie was visibly trembling. 'But you can't be—'

'Look carefully,' Old Man Wood said. 'That's me in all those pictures you've pulled off the walls.'

'I told you so, I told you so,' Daisy said, squealing with delight. 'Does that make you, like... God?' she asked. 'Please say yes!'

Old Man Wood smiled. 'I promise you,' he said 'my situation is nothing more than a terrible curse. A burden that is heavier than you can possibly imagine. I was telling you about the poison...'

But now that he studied the children's expressions, Old Man Wood realised they deserved more of an explanation. 'If you must know, I've watched you humans develop for an awfully long time.'

The children looked at each other and then at Old Man Wood with their mouths ajar, the enormity of these words not lost on them in spite of their young years.

After a long and very awkward silence, Isabella spoke. 'Look, this is a bit of a head-fry, and I'm still not sure I really, truly grasp what you're saying. So let me recap: You're saying that *Rivers* are connections between worlds? Yes?'

'Indeed,' Old Man Wood replied. 'They are the routes between Earth and other planets. Daisy has already experienced one when she visited the atrium.' He smiled warmly at Daisy.

'And you're saying that the Garden of Eden really did exist, right, like a huge laboratory?'

Old Man Wood agreed.

'And the Garden of Eden is a planet, and not actually a garden—with flowers and berries and veg?'

'That's right.'

'And that every living thing came from there?'

He raised his eyebrows.

'And then these other places went to war, and in so doing shut it down. And you've been around for the whole time since?'

The old man nodded.

'And now, we've got to discover three tablets by way of five random poems on five mangy old rugs to get to these other worlds—particularly the Garden of Eden?'

'Hmm, well, yes, I suppose.'

Isabella screwed up her face as though she was on the verge of bursting into tears. 'You've got to agree it is utterly irrational,' she muttered. 'Why?'

'To open the Garden of Eden, of course,' Old Man Wood said. 'It's a source of incredible power. The power of creation is something you here on Earth can barely imagine.'

'But why *now* and, more importantly, *why us*?'

Old Man Wood stretched his arms out wide. 'Something has shifted in the universe and, as a result, you have been given the Great Dream. And it's you lot, because your direct family line happens to have been under my care for thousands of years. It is a test, I believe, like those examinations you have at school, only a little bit more important.'

He rubbed his chin, thinking. 'Not all my brains have returned inside here,' and he pointed at his skull, 'but as far as I remember, this test was put in place to see whether those chosen on the planet were ready.'

'Ready for what?'

'To survive and move mankind on to its next stage.'

Isabella didn't like the sound of this. 'And if they aren't ready and fail, then what?'

'Hmm, good question,' Old Man Wood said. 'Let me think. I believe the species on the planet will be done away with.'

'Done away with?' Isabella said. 'You mean killed?'

Old Man Wood shrugged.

'Like the dinosaurs?'

The old man hummed. 'Yes, I suppose you're right. Those horrid scaly things were a terrible nuisance. But you see, when the universe had something better planned it got rid of almost all of them except crocodiles and birds and a few others. The universe changes—it just does that, you know. A new time is upon us and it's going to try and do it again.'

'Didn't an asteroid hit the earth and wipe them out?' Daisy said, quietly. Her bones ached, and her head throbbed. She remembered the cave paintings, and the final panel. Now, the puzzle was coming together.

Old Man Wood continued. 'It's not the first time, and it certainly won't be the last. There have been all sorts of new types of mankind—'

Isabella butted in: 'Homo habilis, homo erectus, Neolithic man and now us, homo sapiens,' she rattled out. 'Dad taught me. But I thought they came one after the other, in some kind of order?'

'Clever of you to know all that,' Old Man Wood said, encouragingly. 'Then, perhaps it's time for another one—'

'If we don't fail,' Archie added.

'Yes. Something like that,' Old Man Wood said. He stood up and piled the plates together, the candlelight accentuating the grim reality and faces of the siblings. Then he opened the door to the range cooker where the embers sat like small duvets of ash over glowing bodies and added a couple of logs. The children's eyes followed him as he went about his business as though he were a kind of pet alien; freaky, yet all theirs.

'Well now,' the old man said as he sat down again and looked up at the kitchen clock. 'Best get off to bed. There's a busy day ahead finding these tablets and it's already near enough eleven.'

'Shouldn't we be searching for them right now? Archie said. 'If it's so important, we don't have a moment to lose. Daisy, you thought there were seven days in which to do this... I think I can remember the poem:

'You have but seven days and seven nights

'As Earth moves in its cycle
'From first lightning strike and thunderclap
'A world awaits your arrival.

'How long is it since that first lightning bolt?' He rubbed his strange hair in recollection of the event which birthed his spikes. 'Three days... four?'

Daisy screwed up her face as she attempted to recall the days and nights, counting them off on her fingers. 'After tonight, I reckon there are three days left.'

'Over half way already,' Archie said, flatly. 'And, so far, all we've managed to do is pretty much destroy the house, get on the "international missing persons" list, start a Biblical storm, lose three of the animals and set off a global plague—'

'And we only have one tablet.'

'Yes. Is that good, or bad?'

'Shocking,' Daisy said. 'And we don't even know what the other riddles mean.'

Old Man Wood pointed towards Isabella whose forehead lay neatly perched on the table, her hair folding down in front. 'You won't be getting much joy from clever-clogs over there.'

As he said it, Isabella stirred, yawned and moved her head so that it lay on her forearm. 'I'm still awake,' she murmured, 'listening to your incredibly interesting conversation.' She yawned. 'And by the way, if there are any tablets that need finding up by the ruin, count me out. I would rather the world slips to a miserable end than scout around up there again.'

'Thanks for your huge support, as always, Bells,' Daisy said, yawning. 'I'm going to bed. Coming?'

The other two stood up.

Daisy hugged Old Man Wood. 'Are you going to bed too?'

'No, my dear littluns.' he said, 'there are a few things I still need to find out.'

'Like what?' Archie said.

'Like what the poems on the rugs are all about. Since I have no idea what Blabisterberry Jelly means, or where we'll find it, I guess I'm going to have to do some rooting around.' He smiled broadly. 'Before you head upstairs, does anyone know what happened to those poems Archie wrote down?'

Archie sighed. 'They're somewhere next door, probably ripped to bits when we found the tablet. I'll go and find them.'

Daisy laughed, thinking what a terrible state the room was in. 'Wait for me, Arch,' she said. 'I'll lend you a hand, they could be anywhere.'

11 MEMORIES RETURN

Isabella reluctantly stood up and, with leaden feet, followed Archie, Daisy and Old Man Wood into the dark living room where the embers of the fire glowed like dulled molten gold. After watching them poke and prod at the debris in the candle-light, turning over bits of paper here, shuffling others there, Isabella's impatience got the better of her. 'Oh, come on! You're all being completely hopeless,' she roared. 'Stand back, please, and leave it to the pro.'

They backed away and in a matter of moments Isabella's body flashed from one side to the other, up and down the room, her hands shooting here and there collecting up sheets of paper, her feet moving like a blur, her fingers shuffling through the slips of torn paper. When she slowed, she held a large, stacked pile of paper with, at the very top, the sections that made up the strange poems.

'How-the-hell-did-you-do-that?!' Archie said, wide-eyed in shock.

'Easy,' she replied.

Daisy shook her head. 'You know, Isabella, you're really taking organisation to a scary level.'

Isabella cuffed her on the arm. 'On the day of the storm,' she began, 'when I woke up, my feet and hands ached for hours.' She held them up. 'I know I can heal and protect with my hands, like

I did with Old Man Wood, but sometimes my feet move as if they're jet-propelled, I've been zooming about—when I ran back from the ruin I wasn't even out of breath.'

'We noticed,' Archie said drolly. 'Daisy has always been faster than you.'

'Well, not anymore!' Isabella said, her eyes twinkling. 'And the rest you know about.' She drew in a large, satisfied breath. 'It does seem to work better when I concentrate—'

'Same with mine,' Daisy said. 'Though my things are not only seeing kind of weird stuff but hearing it too. You won't believe the odd sounds I hear.'

She caught Archie's eye. 'For example, there's some kind of watercourse underneath the house. I bet you didn't know there's a noise dripping away, did you? And mice all over the place nattering away all the time. They are sooo dull—'

Isabella, Archie and Old Man Wood looked at Daisy with increased fascination.

Archie looked her hard in the eye. 'You mentioned it at the ruin. Read the poem, Bells!' he demanded. 'It's the third one, I think.'

Isabella obliged.

> 'The third you search is underneath your nose.
> 'It's clear, pure and cold.
> 'In order to draw it out
> 'You need to send a rose.'

'I thought it was: *clear, pure and warm,* like snot,' Archie said. '*Clear, pure and cold* has to be water.'

'It's coming from under the house,' Daisy said. 'Drip, drip, dripping-away.'

Old Man Wood suddenly became agitated. 'By all the apples!' he said springing out of his chair.

DOFF!

Old Man Wood's bald head walloped a low beam and the noise echoed around the room.

'**OW!**' Old Man Wood howled. 'OW, damnable beams!' he

rubbed his bald, moon-scaped pate. 'Always thought I'd built the bleedin' house too low!'

He sank down cautiously into the armchair, blinking and screwing up his face and rubbing his head like mad.

'I hope it won't muddle him up again,' Isabella whispered to Archie.

'Hmmm,' Old Man Wood eventually muttered and the children collectively breathed a sigh of relief. 'I'm sure there was once a well in the middle of the house, and if I'm not mistaken there was also, secretly, a tunnel connecting the ruin to this house, which many, many moons ago was a popular inn. You wouldn't believe how different it was...'

'Do you have architectural plans tucked away in your cellar?' Archie asked. 'I mean, you said you'd rebuilt it about thirty times. You must know the layouts like the back of your hand.'

Old Man Wood thought for a while. 'I can't remember... oooh... no. It's been so long, you can't conceive how long, that I've been waiting for all this to happen. So even though I now remember where I come from, which, I suppose, is soldered into my brain, there's an awful lot in-between which is a blur.'

He noted their disappointed faces.

'There was a time, several hundred years ago, when I thought it was time to return to the Garden, but it was a false alarm—even the Universe gets it wrong from time to time,' he smiled at the thought. 'Thinking that my reason for being had passed, memories started to ebb away, like the tide, I suppose. There's a massive amount that I don't think I'll ever get back, but the tide is rushing in again, faster than a galloping horse.'

Old Man Wood smiled kindly. 'We're just going to have to work it out together. If it's any help, I'm sure there was a network of cellar rooms underneath the ruin—like a labyrinth, I suppose. I got lost there for a couple of weeks once upon a time. Most unpleasant it was too, so I haven't been there much recently.'

'When was that?' Archie asked.

'Oooh now. Let me think. Probably a few centuries ago. Back

in the ...' He counted several hundred on his hand. 'About the mid seventeen-hundreds.'

The children looked at each other, dumbfounded, trying to get their heads around this vast stretch of time. A couple of days with Auntie Spoon felt like a few hundred years, so goodness knows how it must feel to be so old.

'Before Australia was discovered?' Isabella pressed.

'Hmmm, well, yes I suppose it is rather a long time for you little things to contemplate. Now, you must have heard about them Aboriginal peoples. Most interesting bunch and they've been there a long time—'

'I know we need to find the well and the tablets and all that stuff,' Daisy interrupted, 'but is the Q'ash Warshbit a real thing, did it *actually* exist?' she asked. 'Were those stories about Iso that you told us in front of the fire, actually true?'

'Oh yes! Most definitely, all those stories really happened. One day you might actually meet Iso—she's out there somewhere, I'm sure of it. You never know—'

'Please!' Isabella roared, giving Daisy a hard stare. 'Would you two be quiet for a moment! How are we going to find the dripping water?'

Old Man Wood paced around the room for a few minutes, alternatively rubbing his chin and his head, and humming to himself. Finally he sat down in his armchair and sighed.

'I think, my little ones, we may have to go up to the ruin and find those old cellars.'

Isabella groaned. 'But what about the "thing" we heard at the ruin?'

'Well, you and your MAGIC powers should be able to sort it out,' Archie said, sarcastically. He appeared disappointed that he seemed to have missed out on the wider, perhaps cooler, distribution of gifts.

The girls looked away, embarrassed.

Old Man Wood leaned in, his brow deeply ridged. 'What kind of *thing* are you talking about?' he asked.

Daisy started to recall how they had heard a strange cough and an evil bark and how, just as the bell had rung, Archie had idiotically jumped out and found nothing there. 'And on the way back we bumped into Mrs. Pye.'

'Are you quite sure the noise wasn't Mrs. Pye?' Isabella said.

Archie burst out laughing. 'Mrs. Pye it definitely wasn't. She's more like a strange looking angel than a monster—isn't that right, Old Man Wood?'

Old Man Wood looked shaken, his face pale and withdrawn. He waved a hand in the air.

Isabella rolled her eyes. 'You know perfectly well that monsters don't exist here in Yorkshire.'

'Are you absolutely sure about that, sis?' Archie said. 'Coz the panels on the bed didn't really exist, did they?'

Daisy caught his eye. 'Nor the exploding toadstools,' Daisy added, 'and the tablet coming out of the fire was pretty imaginary.'

Archie clapped her on the back. 'Come on Bells! *Anything* is possible. Don't you understand; our dreams—these strange events—are leading us to this Garden of Eden place. We're inexplicably linked to it, and nothing can stop it.'

Isabella looked crestfallen. 'Look, I know, alright. But if we have to find one of the tablets at the ruin, I'm not going.'

Old Man Wood noticed her anxiety and draped an arm around her shoulders. 'Bells, together we'll be fine, I'm reckoning. Nothing like a good night's sleep to stamp out your worries.'

'Are you sure we shouldn't start right away?' Archie said, persisting.

'No. We have to find Blabisterberry Jelly next,' Old Man Wood began. 'My friends, the willows, may just have the information we need. I'll head down there shortly. Tomorrow will be quite a day so I suggest you grab every moment of sleep you can.'

Archie nodded. 'So that's it then,' he said firmly. 'Tomorrow, at dawn, we find Blabisterberry Jelly,' he said, looking at the poem as though it would be dead easy. 'Let's meet at six for breakfast.'

12 THE TRUTH OF KEMP'S MOTHER

'As I said,' Cain began, 'I am simply telling you the truth. That woman is your mother.'

'Then take me to her,' Kemp demanded, 'this minute. We'll settle it once and for all.'

Cain was beginning to regret ever having mentioned the boy's mother. The ghost hovered away and let the overcoat slip to the floor. A body of dust puffed up and the specks played briefly in the light as tiny particles of glitter.

'What benefit will it be for anyone?' Cain said. 'The woman will not see you as her son as much as you do not wish to take her as your mother. Why complicate? Why muddy the waters? What can you possibly gain?'

'If you're saying Mrs. Pye's my mother, fine, let's go and ask her. If she denies it then I know you've been lying,' Kemp said. 'If she says that she is, then so be it. But if you're telling me lies, I will never go with you again.'

'You are not listening,' Cain responded, angrily. 'Of course she will deny it. She will deny ever knowing you because she doesn't know you exist, boy. Then what? Would you like me to present a fake, to make you *feel* better? So you can live out your fantasy of having a mother?'

Kemp didn't have an answer, but something troubled him. 'Why won't she remember me?' he said, staring at the floor.

'When your father died,' Cain said, as a brilliant idea popped into his mind, 'your mother escaped the accident, but not without terrible injuries. Because of them, she has no recollection of anything before that time. What I am about to tell you may be hard to stomach.'

'Go on,' Kemp said.

'You might think this is not possible, but it is,' Cain began earnestly, 'the old de Lowe helper—'

'Old Man Wood?'

Invisible to the boy, Cain beamed. 'Yes, I believe that is what they call him. He found her and seeing her broken took her back to the de Lowe cottage to care for her. But as he attempted to heal her, that old man did a terrible thing. I'm afraid, boy, that what you're about to hear won't be easy to digest.'

'How do you know this?'

'Your father's ghost told me this, so it must be true.' Cain grinned and thumped the air.

Kemp prickled. 'What did my father tell you?' he said, quietly.

'That Old Man Wood, for reasons I expect of pure bloodiness, cut into her head with a large, sharp knife and removed a section of her brain, a piece of her memory.'

Kemp's eyes bulged. Then a shadow of doubt passed over his face. 'I never thought the old man was the blood-thirsty type,' he said. 'Always seemed as soft as putty to me.'

Cain responded swiftly. 'One of the biggest lessons I can give you is that there's always, always, more to people than meets the eye. Take me, for example. At first you found me reprehensible and vile, didn't you? And with good reason.'

Kemp nodded, slowly.

'And now we're quite the best of friends, aren't we? You're learning fast, boy. I've heard stories about that old man from various ghostly friends of mine and I'm told that he harbours a terrible past—'

'Really?'

'Absolutely! Of bloodletting and gore. Unmentionable cruelty.

There's little doubt that the old man thinks nothing of cold-blooded murder.'

'Old man whatshisface? Are you sure?'

'When I heard he was in charge of the Heirs of Eden, I wondered for the safety of those poor de Lowe children.' Cain wondered if he'd gone too far.

'Have no fear though, boy. You are with me now, and safe enough. I will take you to your mother. But do not say later that you did not heed my warnings.'

Kemp sat deep in thought, twisting a knife around his fingers. 'I think I need to get it over with,' he said at length. 'I need to know, one way or another.'

'Very well,' Cain said. 'In the morning, at first light on Earth, I will summon Asgard. He must sacrifice two of his dreamspinners for us to travel there and back. They will need forewarning.'

Cain called into the air, 'Dreamspinner, dreamspinner, dreamspinner.'

Seconds later a tiny flash was followed by an opaque, white, almost arachnid creature, standing in mid air.

'Asgard, tomorrow at first light I must honour my promise to the boy. We go to find his mother at Eden Cottage. Can you give us transport within your brethren?'

Asgard tapped the air beneath him. 'There are many who are old and would rather die than see the demise of the dreamspinners. They are yours, for now. But be warned, Cain. Genesis, our mother, has returned from her self-imposed exile. She draws many dreamspinners to her. Even those who are old.'

Cain smiled. 'But as we know, Asgard, there are but three days left to open the Garden of Eden. The Heirs have but one tablet. The task is beyond them and all the while the Earth cries out of its own accord.'

Asgard stared at Cain, the dreamspinner's three black eyes boring into the ghost. 'I will be here just before dawn for your trip to Earth.' And in the next moment, he had vanished.

Cain turned to Kemp, who was cramming a chocolate-coated strawberry tartlet into his mouth. 'Now, rest, boy. Tomorrow you will discover the truth and it may not taste quite as sweet.'

13 GUS ESCAPES

Gus beamed his biggest, toothiest grin at Sue as she walked through the door, a big suit covering her from head to foot like a spaceman. She ran over and, without thinking, jumped up into his arms.

'Missed you,' she said, as tears formed in her eyes.

'Me, same,' he replied. 'Though it's not quite the same kissing a plastic helmet.' He put her down and stepped back. 'Cor! I'm digging the sexy outfit,' he joked.

Sue hit him playfully on the arm.

'I'll leave you two to it, then,' said the nurse who'd accompanied Sue in. 'To be perfectly honest with you, there's nothing wrong with you, is there, Gus?' The nurse looked her up and down. 'I have a strong feeling, young lady, that you'll survive without the suit,' she added, winking.

The door snapped shut.

'When are they letting you out?' Sue said through the protective helmet.

'Don't know. No one knows anything round here. They're all shit scared, apart from that nurse. She's totally chilled, but if I go "BOO" to the others they shriek and run away!'

Sue held his hand.

'Thing is, I'm fine, one hundred percent. All I had was a

twenty-four hour bug, nothing serious. Certainly not this Ebora, otherwise, by the sounds of it, I'd already be dead.'

'Thing is,' she said, 'you're a survivor. So they'll want to know what makes you so special.'

'You don't know?'

'Course *I* do,' she smiled. 'Just the other numpties round here.'

Even though her surveillance bug was pinned to her clothes in the changing room she knew she should keep her voice down. 'Gus. Do guards watch over you?'

'Not really,' he shrugged.

'What about doctors?'

'Nah. The nurses are alright. There's a camera over there and someone outside, but I'm pretty sure they're asleep half the time. Last night whoever it was slipped off at about ten o'clock. When I popped off to the toilet there was no one around. But they do the rounds in roughly four-hour cycles. Yesterday they came in to take blood three times, urine twice and... it's a wonder there's anything left. Do I look a bit pale?'

Sue laughed. 'Very—'

'Anyway, for the last twelve hours I've been the last thing on their minds. They're trying to make a serum or something. They're really not interested in me.'

'Good,' Sue replied, moving close. 'That creepy Commissioner is close to finding out about Archie and the others. We've got to help them. So I'm getting you out.'

'Cool,' Gus said. 'How?'

'I don't know.'

'What you've come here without a plan?' Gus said feigning shock. 'How very un-Sue like.'

'Actually,' she said as an idea rocketed into her head, 'I have. Where are your clothes?' He pointed at the cupboard. Sue marched across, took them out and, as subtly as possible, placed them on the bed.

Sue searched the small room and pulled up a privacy screen at the far end spreading it around the bed as far as it would go. She sat down on the bed and beckoned Gus to do the same. She unzipped her headpiece, detached the poppers and pulled it over her head. Her hair tumbled out.

In the confines of the small bed, she began to slip the remaining part of the protective suit down her body. 'Give me a hand, please.' Her eyes twinkled.

Gus' smile spread across his face, a mix of glee and nervousness. In a short while, Sue lay naked on the bed save for her underwear. She looked up at Gus beside her who was painfully trying not to look.

She giggled. 'Kiss me.'

Gus hesitated, stunned by Sue's directness. 'You're kidding!'

'Go on,' she whispered.

Gus hesitated.

'Don't worry—it's all part of the plan.'

'This is your plan?'

'Yes, and you're on camera, so it had better be good!'

Gus didn't need to be asked again.

In the corridor outside, the nurse hurried down to the desk outside Gus Williams' door and checked the clipboard.

Time to get the girl out. She looked up at the screen and for a moment couldn't think what she was looking at. Then it dawned on her.

She readied herself to march in but then she remembered being fourteen and the feeling of being kissed. She smiled. If the news was as bad as everyone said, how many more youths would miss out on this simple pleasure?

Better to gently warn them.

The nurse knocked on the door. 'Miss Lowden. Time to go! And don't think I don't know what you two are up to!'

From behind the door she could hear giggling followed by hysterical laughter.

Oh, to be young and in love, the nurse thought. 'I'll be back in five minutes,' she said and then called out. 'And when I come back, I want you out of there.'

The nurse smiled. There's absolutely nothing wrong with that boy. Cheeky lad and all. She'd give them their last few minutes alone. She sighed. There were more important things to be getting on with than peeping at them on the monitor.

Sue listened as the nurse's footsteps tapered off down the corridor. 'Right, Gus. Get in the protective suit.'

Gus leaned in again. She moved away.

'Uh?'

'Get in that suit, NOW!'

Gus looked confused.

'It's your way out, silly,' she said, her eyes sparkling. 'People round here know who I am, but we can't have you just wandering about. If you put the suit on, no one will know any better.' She pulled his t-shirt on. It smelt entirely of him and it felt strangely reassuring.

'I'm going to make a run for the toilet while you get changed. You'll need to make a dummy in the bed with the pillows—make it look as realistic as you can. As soon as you hear the nurse return, open the door in your protective suit, turn to the bed and blow a kiss, switch off the light, pretend to snivel like a girl and head down the corridor.' Sue smiled at the thought of it.

'Go directly outside and walk to the right. I'll join you. There are loads of people milling about and tents dotted here and there. Just walk like you mean it.'

'You're mad!' he said.

'I'm not, Gus. We need to help Archie and his sisters and I need you. And besides,' Sue said with a sparkle in her eye. 'If you ever want to see me nearly naked again, you'd better do exactly as I say.'

14 OLD MAN WOOD'S PROBLEM

The willows, Old Man Wood thought, *may not know about the water under the house but they are sure to know how to eat Blabisterberry Jelly.*

As the children headed up the stairs to their attic room, the old man donned his coat and boots and slipped quietly out of the back door, down the path to the potting shed, selected a clean, plastic, water-tight bucket and, using his torch to help him find his way, he trudged down the steep, treacherous terrain past the decimated remains of vegetables and ruined fruit trees. When he found the brown water line, he followed it, just as he had with Archie, until he came to the impenetrable willow barrier—the Bubbling Brook.

'Bethedi,' he whispered. 'You awake?'

'Uh! Eh! What time d'you call this?'

'Who's there?' said another voice. More voices joined in and shortly Old Man Wood found he could see the figures of sleepy elf-like tree-spirits rubbing sleep out of their tiny eyes and leaning out from their respective boughs or dangling from branches like bats.

'It's me,' Old Man Wood said, shining his torch around. 'I need to ask about a few things.'

Bethedi's gnarly old tree spirit bounded down the tree and perched near his head. The tree-elf stretched his arms wide and yawned. 'For sure, my old friend. We've all got good memories, hum-hum. Ask away.'

'I've discovered many things,' Old Man Wood began, 'like those little rugs with verses written on them. And you're right, time is running out on us.'

The wind picked up and blew heavy drops of water off the branches where they sprinkled down into the pool. In the torch light, Old Man Wood watched the water rings spreading out and beyond. In the corner of his eye, he noted that, attached to each tree, little elves moved along branches and stems to listen.

'Now before you start, hum-hum, make yourself comfortable,' Bethedi said. The old man wiggled his bottom onto a stump and leaned back on a tree trunk. 'You have questions? Well, good. I am pleased to hear it.'

'Tell me,' the old man said, 'what in the apples is Blabisterberry Jelly? Where would I find it and what do we do with the three tablets if we find them?'

Bethedi roared with laughter.

'Oi—you—cut it out!' sang a thrush from higher up. 'We're sleeping. You know the rules: no talking after nightfall.'

'Hum-hum. You are a right one,' whispered Bethedi. 'It's lucky that in the deep roots and folds of our bark we hold your secrets close. You told us Willows about three tablets and a very cunning plan, hum-hum. Well, do not be a-worrying; we remember. Your secrets are safe, even from those a-blasted birds, hum-hum. You want to know about Blabisterberry Jelly.' Bethedi took a deep breath.

'Blabisterberry Jelly, my old friend, is the most amazing, cunning, hilarious and terrifying potion ever created. Made from about three hundred ingredients—each one doused in magic—so that even the great wizard, Merlin, your old friend, didn't like to use it, hum-hum. Remember how you told us that he never really understood it, or how to control it?'

For some time, Bethedi told a few stories about Blabisterberry Jelly and, as he spoke, the nature of the mixture began to come back to Old Man Wood.

'But why is it dangerous?' he asked. 'And how does one of the stone tablets come from it?'

Bethedi hum-hummed. 'Now here's the thing, hum-hum,' the little elf began. 'If used in the wrong way, Blabisterberry Jelly is lethal. Too many grew frightened of it because they couldn't trust it. This was the reason you used it to protect the stone tablet. The riddle you found will reveal the tablet, but only to those who truly believe, hum-hum.'

And so, as the night drew on and the rain came and went, Old Man Wood rediscovered some of the mysteries of Blabisterberry Jelly, and bits and pieces of his long life and adventures. Finally, he asked about the water source under the house that Daisy had mentioned. 'Did I ever tell you of a well under the house?'

Bethedi thought for a while and hum-hummed, knowing what to say, but not quite knowing how to say it. 'Yes, dear old friend,' the tree-elf said at long last, rubbing his tiny, long beard. 'Once you talked of a well, deep in the hillside. The only route to it was through a labyrinth beneath the old castle. It was guarded by a fearsome beast you saved from execution when the Garden of Eden closed.'

'Why would I do a thing like this?'

'When the tablets and their riddles were put in place for the new time, the beast would have suffered an eon of sleep and, on awakening, either it would die or the new Heirs of Eden would prevail. Never was there a better test of bravery and cunning than to outmatch and outwit the monster.'

'Apples-alive!' Old Man Wood said, shocked.

'Oh yes, hum-hum,' Bethedi said, leaning back and gauging Old Man Wood's reaction. Then he continued, selecting his words carefully.

'When you put these spells in place many thousands of years ago, you did it to deter impostors who might stumble upon the secrets, but no one wanted you to go so far, hum-hum. The clues were too difficult and we knew you would never be the same person as the energetic youth you were then.' Bethedi's voice was deep and sincere.

'And now, my dear friend, you are old, humanised and soft. You have lost your magic and your youth. You fooled yourself that you would be young forever. You see, we trees understand the ageing process better than most things borne of Mother Nature. With great age comes wisdom and understanding, but also a loss of skill, courage and clarity.' Bethedi ducked behind a leaf and momentarily rubbed the corner of his mouth with it.

'I know the water is up and you have to find the tablets and try and get into the Garden of Eden—everything is talking about it—but you will struggle, if indeed your Heirs conquer Blabisterberry Jelly. You told us it was your finest riddle—and your hardest. And you were quick to tell us Willows how clever you'd been, but, hum-hum, unfortunately you kept it from us. Sorry, dear friend, but we cannot help you further. For this, you are on your own.'

Old Man Wood slumped further down the trunk. He, more than anyone, should have known better. Living things never remain the same, they change and evolve. Why would he be any different?

Old Man Wood thanked them and, feeling quite stiff from leaning so long on the tree, bade them goodnight.

He lowered the plastic bucket into the Bubbling Brook and watched as the water filled it. And with his mood as dark as the night surrounding him, the old man started home, slipping up the wet, muddy slope careful to keep as much water in the bucket as possible.

Deep, troubling thoughts filled his mind. From what he'd heard, he was almost certainly leading them to a violent, terrible death. He needed his wits, and a bit of magic wouldn't go amiss, he thought. B*ut where the apples would that come from?*

He heaved the bucket up, feeling the weight in his arms. And how would he explain the secrets of the Beast—or whatever it was—when he didn't have a clue?

15 KEMP GOES HOME

'Now when we arrive with the woman,' Cain said, 'her reaction may be one of profound shock. She will not understand what she sees and nor should she. Together, our appearance is that of an ash-covered human, as if we have climbed out from a foul, sooty chimney.'

Cain mused on his description and wondered whether this was the right approach. 'Perhaps I should let you talk to her alone,' he mused. 'Seeing an ashen man will almost certainly make her nervy.'

Cain lunged athletically and jogged up and down on the spot as if to remind the boy who was in control. 'If I do this, under no circumstances must you make her scream or wake the others. Understand? We do not want to be found. Furthermore, these dreamspinners are a cautious breed, my friend, and we would not want to be accused of being caught meddling with the prophecy. Goodness knows what might happen. I would be stranded and you, dear child, would more than likely lose your life.'

"Yes, yes, yes,' Kemp said impatiently and he pushed his wet arms up and through the arm-holes of the overcoat that hovered in front of him. Then, as before, he donned the trilby hat that the ghost preferred. Pain prickled through him but, in comparison with the first time, it was like a mild case of pins and needles.

Cain sensed the boy had settled and called out into the dark sky. 'Dreamspinner, dreamspinner, dreamspinner.'

Seconds later, two tiny flashes appeared. Asgard, along with another, even more grey-ringed dreamspinner hovered above them, their flashing magholes reflecting blue light on Cain's ashen body.

Cain clapped his hands and a puff of ash exploded into the sky. 'Excellent. As quick as ever, Asgard. Good, good.'

Asgard floated upon the air as though standing on an invisible cloud. 'This is Avantis. She travels one last time.'

An ashen Cain bowed low in front of the dreamspinner. 'We are humbled by your sacrifice,' the ghost crowed.

'My sacrifice is nothing in comparison to yours, Master of Havilah.'

'Time to go. Light breaks on Earth shortly,' Asgard said.

Avantis moved in front of Cain. 'I am ready, when you are.'

'Good,' Cain replied. And without further ado he dived through the extended maghole.

In the blink of an eye, Cain and Kemp lay on a cream carpeted floor.

Slowly they picked themselves up and Cain looked around, noting how the woman slept soundly in her bed.

The room, Kemp noticed, was simple, uncluttered and painted in a soft pink. Photo frames of the de Lowe children in various holders and old wedding pictures of their parents crowded the table and dresser tops. A scrap book on her desk stuffed with local newspaper mentions of the children, and a recent picture of Daisy and Archie in the football team lay on an open page ready to be glued in. On another table sat a couple of trinkets, a small silver cup, a necklace and a glass jar with an ornate silver top.

At the far end of the room, in the corner, was the television facing a comfortable armchair with floral pink cushions and a matching blue cover-throw.

Cain stood up as the woman stirred—this was his chance. He moved towards her and sat down almost weightlessly on the bed, close enough to place a hand over her mouth if she were to scream.

Then, true to his word, Cain removed himself from Kemp, his spirit flying freely into the room. 'Take your hat off, boy. It doesn't really suit you. And the coat. I'll hang them up outside the room and wait there for you when the hand on that time-piece moves to here,' he said, pointing at the clock.

'Good luck, boy. And if it's any help,' he whispered, 'you are the son of Tobias and Lucy Kemp.'

'Forty minutes?' Kemp said.

'You are on your own now. I need to pay someone a visit.'

Dickinson killed the engine and let the RIB drift in towards the makeshift shoreline. A huge beam of light scoured the scrub for a suitable landing area and within a few moments one of the men, a compact, shaven-headed man with a crooked nose, named Geddis, thrust an oar in so that the boat swung round and beached perfectly. Four of the five jumped out and, water up to their knees, pulled the boat until it slid noiselessly onto the bank.

'It's mud, sir,' Geddis announced. 'Damn hellish amount.' He sniffed the air. 'And fog closing in fast. Might take some while to get up that hillside, sir.'

Dickinson stared through the misty early morning darkness, a hint of light growing in the east across the hills. 'You two head right. Two left. Back here in five minutes,' Dickinson said. 'Look for tracks—signs of anyone coming or going. And if you spot anyone, take them. Under no circumstances maim or kill. I need these people alive.' He clicked his radio, snapped his headphones open and pushed them over his ears. 'Dickinson reporting in. We have touched land.'

Dickinson listened, then replied. 'Thick fog, sir. Visibility approximately ten metres. Not sure how much use the camera will be until we get close to the house. Scouting the perimeter area at this moment.'

Shortly, Dickinson's radio burst into life. 'Sir,' came the metallic tone of one of the soldiers through the radio. 'Foot-prints. One, two days old. Hard to tell—prints saturated by mud and water.'

'What sizes?'

'Some big, some small, sir.'

'Can you tell where they lead?'

'No, sir. Looks like they lead into the flooding. Impossible to tell, sir.'

Dickinson rubbed his chin. *Maybe they've already gone,* he thought, *exactly as that girl Sue said.* Perhaps they really had gone to find an electronic tablet. There was only one way to find out.

Dickinson buzzed his radio. 'I'm coming over. We'll wait for more light before we begin the ascent. No-one will see us in this stew.' He paused and pressed the button again. 'Reconvene at the boat in five minutes.'

Archie woke up sweating.

He'd dreamt of Cain. Cain laughing from under a cloak with such bitterness that his blood boiled and pulsed in waves around his body. Then, Cain merged into Kemp, becoming a monster before spitting ash in his face like a fire-breathing dragon. Archie's head throbbed. He sat up and wiped his brow, then opened his eyes and stared out from under the huge drape at the dark, silent room. His chin stung, from where the ghost had nicked him with the dagger only three nights before.

He rubbed the newest cut, a thin clear liquid moistening his fingers.

Archie checked his watch, then climbed out of bed and, treading lightly on the creaking floorboards, found his way to the table where he lit a candle and slipped down the stairs. In the bathroom, he held the candle up to the mirror and inspected the cuts. There they were—not more than a centimetre long, open, hot, angry and sore, and in exactly the same position either side of his chin. Cain's doing—to remind him, perhaps?

And anyway, why, hadn't Resplendix Mix cleaned it up, like it had with everything else?

Archie tried to forget about Cain but this was easier said than done. Those haunting words of his kept reverberating round his brain. '*Courage, young man, so you are feared and respected,*' and '*Your strength will be without doubt. I assure you these rewards will be genuine*.'

The iciness in that cold, deep voice swished around his head. Archie needed to wake up. He splashed cool tap water over his face and looked back at his curious reflection. His crazy hair, gelled into wire-like points, was tight and strong and he realised that his follicles somehow reflected his mood. When he relaxed, a softness came to his spikes which might, in a very tiny way, be shaped or sculpted.

He prised open the most recent cut with his fingers, and then picking up a nail brush on the side of the bath, scrubbed the gash hard, as if it were an ink mark. He winced as the wound opened and blood dripped out, decorating the white ceramic basin with deep crimson drops, each one splashing over such a large area, fixating him.

He was snapped out of his daze by Daisy calling down the passageway. 'Winkle, get a move on! I need to go!'

Archie grabbed a handful of toilet roll and pressed it firmly to the cut, hoping the wound would congeal. Daisy walked in, her hair stuck to her face in a gigantic mess.

'What are you doing?' she said, moving a clump of curly blonde strands from her forehead.

'Random cut that needed a bit of a clean,' he said.

Daisy screwed her face up and grunted. 'Your hair's still crap,' she said, as she stared at her face in the mirror, moving closer and closer so that in the candlelight her eyes looked particularly ruddy.

'Awesome. Wonder what else they'll do today?' she said, as she opened her eyes as wide as possible and pretended she was a vampire, snarling and clawing randomly at her reflection.

Archie laughed. 'Don't be a fool. And hurry up. We've got Blabisterberry Jelly to find—or had you forgotten?'

'Forgotten? Nah. I can hardly wait,' she said. 'Off you go.'

A cold chill hung about them in the dark kitchen. Isabella lit three further candles to offer a bit more light and Archie scrambled around for some newspaper and kindling which smouldered before igniting on the old embers of the fire in the belly of the old range cooker.

Daisy sat in a heap next to the table. 'What do you reckon it is?' she said.

'What is?'

'Blab-ista-stuff, or whatever it's called?'

'Blabisterberry Jelly?' Isabella said smartly. She turned her head skyward as if deep in thought. 'By the sound of it, it may well be some kind of fungus or tree-growth or pus-filled plant. Or perhaps the "jelly" refers to a kind of gelatine mineral deposit, like oil.'

Archie lowered four plates onto the table. 'What if it's some kind of jelly fish? A weird creature from out there in the flooding.'

Daisy looked horrified. 'Oh God, I hope not. I hate jelly fish. It'll be full of disease and dead stuff. Bells, can I have an extra helping of cheese on my Mrs Pye Special sandwich and a double egg? I'm starving.'

'Give me a chance,' Isabella shot back. 'The oven's not hot enough. Anyway, stop being a slob—get some apple juice out and lay up,' she ordered. 'Has anyone seen Old Man Wood?'

'I heard him snoring from Mum and Dad's room earlier,' Archie said. 'He's moved in.'

Isabella sliced the thin loaf of crusty bread that Mrs. Pye had left out, added ham and several slices of cheese to each, followed by a chunky wedge of tomato on top. 'You'd better go and get him. Make sure he hasn't gone mad or died again.' She dripped three drops of sauce on top. 'Anyone know where Mrs P is? Very odd that she's not put in an appearance.'

Daisy smiled wickedly. 'I'll go and kick a ball around in the courtyard. If that doesn't wake her up, nothing will.'

Archie tore off up the stairs in one direction as Daisy shot out of the back of the house and on to the courtyard where she found a ball and began to kick it against the wall right beneath Mrs. Pye's apartment.

As the water boiled, Isabella turned into the kitchen where she realised the quiet wasn't in her imagination. She was on her own, so she opened the oven door and slipped the first of the Mrs. Pye Specials onto the top shelf, and soon the smell of melting cheese made her mouth water like crazy.

Beneath them, in the courtyard, Kemp could hear a ball being kicked; its thudding reverberating annoyingly through the window panes.

Kemp stared at the plump woman waking in front of him. She tossed from side to side and groaned. Could this odd looking woman really be his mother? He didn't know whether to laugh or cry, to scream with annoyance or with delight, as a horrible doubt lingered. No—impossible. She couldn't be. Suddenly Kemp wanted to be as far away as possible, not in this room, not even within a hundred miles of here. Kemp stood up and gingerly crept towards the door.

He turned his head back to the woman, just as she stretched her hands out, drew them together and fanned them out, flexing her pink digits in front of her face. A snapping, cracking, popping sound came out of each little joint, but one thing caught Kemp's eye.

He stared hard at Mrs. Pye's hands. There, again. As she did it, now he did the same.

One odd, strange movement.

He pushed his arms out and flexed his fingers and then pushed his thumbs together, which, just like Mrs. Pye's, bent back at a quite extraordinary angle.

He'd never met anyone who could get even close to this level of dexterity, this bendiness, the way the thumbs pushed flat on their pads at ninety degrees.

Mrs. Pye opened her eyes, stared at his thumbs, then at her hands, doing the same motion. Slowly, she fixed her gaze at him, her initial reaction betraying shock and fear and now curiosity.

Kemp stared back, mid stretch, his thumbs bent back and for what seemed like an eternity, the room filled with silence.

'Please, don't scream,' Kemp implored.

Mrs. Pye scrunched up her face and eyed him curiously.

Kemp stood stone still, not sure what to do next.

'What do you want?' Mrs. Pye forced out.

'I just wanted to see you.'

'You're Archie's friend, now, aren't you?' Mrs. Pye finally said, and she shifted up the bed to see him better.

Kemp nodded.

Mrs. Pye tutted. 'And you've lost your lovely hair. If I remember, it was bright—'

'Ginger,' Kemp butted in. 'Just like—'

'Mine,' she said and, as she did, she smiled, although it looked every bit like a scowl to Kemp.

'Yeah,' he said.

The long silence returned. Kemp stared at the woman, her funny scars, her fat lips and her slightly long nose and, in particular, those sharp, light blue eyes. It was like looking at a distorted mirror.

Maybe Cain was right.

'I need to get up, young man,' Mrs. Pye said. 'So unless you've other business ...'

Kemp hesitated. 'Yes. I mean, no. I mean—'

'What's the matter? You got a problem with one of my lot?' She shot a look towards the desk with the scrapbook and photos of the de Lowe children.

'No, no. Not them,' Kemp said.

'Well then, be off with you. Don't know what you're thinking, creeping into people's houses. I've a good mind to telephone them police.'

But Kemp's feet remained glued to the floor. 'Mrs. Pye,'

Kemp stuttered, trying to find the right words and then, summoning every ounce from a place deep within him, he said: 'How did you, er, how did you get those scars?'

Mrs. Pye shot him her most dastardly look. 'None of your business.'

'The thing is,' he replied, as tears filled his eyes. 'I do believe it is.'

16 A SIP OF WATER

If his theory was correct, and the virus was being spread by something in dreams, Solomon thought his chances of survival were probably greater than most. After all, he'd been a light sleeper for years and he rarely, if ever, dreamt.

He woke before dawn, dressed and headed outside to find Dickinson with his team preparing to take a Land Rover down to the water. From there they would motor across the Vale of York to the edge of the Yorkshire Moors and then climb up to Eden Cottage.

They exchanged pleasantries.

'Dickinson,' Solomon began. 'Please keep me updated. If they're not around, I'd like to drop in as soon as I can to tie up some of my research.'

The officer nodded. 'We should be in and out in no time. With any luck we'll be back at lunchtime.'

'I've been given a radio. What frequency are you on?'

Dickinson gave him the information and gathered his protective helmet.

Solomon smiled. 'Good luck. Let's hope they haven't caught the Ebora virus, huh?'

As they departed, Solomon went back to his lodgings and then on to find Sue in the room above his. He knocked on the door. When he knocked again, the noise told him a good deal of scrambling was going on. Sue wasn't alone.

'It's Solomon, Sue. Can you let me in?'

More scrambling from inside. Finally the door opened. Sue's head peeped round the door. 'Morning, sir,' she said gaily, a twinkle in her eye.

Solomon moved in and shut the door behind him. 'Stone's obedient dog has gone to sniff out Eden Cottage,' he began. 'He reckons he'll be back by lunchtime, so we'll need to be ready to go.'

Sue looked up from her perch on the bed. 'OK,' she said. 'What do we need to do?'

'First get your hands on some of the protective suits. Three of them.'

'Three?'

'Yes. One for you, one for me and one for Gus.'

'Gus?'

'Yes. Gus who is hiding in the cupboard.'

Sue reddened. 'Sir?'

Solomon smiled at her. 'You must think I was born yesterday,' he said. 'Besides, I'm a schoolmaster. Come on out of there, Mr. Williams.'

The door swung open and the large figure of Gus tumbled out over the floor in a muddle of arms and legs.

Solomon helped pick him up. 'Right now, I am your friend, not your headmaster,' Solomon said. 'So let's be grown up about this.' Gus sat down beside Sue and stared, red-faced, at the floor. Solomon moved over to the radio and turned up the volume. Then he sat down next to them on the bed.

'We know,' he began quietly as the song crashed into the chorus, 'that the de Lowes are on to something quite astonishingly important. There are clues littered everywhere; in the old books in the library, the stained glass and, I'm sure, in their house, but what it is they have to find, I don't know.'

Solomon rubbed his hands. 'However, the world is falling apart at an alarming pace and until they get hold of this thing, I have a terrible feeling that this deterioration will continue swiftly and without mercy.' Solomon looked from Sue to Gus and back again. 'From the chaos out there, they may already be running out of time.'

The headmaster raised his eyebrows. 'I am increasingly certain that we must keep Archie and his sisters away from Commissioner Stone and his cronies. Officialdom will only hinder the children, and my instinct tells me is that it is up to the de Lowes, and only the de Lowes to find what they have to find. If not, then I am quite sure Isabella would somehow have managed to bring this to the authorities' attention.' The headmaster removed his spectacles and rubbed his eyes.

'I cannot begin to tell you how much pressure Stone is under. I'm talking pressure on a massive, global, governmental scale. And the problem is that he thinks finding Archie de Lowe is the answer to all his woes. As such, that man will stop at nothing to find them. He will want to extract every grain of information out of Archie and indeed his sisters.'

The music went quiet as the song ended, and Solomon did the same.

'Here's what I think,' he said as the next song burst into life. 'We need to be ready for two situations.'

'Two?' Gus queried.

'Indeed. The first is the eventuality that the children are at the cottage and are brought back here, in which case we'll need to set them free, at all costs. The second option applies if they are not at home. If that is the case, then we need to get into Eden Cottage and find out whatever we can in order to protect them. But it is vital that we keep this from Stone and send him and his boys on a wild goose chase.' He smiled at Gus and Sue. 'And to that effect, to get you both to Eden Cottage with me, I have a plan.'

Old Man Wood came downstairs holding a large bucket filled with water. He placed it in the hallway and made his way into the kitchen. '*Stop eating*!' he shouted, waving his arms in the air. '*Please! STOP, NOW*!'

'Why?' Isabella said. 'Is it the Havilarian Toadstool Powder?'

'No, no. You must be ravenously hungry for Blabisterberry Jelly—'

'You *eat* Blabisterberry Jelly?' Archie said as he chewed on a combination of ham, egg and cheese. 'Are you sure?'

'*YES!*'

'I hope it's as good as this,' Daisy said, forking in a huge mouthful.

'*NO*!' the old man begged. 'Daisy... please don't.'

Daisy lowered her fork and fixed him with her red eyes. 'So what does this jelly look like?'

'That's the thing. I don't know,' he began, 'but you'll find out, I can assure you. Believe me—but it really is vital you're starving.'

'I'm always starving!' Archie said, as he made to help himself to more.

'NO!' the old man roared and he reached onto the table and tossed Archie's plate into the corner of the room where it smashed into fragments.

'Archie,' the old man said firmly, 'I am deadly serious. This is no game, it is not a joke. Blabisterberry Jelly is lethal, it will kill you.' He turned towards the plate in the corner. 'I am sorry about your wasted Mrs. Pye Special, though.'

Daisy stared at her plate, desperate for another mouthful, but instead she stood up and tossed her plate across the room where it too smashed into little pieces.

'Daisy!' Isabella cried.

Daisy shrugged.

'Why couldn't you put it in the bin like an ordinary human being?'

'Bells,' Daisy said, flipping her pink glasses from her forehead to the brow of her nose, 'this is no time for rubbish bins. And besides, we aren't ordinary human beings.'

'Clear it up,' Isabella demanded.

Daisy snarled. 'Don't you ever listen? We are about to go and eat Blabisterberry Jam or whatever it's called and we may well die and you want me to clear up a plate?'

She grabbed Isabella's plate and threw it like a Frisbee across the room, where it too smashed into tiny pieces.

Isabella's face turned puce and she stamped her foot.

'*Enough*,' Old Man Wood roared.

The girls sat down, a little bit in awe of his raised voice.

'I learnt about Blabisterberry Jelly from the Willows at the Bubbling Brook last night. It's a good deal easier if you're hungry, but impossible if you're not.'

The children looked at him with concerned faces. 'Now, my littluns, first things first, we need to find it.'

'Find it?' Isabella said. 'Where? In the house, outside the house, by the ruin?'

'Why,' the old man began with a smile, 'somewhere round here I'm reckoning. But first,' and his face grew into a smile, 'follow me. I've got a little something you'll all be needing.'

They followed him out of the kitchen and into the hallway.

Old Man Wood produced a mug, bent down and filled it with the not entirely clean water from the plastic bucket. 'Now, drink some of this. It's a wee bit special.'

Isabella knelt down and sniffed it. 'Smells funny. Slightly sulphuric. Are you sure it hasn't been infected? If it comes from the flooding, you do realise it's almost certain to kill us.'

'My dear Bells,' the old man said, 'it's from the Bubbling Brook—'

'But your Bubbling Brook place is within the vicinity of the flooding, is it not?' Isabella said, knowingly. She stood up. 'This sample needs testing and at the very least boiling before anyone touches it—'

'It is *special water*, Isabella,' Old Man Wood said, his tone exasperated.

'But why is it so special that it doesn't require treating?' Isabella insisted.

Old Man Wood looked at her stunned. Then he turned to the other two for support.

Isabella noticed. 'All I'm trying to say is, why should this sample be absolutely fine in contrast to a sample taken from anywhere else in the floodwater because, to all intents and purposes, they must be from the same source and therefore infected?'

He shook his head. 'Because this water will enable you to speak, read and write in any language,' the old man said. 'Don't ask me how it works. It's an appley-funny-peculiar sensation at first, but you'll get used to it.'

Daisy shrieked. 'Ooh! I get it. I had some when I went into the glade—remember?' she said. 'I've had the coolest conversations with things. Did you know, this house is full of little notes from lovey-dovey mice?'

'Those are droppings, Daisy,' Isabella said.

'Depends on how you read them, Isabella,' Daisy said. 'All they go on about is food and sex. They're at it all the time and they go on and on and on ...'

'Like someone else we know?' Archie said.

Daisy hit him. 'Here, give it to me.' She grabbed the glass of water from out of Old Man Wood's hand, raised it to her lips, sniffed it and then, as she stared Isabella in the eye, downed it in one. 'Ah,' she said, and she belched and sat down with her eyes shut tight.

'You are quite disgusting,' Isabella said, wafting her hand in front of her.

Old Man Wood passed the mug to Archie. 'A couple of mouthfuls should do it,' he said, his eyes raised in earnest. Archie did as the old man recommended and passed it on to Isabella, who very reluctantly and only after popping in a finger and licking it, took a couple of small sips.

'Come on, Bells,' Daisy said. 'That's hardly going to work.'

'Just because I'm not as greedy as you,' Isabella said. She fixed her sister's eye and drained the glass. 'Urrrggh!' she cried, pulling a face as Daisy laughed.

'Disgusting... pheteucx!' Her eyes watered and instantly it felt as if her eyeballs were walloping about her head like pinballs.

As their brains fizzed and their ears crackled and eyes spun, Old Man Wood explained how it worked. 'When you concentrate on something you'll find there's a difference. But when you concentrate *an awful lot,* that's when it starts happening; you'll see and hear things... well, you'll find out soon enough. Don't worry,' he reassured them, 'you won't whoosh up into the air or grow a moustache or anything like that.'

He led them out into the courtyard where sunlight was attempting, rather sadly, to break through the thick white fog coming up from the valley. 'Now, littluns,' he said, smiling, 'somewhere around this courtyard, according to my old friend, Bethedi, there's a sign on a wall or a stone on the floor. It'll tell us what to do.'

'What sort of sign?' Archie asked.

Old Man Wood shook his head. 'If I knew, young man, I reckon I would tell you. Perhaps it's like peculiar writing you find on walls in the towns ...?'

'Graffiti?'

Old Man Wood appeared confused. 'I suppose,' he said, 'it could be graff... whatever that is. But you'll need to look carefully—it could be anywhere. Now, for apples' sake concentrate, the lot of you.'

17 DAISY'S DISCOVERY

Daisy's search faltered immediately. Instead of looking for the writing or the sign outside, she had been distracted by a peculiar, strange, high-pitched squeaking sound coming from somewhere inside the house, which had been bothering her for a couple of days. She went back in to the house to investigate and ended up back in the kitchen, rooting through the condiment jars and flour pots and herbs. Eventually she honed it down to one particular area and, now concentrating at her utmost, she could see the offenders through the cupboard door.

She ran back outside. 'Old Man Wood, you'd better come and check this out.'

Soon the others joined her. And even though Daisy's hearing was a hundred times greater than theirs, Archie and Isabella also heard a strange noise coming from within the cupboard.

'It's a trapped mouse,' Archie volunteered.

Daisy shook her head. 'Nah. Too many. Sounds like a whole load of them—'

'An infestation?' Archie said.

Daisy nodded knowingly as Isabella took two steps back. 'Actually, by that scurrying noise, I wouldn't be surprised if it's a whole load of rats trapped behind the door waiting to rush out.' She caught Archie's eye and winked, trying not to laugh.

'Yeah, definitely rats,' Archie said, waiting for the explosion. 'I hope they don't bite too much.'

'Oh, shut up, you two,' Isabella said from behind the door. 'Stop it! Stop being so childish. You know I hate them.'

The twins thought this was brilliantly funny. Daisy opened the door and both of them started shrieking, and then they howled with laughter at Isabella's terrified reaction. 'Oh chill your pants, Bells,' Daisy said, pulling the sugar bowl out. 'The noise is coming from here. I promise you there are no rats.'

Now that they were concentrating on the bowl, the high-pitched commotion grew. Daisy placed the bowl on the work surface as four pairs of eyes peered into it, baffled. For a while, all they could see were the granules of sugar. But it quickly became clear to Daisy that this wasn't entirely sugar. She found herself looking at a mixture of microscopic toadstools that kept on morphing into granules like miniature Christmas lights in a random flashing sequence.

She stood up and took a step backwards. 'These are microscopic mushrooms,' she said.

'Are you sure?' Isabella said. 'Not sugar?'

'Definitely not. Try one. I dare you.'

Isabella shook her head. 'Fungi? Here?' Isabella's expression dropped. 'What if this is the Havilarian Toadstool Powder?!' she cried.

'The stuff that nearly killed you, Old Man Wood.' Daisy added. 'What do you think?'

Old Man Wood studied it, but it was hard to tell from his expression if he could even see the fungi let alone hear them. 'If it is,' he began, 'it's lethal stuff, especially to me.' The children backed away as Old Man Wood shot off out of the room.

'What's it doing here?' Daisy said. 'It's a very odd place to live—'

'No, it isn't,' Archie cried. 'It makes total sense.'

Daisy looked confused. 'Go on, Sherlock. Reveal all.'

'I added a spoon of sugar into the tea full of rum that sent Old Man Wood bonkers,' he said. 'At the time you two thought it was a bit funny.'

Old Man Wood returned wearing a pair of rubber gloves and holding a small glass jar.

'Havilarian Toadstool Powder can't escape from this old thing,' Old Man Wood said. 'Would one of you mind pouring it in? If it touches me, I might end up a bit like last time.'

Isabella carefully jigged the sugar and slowly the powder emptied from one container to the other. As Old Man Wood sealed the latch, the screeching howls from the tiny toadstools ceased.

The children exchanged glances. 'But why only you, Old Man Wood?' Archie asked.

'Because the toadstools only poison those from the Garden of Eden, that's why,' the old man replied. 'Which reminds me—if we ever get there, the only way to dispose of these horrible things is in the River of Life.'

Old Man Wood slipped the jar into his coat pocket.

'You sure you don't want me to take it?' Archie said. 'What if you fall and it breaks?'

Old Man Wood smiled. 'Need to be some strength for this to break. In any case, it'll remind me to be a little bit more careful.' He ushered the children out. 'Come on, come on. We have the urgent matter of finding Blabisterberry Jelly.'

After a few minutes, it became clear that what they were searching for was akin to finding a needle in a haystack. Hundreds of stones from the cobbles on the floor to those in the walls, and even the roof, bore some kind of writing or message. And worse still, many had messages on that were so old and scuffed that they took considerable deciphering.

"... NOT HERE. SORRY," said a weathered grey stone that Daisy found. And then, as she neared Mrs. Pye's flat, she found another three similar messages. Irritated, she opened the door of one of the shed doors beneath Mrs. Pye's flat, let herself in and lay on the floor.

This old stable, used mainly by Old Man Wood, was

crammed full of things to mend. Dotted on the floor and hanging off the walls were an assortment of old chairs and picture frames and lamps and parts of old bicycles and even an old piano, its ivories removed. To Daisy's left sat a colourful carpet with a big hole in the middle and, to her right, a doll she recognised from her childhood that was missing an arm, a leg, and an eye.

Daisy rather liked it in here and sat down among the odds and ends as the dappled daylight filtered in through the dirty, cobweb-filled windows. For a minute the quiet allowed her to empty her mind. She closed her eyes, oblivious to the cacophony of new sounds and images around her. She breathed deeply and for a while sleep called her.

Suddenly she heard a familiar kind of noise, which was neither a squeak nor anything unusual. She roused herself. Perhaps the wind had pushed the door, making it groan. But as she thought about it, she realised there was no wind only the gently swirling cloud down in the valley swamping the vale.

She listened again and heard a voice. A boy's voice talking slowly, whispering and... weeping. It wasn't Archie and it certainly wasn't Old Man Wood. She listened harder and realised the words were coming from Mrs. Pye's flat directly above her.

Then she heard, unmistakably, Mrs. Pye's distinctive tones.

Who the heck was it?

Quietly, Daisy slipped out of the mending room, ran down the courtyard and bounded up the stone stairs on her toes, barely making a sound. At the top, she prised open the door to Mrs. Pye's apartment, slipped inside, tiptoed down the narrow, dark corridor and stopped outside Mrs. Pye's bedroom door.

She caught her breath, her senses on high alert. She listened. Nothing. Just muffled sounds, like... sobs, crying. Daisy desperately wanted to look inside but something told her not to. She stared hard at the door as if willing it to move aside. Then, much to her astonishment, she found herself seeing right through the wooden door, as though she had somehow opened up a large porthole of glass. And the harder she stared, the clearer the image.

There, in front of her, was the large figure of Mrs. Pye sitting on the bed with her eyes closed and a wide grimacey-smile traced across her face, a smaller figure folded into her bosom.

Astonished, yet intrigued, and nervous that she was seeing things, Daisy tip-toed down the passageway and, as her concentration moved from seeing to keeping quiet, she found herself staring at the dark magnolia-coloured wall. When she regained her concentration, the see-through portal reappeared and she found herself looking at a boy. A boy she'd definitely seen before. But who was it?

Suddenly it came to her, though it made no sense. It looked like the boy from the TV, the boy who survived the storm, the miracle child, the boy otherwise known as... Kemp.

KEMP!

She swore, under her breath. What was he doing here! Isabella's greatest enemy... here... with Mrs. Pye... how? Had the world ended already? Was she in a parallel universe or something?

She watched. For ages, they didn't say anything, just held each other as though *they had just found each other and didn't want to ever let go,* she thought. Daisy noticed tears streaming down Kemp's face and then she began to see the similarities.

The hair, the lips, the piggy blue eyes.

Daisy was filled with a strange prickly sensation. She shuddered as she remembered what Archie had told her about Kemp losing his mother when he was a baby. And she recalled Old Man Wood's story of how he had found Mrs. Pye in the hills, as near to dead as you could get, mangled and scarred with no memory.

The whole truth of the matter came to her: Kemp and Kemp's mother, Mrs. Pye. And at that moment, as she watched the boy through the wall, her heart pinched and ached for him.

And for the first time in her life, Daisy de Lowe felt ashamed of her behaviour towards Kemp. This sad boy, who hadn't had the best of luck in life, a boy who'd never known his mother or father, a boy they'd pushed aside and turned into a monster.

Daisy shook her head and moved down the corridor. How did Kemp get here? After all Eden Cottage was stuck out in the middle of nowhere. Furthermore, wasn't Kemp in hospital? He had to be, unless the TV interview had been pre-recorded. Maybe he found out and escaped? But it was miles and miles over terrible flooding.

It didn't make sense. But, then again, nothing made sense any more.

Daisy crept along, deep in thought. A shiver worked up her spine, a feeling as if something was watching her. She shook it out.

At the top of the stone staircase she noticed a strange overcoat hanging on the wall.

She looked back down the corridor. Kemp's coat? No, too big, but then again, too small for the voluptuous figure of Mrs. Pye. Perhaps it had been there all along, for years? Perhaps, Mrs. Pye had left it there as a reminder that she might one day find a man in her life?

Daisy lent in and smelled the fabric. Old, like moths and soot and peat combined, she thought. She sniffed again. More like the ash that drifted about when Dad cleaned the fires. She fingered the fabric, noting how intricately the patterns ran together, and as she did she heard a soft, deep voice, almost purring. Her arms freckled with goose bumps.

Daisy wondered if she should put it on, to warm her up. All she had to do was reverse into it.

She turned around and put her right arm behind her, searching for the hole that led down the arm of the coat. There. She thrust her arm quickly down into the coat and, as she did, she gasped.

An intense, cold rush sped into her arm, like icy treacle. She moaned. It felt so cold, but yet so warm and electrifying.

She twisted her body around as if to push her other arm in when the door flew open.

In front of her stood Kemp. His mouth open.

Daisy, in shock, let the left arm of the coat swing.

'Daisy,' he said, moving quickly towards her. 'I know you generally do the opposite of anything I say, but I absolutely urge you, in fact I'm begging you, not to put that coat on.'

Daisy shrugged and looked him up and down. Kemp had lost

weight and his baldness made him different; less childish, she thought, as a curious tingle ran through her. 'Give me two good reasons,' she said.

'Please don't,' Kemp said. 'For once in your life, just believe me,' he said. 'You really don't want to do it.'

Daisy felt for the other arm-hole. 'That's not even one reason,' she said, as she slid her arm into the coat. She closed her eyes as the freezing syrupy feeling swam through her arms and into her chest.

'Don't do it,' Kemp said, his voice betraying his worry. 'Get out of there, Daisy. *Get out of there NOW!*'

But already Daisy's eyes were shutting, and the sound of a man's laughter filled her ears.

18 BAD NEWS FROM AMERICA

'It's impossible, sir,' Dickinson said. 'Visibility is down to no more than a couple of metres.'

The radio crackled back. 'I don't bleedin' care if you can't see your effing noses, you're going to get up there and then back here, with or without those children.' Stone's voice calmed down. 'Dickinson, I need to know. And fast. We can't risk the helicopters. You're on your own. Do you copy?'

Dickinson shrugged. 'All I was saying, sir, is that we will not be able to proceed at the speed we anticipated.'

'What the hell do they train you for?' Stone yelled down the radio. 'Sunning yourselves? It's not a bloody holiday.'

Dickinson turned to the unit. 'You heard the man.' He pulled out some instruments from his rucksack. 'We need to move.' He delved into his bag. 'Compass, map, heat sensors. Everyone should have the same, if you haven't, I need to know. Understand? It's like semolina out there and if you get lost don't expect us to come looking for you.'

Dickinson had served in four tours: Afghanistan, Syria, the Balkans and Iraq. But never had he encountered conditions like this. A white-out as thick as custard spread out over a wasted, destroyed landscape. It gave him the collywobbles just thinking about it. Going in blind. Utterly devoid of sight. At least, he reasoned, there wouldn't be land-mines or IEDs or sniper fire to worry about, only bogs and brambles and random pools.

He never imagined he'd be plucking three children out of a remote hillside cottage in the midst of a global meltdown.

The country was already out of control. In places, reports said that the army were shooting anyone suspected of having Ebora. Elsewhere, the dead were being laid out on the doorsteps, exactly as they'd done at the time of the Black Death.

The difference being that this was viral, and back then it was bacterial. Both were horrible, nasty, silent killers. Both terrifying, unknown enemies.

They'd had the best of it tucked away at Swinton Park, trying to hold things together. But that would change and Dickinson knew it wouldn't take long. And he had half a mind to see if he could engineer a way of staying.

He shone his torch into the white wall of cloud and the light bounced back. The bottom line, according to Stone, was that they were doomed unless these kids came up with the answer.

That's how Stone operated, he supposed. As a predator sniffs out a weakness or a flaw, he'd chase and chase until he pulled his prey down, extracting whatever information he needed. And nearly always he was proven correct. He'd done it time after time, over and over again.

But, Dickinson thought, *kids on the search for tablets—electronic or otherwise—to stop the world's greatest catastrophe?* It just didn't stack up.

Unless you added in the Headmaster's idea that the disease was being spread by dream-giving aliens, then they had nothing to work on. Nothing whatsoever aside from the suspicions of every nation that it was some kind of hideous biological weapon attack.

Maybe they should bomb the hell out of Upsall and be done with it, he thought.

They had barely started before Simonet, operating the tracking system, came bustling over. 'Bad news, sir.'

Dickinson halted. 'What now?'

'The tracking device has frozen, sir. Satellite down. We can wait for them to come on-line again, but no guarantees.'

Dickinson kneaded his temple. 'No. We need to keep moving. Let's get up this hill and work it out from there.' He turned to the four others. 'Keep tight and don't wander off. If you do, you'll get lost. If by a miracle you manage to spot a significant feature, like a waterfall or cliff face, call a halt and we'll see if we can locate it on the map.' Dickinson stared at the Ordnance Survey map.

'If we head directly up from our landing point, we should be there in twenty to thirty minutes. Any deviation by the smallest degree and it'll take significantly longer.'

Dickinson's radio buzzed into life.

'Corporal,' crackled Stone's voice from the command centre. 'You may have noticed a satellite failure.'

'Affirmative, Commissioner. The imagery disappeared less than a minute ago.'

Dickinson could have sworn he heard the Commissioner sigh. 'Good. Well, you should know where you are.' The crackle of the radio cut out and then came on again. 'I, er, have news just in.'

'I take it this is not good news, Commissioner.'

The radio went silent for a while.

Dickinson didn't like the sound of this one bit.

Stone's voice was softer. 'I mentioned before,' he began, 'that various nation states believe that this area of Yorkshire is the originator of this global catastrophe. Well, the United States tabled an emergency proposal to destroy the entire area.' The radio went silent. 'I'm talking pretty much the entire northern half of the country in what they are calling, *a global action of absolute last resort.*'

'When?' Dickinson said.

Stone's voice betrayed his emotion. 'They wanted to detonate at midnight tonight, leaving a chance for the top brass to get out. But we told them our situation and, to my surprise, we managed to get an extension. So, gentlemen, we have approximately three days to find out what the hell is going on. I need you in and out of there, like yesterday, fog or no fog. If the children aren't there, let me know... in fact I think I'm going to send the headmaster towards you as fast as possible to see if any of his findings from the church at Upsall match up. Might be worth having you lot about to help him up to the cottage. Then I need you back. There's trouble kicking off everywhere. I think the news leaked.'

The soldiers stared at one another, stunned.

'For Queen and country,' Dickinson said quietly, 'and for this entire planet. Lads, you're now on the world's most important mission: to find these kids. Fail, gents, and we've all had it.' He patted a couple on their backs. 'Time to get a move on.'

19 A STRANGE NEW LANGUAGE

To the common eye the insignificant scratches or scuffs littering the walls were scribbles of one sort or another; love notes, bits of information, travel updates, even stories. Some had been added years and years ago and said things like: 'PLAGUE, KEEP OUT!'

Other inscriptions had been painstakingly crafted. Many were recent, and where it was dry, like under the extensively wide eaves, considerable bird scribblings made for compulsive reading.

Archie felt faint, and starving. He climbed the stepladder and sat reading the graffiti, mesmerised and slightly forgetting that he was looking for clues as to how to find Blabisterberry Jelly. A small part of him wished that his eyes and brain would stop and, when that happened, his concentration withdrew so he saw nothing bar scuffs and scratches.

Old Man Wood had been searching the house around the front and came back to see how they were getting along. 'Any luck, Archie?'

Archie buried his face in his hands. 'I never knew other THINGS could write!'

The old man chuckled. 'You lot don't know much, I suppose,' Old Man Wood said. 'It's a secret that's been kept back from human types. You see, humans have one way of communicating, everything else another. That's just the way of it.' He clapped

Archie on the back. 'It happened a long time ago, part of the Great Deal. I'm sure you'll learn about it one day.'

Archie's eyes rested on a message on the dry windowsill which otherwise would have looked like a series of distorted birds' messes. He concentrated hard and shortly a message came out. He read it out to Old Man Wood.

WANTED: SINGLE GEESE FOR LOVING HOLIDAY CRUISE TO SOUTHERN HEMISPHERE. SEE ORAVIO AT THE GRAVEL PITS—TWENTY FLAPS SOUTH-WEST WITH THE WIND. IF IT TAKES YOU MORE THAN THIRTY, I'M TOTALLY NOT INTERESTED.

Archie rubbed his foremost hair spike whose texture was comfortingly smooth. 'That wouldn't be the fat goose that waddles around out here looking a little bit pleased with himself?' he asked.

Old Man Wood shrugged. 'Suppose it could well be.'

'That Goose calls himself Oravio?' Archie said.

Old Man Wood nodded.

'And he comes up here, to... to find a date?' Archie sounded put-out. 'Like all the other animals in the area. Our house is like an enormous dating magazine. It's animal "Tinder",' he laughed, 'a giant community notice board.'

'What did you expect?' Old Man Wood said, putting a comforting arm around his shoulders, 'that other living things don't communicate?'

'But what do you mean by *communicate?*' Archie said. 'Animals don't talk like we do—all they do is sniff each other's bums or twitter or quack or baa or moo. They aren't smart, like us.'

Old Man Wood's deep laugh boomed out. 'Ooh, you're right there, they're not clever—like humans! Clever at putting themselves first at the expense of everyone else and all that, but it doesn't mean other living things can't and don't talk.'

The old man scratched his chin as he gathered his thoughts. 'You see, Archie, one of the flaws of the human race was to fail to recognise that living things do actually converse with one another. All these animals, these creatures and trees and insects and plants, *they know*. It's just that, after a while, the humans couldn't be bothered. Which is hardly surprising, I suppose, because the population of man grew and grew and there were other things to worry about, I'm sure. But it's a shame, nonetheless. Some of those birds are mightily entertaining. Look at those pigeons ducking out the way of cars. To them, it's a mighty fine entertainment—'

'Except when they get hit.' Archie added.

Isabella had wandered over and was listening intently to the old man. 'Don't tell me that trees actually talk?' she scoffed. 'Creatures, TREES actually chatting away to each other. You'll be telling me they watch TV next. You are joking, right?' Isabella said.

Old Man Wood raised his wrinkly brow and shook his head.

'See, Archie?' she said. 'He's making it up.'

'No I am not, Bells,' Old Man Wood said. 'Take your cat, Psycho-cat. Look at the way he moves, swishes his tail, paws his face, rubs against you and opens his eyes when he's cross. He's talking away to you—but you have no idea what he's really saying. You call it "body language" and that's what creatures do to give you clues. The next time you see Psycho-cat, just remember that.' The old man raised his dark eyes to the sky as if remembering things from a long time ago. Then he exhaled slowly. 'The great divide in communication is something that took me hundreds of years to get used to, especially with trees—'

'With trees?' Archie said.

'Yes, Archie, like those Willows which I wanted to show you.'

'But they don't *really* talk, do they?' Isabella said.

'Of course they do,' Old Man Wood replied, his tone a little more upset than usual. 'Trees are the greatest living things on the planet. They are way older than humans and far cleverer. Their roots stretch deep into the earth, their branches high into the sky. They listen out for every season; they play with the winds, with the air and the birds. They clean the waters and filter the air and they sing songs when they swish and they sway and they are funny and sad and beautiful.'

The children listened silently as Old Man Wood continued. 'Each living thing has energy and this is otherwise known as *spirit.* It's strong in some and dim in others and it is this spirit, this energy, which binds us all together. It is the energy we get when we love and when we care and when we feel. It is this energy that allows us to be.'

The old man sighed as he remembered. 'But the trees had a terrible time, especially after everything they had given up.'

'You're talking in riddles again, Old Man Wood,' Isabella said. 'What do you mean, "given up"?'

'Now let me think,' he said as he rubbed his chin. 'In the Garden of Eden, most of the trees moved, some faster than others. But when they came to Earth they had to give up their mobility. There wasn't really room for them all to be running around. So they found a suitable place and dug in their roots—like anchors I suppose—to support the planet, hold it together, help us breathe.'

Isabella shook her head. Her belief system was being mightily challenged. Unless she remained calm, she could see herself slipping into madness.

'So you're saying humans are rubbish?' Archie quizzed.

Old Man Wood laughed his booming laugh. 'No. Humans are wonderful. Smart, clever, resourceful. But they look after themselves first at the sake of every other thing, even though they tell themselves they don't. They always have and that, my boy, is why they've been so successful. And it's why you must succeed,' he said turning to them.

Old Man Wood noticed their perplexed looks.

'I'm afraid the water from the Bubbling Brook will shock you,' he said sweetly. 'But from now on, it is essential that you open your eyes, your ears—and your minds!'

20 DAISY AND CAIN

Daisy closed her eyes and groaned as an immense feeling of power grew inside her.

She could trace where the sensations of the cold, an almost painful icy flow, ran through her sinews like thick oil. A powerful, strange, exotic feeling began to build as a wave slowly swept over her, through every little vein, down every artery, into her hands, teasing the nerves in her elbows, her breasts, her genitals and into her knees and then to the end of each toe. The sensation tingled parts of her she never knew even existed. She gasped and cried out.

She could hear a low, silky voice talking directly into her brain. 'There is so much more,' was all it said.

Daisy moaned, but something wasn't right. She forced her eyes open and saw Kemp. 'What... what's happening to me?'

Now the voice came back at her and the feelings intensified. 'Come with me,' it said, 'willingly, like the boy and you will have everything. Say "Yes" and it will be done.'

Daisy almost gave in then and there as a slither of cold ran through her body and circled her midriff before plunging into her groin. A blinding flash blew through her brain and the feeling grew and grew before rocketing through her body.

She breathed deeply, trying to regain control. *Too much.* She opened her eyes. Kemp, again, a look of deep concern plastered on his face, pulling at her arm, pleading, yelling. Had he noticed?

Daisy gathered herself but her arm was stuck. Something in the coat held it.

She thrashed one way, then the next, but the more she did so, the more a curious sensation built in the fingers of the trapped arm. At first it felt like pricks from small, sharp pins but soon these joined together until collectively they hurt more and more as if thousands of pins were thrust in. Soon it burned. She gritted her teeth. Her hair was singeing.

'Let go of me!' she seethed.

She tugged, but it stuck, as if caught in a vice. 'Let go of me, now!' she cried.

'Let her go!' Kemp said, his voice firm. 'She does not go willingly.'

The pain receded.

'Let her go now, or I will never go with you again.'

Suddenly, Daisy lay on the floor, her arm red and tender halfway to her elbow. The delicate hairs on the backs of her fingers were singed.

Instantly, she knew that Kemp had suffered the same fate.

'Please, go... now,' said a soft voice above her—Kemp's voice. A voice so gentle, she'd never have believed him possible of uttering it.

In a millisecond, Kemp had taken her place and his arms pushed into the sleeves of the grey coat. From out of the coat pocket he pulled out a curious-looking trilby hat. He boxed it out and, with a tiny smile on his face, slipped it over his head. As he did this, not once did he take his eyes off her. Not once did his expression alter.

Then, as if by magic, underneath the long coat, Kemp suddenly morphed into a human figure of ash. But the person the ashen features revealed was an older-looking human with sweptback hair and scabbed skin marks. Daisy scampered backwards as the figure loomed over her and then pounced towards her face, ash falling from it.

'Come with me,' it demanded. 'Come. You know you want

to.' Ash fizzed out of its mouth showering her like a fountain. And then, with a windy chuckle, the grey-coated ash-man stood up and dived headfirst down the stairwell, vanishing in a tiny blue flash.

Daisy's heartbeat raced and she looked down at nothing but a tiny pile of ash on the stone stairs below.

21 DECIPHERING THE CODE

Daisy sat in stunned silence. Her red eyes shone brightly, like the depressed brake lights of a car. Her heart thumped. That, she thought, was weirder than when she'd landed in the Atrium or whatever place that was.

What sort of monster lived in a coat? Was it a ghost? She shook as she thought about it, her whole body resonating at the memory. Those feelings—so cold and painful and yet hot and exhilarating—at the same time. Like her dreams.

And how come Kemp was with it? In fact, was Kemp actually dead, or alive, or now some kind of spirit? But she'd felt the flesh and blood of his arm pulling at her, trying to release her from the creature and thinking of that, she'd sniffed the sharp smell, the distinctive pungent tang of his burned hair.

Kemp had warned her, so why didn't she listen? Was she simply so bloody against him she wasn't prepared to give him a chance? And then she thought of Kemp talking to Mrs. Pye. His tears and their soft, loving words. Inside, Daisy felt terrible and her heart wanted to reach out and tell him that he was OK, and that she understood.

'Mrs. Pye,' she said as she leapt up and ran along the corridor. She stood outside Mrs. Pye's bedroom door and swallowed. *What should she say? What words would be comforting enough for Mrs. Pye or... simply, right?*

She knocked on the door and, with a deep breath, walked in. Mrs. Pye sat on the bed, her body swaying from side to side, tears rolling down her cheeks.

Daisy ran up and threw her arms around her. But although Mrs. Pye reacted by closing her eyes, she continued swaying, murmuring incoherently.

When Daisy pulled out of her embrace and took a step back, Mrs. Pye carried on doing the same thing, her eyes staring, lost across the room, her voice like a slow chant, her body rocking back and forth, to and fro.

Daisy waved her arms in front of her face.

Oh no, she thought. *Mrs. Pye has slipped into a mental state of shock.*

For a little while, Daisy did everything she could think of to try and snap Mrs. Pye out of her state. She tried yelling 'BOO' suddenly and very loudly in her ear, she pinched her cheek and gave her a mild Chinese burn, but Mrs. Pye was immovable. Daisy then did a dance right in front of her, which in normal circumstances would have had Mrs. Pye chortling and telling her to "stop it, you daft brush".

Finally, Archie appeared. 'What are you doing?' he said, as he popped his head around the door.

Daisy shrugged. 'It's Mrs. Pye. She's away with the with the bleeding fairies. Watch this.' Daisy then proceeded to swirl like a Spanish dancer right in front of Mrs. Pye before clapping her hands loudly right in front of her face.

'I see what you mean,' Archie said, a frown ridging his forehead. 'Any idea what's set her off? Something must have happened.' He frowned. 'Maybe she saw that the authorities were looking for us on TV, that we're wanted. Or maybe it's because we've smashed up the house—'

"Nah. I found her like this. And we do look a bit weird,' Daisy said.

Right now, she needed to get her head together about what

had happened with Kemp, and how he'd discovered that Mrs. Pye was Kemp's mother, and how she'd been manhandled by a ghost let alone explain it all to Archie. She shook her head.

Archie put a hand on her shoulder. 'Sorry to drag you away, Daisy, but we could do with a hand out there... it's a bit complicated and we're getting nowhere. We'll check up on Mrs. P later, OK?'

Archie first of all gave Mrs. Pye a hug and then Daisy moved over to Mrs. Pye and, looking into her eyes, planted a small kiss on her forehead and said, 'we'll be back shortly to make sure you're alright, I promise.'

'So, here's the problem,' Archie said. 'When you concentrate the whole place turns into of a nightmare of notes and letters.'

'I know. Irritating, isn't it?'

They met up with Isabella and Old Man Wood in the middle of the courtyard.

'You know something,' Daisy said dreamily as she stared at the wall next to the front door, 'it's probably a good thing that humans don't understand any of this. Listen to this classic.' She moved in and pointed to the windowsill.

'NEST VACANT,' she read raising her eyebrows.

'FAMILY EATEN. NEST WILL ROT IF NOT OCCUPIED. LOOK IN THE HAWTHORN BY THE BUBBLING BROOK. ASK FOR SPRINKLE THE THRUSH.'

Daisy shook her head. 'And there's more. Listen to this one.

'PREDATOR EVASION COURSES: PROTECT YOURSELF AND YOUR FAMILY. BASED ON GROUND BREAKING RESEARCH BY DR. ROB ROBIN, GUARANTEED 35 PERCENT SURVIVAL INCREASE.

'And then, in smaller writing, it says; *Conditions apply.'*

Isabella burst out laughing. 'They're adverts!'

Archie kicked a loose stone, which flew out of the courtyard towards the path. 'But it isn't helping us find Blaster-whatever-it-is Jelly. And I'm starving. Are you sure we can't eat something?'

'Certainly not,' Old Man Wood replied, groaning as he attempted to move some loose stone slabs from the corner of the yard.

Daisy shook her head. 'What did the willow trees say? Are you sure they meant this courtyard, not the ruin?'

'Oh yes, this is the right place alright.'

Daisy sat down. 'Have we checked everywhere?'

'Twice,' Archie said, settling beside her. 'Can't your eyes find it?'

Daisy looked incredulous. 'No, Archie, apparently they can't,' she said flatly.

Archie's stomach rumbled. It he wasn't allowed to eat any food at least he could look at it. He decided to nip inside and sneak a peek inside the fridge.

He stood up, walked across the steps and, just as he opened the front door, he looked down at the metal foot-grate. Bending down, he moved it aside and there, in large letters, were the words:

'BLABISTERBERRY JELLY'

'Over here! I think I've found it!' he said. In no time four faces were peering over the stone.

'There's small writing beneath it,' Daisy said. 'Bit worn out—looks like instructions.'

Archie sniffed. 'I'll pull up the slab? It'll be underneath.'

'I don't think so—' she said, but already Archie was on his hands and knees trying to squeeze his fingers into the gap on one side. He groaned and pulled and heaved until his face started to sweat.

Daisy watched Archie straining. 'You haven't lost your strength, have you?'

Archie bristled and he made an even greater effort.

Eventually he relented.

Daisy smiled. 'Now, let me read the instructions to you,' she said, in a very irritating kind of school-mistressey manner. She adjusted the pink glasses on the bridge of her nose and cleared her throat.

'*TO OPEN ME,*' she read, '*KNOCK THREE TIMES* AND *PRESS ON EDEN'S*... and the final word is scuffed. It goes something like, blank, blank, blank, maybe blank, then a P, blank, blank. I think.'

_ _ _ ? P _ _

They all looked at each other quizzically.

'Gatepost?' Isabella said, getting excited. 'It could be a... gatepost?

'We don't have a gatepost, we have a rock,' Daisy said.

Archie rubbed a hair spike. 'The rock does look like a gatepost,' he said hopefully. 'But it's missing a "T".'

'It's a massive grey rock, or obelisk, with *"Eden Cottage"* etched into it.' Daisy said. She ran to the top of the yard and concentrated hard on the gate-rock and just as before all sorts of writing started to appear.

A fresh one, not yet blurred from the rain read:

"NOPPY LOVES SCROPPY. BUNNY KISSES."

Further up were watered down names from a deer called Lush, a fox called Sand and a badger called Leaf. Perhaps they lived here too. Then one caught her eye, nestled under the dry overhang of the stone.

"RED TO THE RABBITY FAMILY. SORRY ABOUT FLOPPY BUT I AM A FOX. THE FLOODS HAVE MADE IT VERY DIFFICULT TO EAT ANYWHERE ELSE. DON'T HOLD IT AGAINST ME."

'Wow!' Daisy said under her breath. 'Incredible.' And then she just made out a very recent addition beneath it:

"BEWARE. EVIL SURROUNDS THE OLD RUIN FOR ALL."

Daisy swallowed. 'There's nothing!' she shouted.

'Nothing?' said Archie. 'Are you sure? I mean magic eyes or not, were you concentrating hard enough?' he said sarcastically.

'Shut up, Arch—what's got into you?' Isabella said. 'You're getting really nauseating.'

'If it's that irritating, zap me with your hands?'

'I'm very tempted, Archie.'

Archie didn't react. He stood dead still. A brilliant idea had suddenly leapt into his head.

'I think I've got it!' he cried. 'Listen. It's got nothing to do with the gatepost. It's *carpet*—you know: blank, blank, blank, P, blank, blank.'

'The hand-mark on one of the rugs,' Isabella cried. 'Archie's right!' She ran inside and, moments later, returned with the carpet rolled under her arm.

She re-read the riddle: *'TO OPEN ME, KNOCK THREE TIMES* AND *PRESS ON EDEN'S CARPET.'* Isabella looked delightedly at her siblings. 'Well, there's only one way to find out. Who's going to press and who's going to knock?'

'I'll press on the hand mark. Archie knocks,' Daisy said. 'Are you ready? On the count of three.'

'One, two, THREE'

Daisy moved her hand in alignment with the smaller outline of the hand on the carpet.

KNOCK, KNOCK, KNOCK.

They held their breath.

Then, ever so slowly, the paving slab with *'Blabisterberry Jelly'* written on it started to fade away and in its place appeared a stone stairway.

The children and Old Man Wood exchanged glances. 'We did it,' Isabella said, nervously.

From the bottom of the steps a sweet perfume wafted up to them. They stared down. Then a lovely, sweet voice came up to them.

'Hello there!' it said. 'Well, now, there's no time to dally. Come along, come along.'

Isabella cringed, her body filled with trepidation. 'Oh hells-bells,' she whispered. 'We've really got to go down there, haven't we?'

22 TROOPS ARRIVE AT EDEN COTTAGE

'Look, sir, buildings,' Geddis said, relieved. 'The fog's a little thinner up here.'

The stony corner of a building, like a ship, quickly emerged out of the white, creamy soup.

'OK, quiet. Protective clothing on, please.' Dickinson said.

Without hesitating, the troops donned the white protective helmets and gloves.

'Call in on your MICs please.' The troops responded. 'Geddis, anything on the sensors?'

Geddis shook his head. 'Nothing, here, sir.'

Dickinson waved them forward. 'Remember, if you see them, do not shoot—is that perfectly clear? Shoot as a very last resort and not to kill. Did you get that, Talbot?'

The four soldiers responded to their commander in the affirmative. At least there were no problems with the microphones and earpieces.

By now the fog had caught them up and, in order not to get swamped by the huge blanket of white cloud, the troops moved silently, hugging the wall, moving in a line of five.

Dickinson stopped near the front door. 'Geddis, do you read anything?'

'Negative. Nothing in the courtyard area. And as far as I can tell nothing through these three windows on this side of the house.'

'Inside,' Dickinson commanded, tipping his head.

The men moved fast, opened the door and entered the hallway.

'Looks like someone's been in here already, sir,' said Pearce, the tall, wiry commando, as he inspected the mess of frames, canvasses and pictures lying in heaps all over the floor. 'Someone's given the place a good going over. I reckon they've already been and gone.'

Dickinson sucked in a breath as he inspected the pictures. 'Maybe they searched the house and took the kids.' *After all,* he thought, *the helicopter hadn't reported any sign of life during its reconnaissance mission.*

His earpiece crackled. Geddis' voice came through, breathing hard. 'Better make your way upstairs, sir. There's been one hell of a struggle up here. It's riddled with bullet holes.'

Dickinson instructed Talbot to come with him, leaving Pearce and Mills downstairs to search the remainder of the downstairs.

At the top of the stairs, signs of a battle could be seen on the landing where a burned rug lay on the floor.

Dickinson inspected it. 'Over a day old, maybe they've been gone longer than we thought.'

'In here, sir.'

Dickinson moved in and looked around. The room, as Geddis said, was a wreck. Small holes littered the wooden panels on the walls; the four-poster bed lay in a heap, the bottom end in bits, splinters scattered over the floor. 'Jeez, what happened here?'

'First impressions would be a gunfight. By the look of it, a hell of a lot of rounds. Machine gun, possibly a grenade or two.'

Dickinson ran his hand over the carvings on the bed. 'Any ideas who was involved?'

The pair searched the room.

'Have you noticed something?' Dickinson remarked. 'It doesn't really stack up. Masses of bullet holes but no—'

'Shells.'

'Precisely.'

Geddis whistled. 'You're right. There are no shells, sir, anywhere,' he said, scouring the floor. 'And, if I'm not mistaken, looking at the holes, they've used one helluva strange gun.'

Dickinson took out a tiny camera and began filming.

The headphones in his helmet crackled. 'Sir, Pearce here. We're going across to the other buildings. No sign of life in the main building. A few smashed plates, but the oven is warm. Did you say there was a housekeeper, sir?'

'Affirmative. Apparently she lives on site, in one of the outbuildings. Call me when you find her.'

Dickinson checked his phone and wondered whether to call Stone. No, perhaps he'd do it when he had a proper feel for what had gone on.

He shook his head. Clearly there had been a terrible struggle, but there had to be a clue—something—that gave them a chance to find out where they may have gone. Surely, they would have left a message somewhere?

'Commander,' the radio blared.

'Dickinson here.'

'You'd better come over. We've found someone. I think it's the woman you were talking about.'

Dickinson clenched his fist. 'Excellent. Coming over.'

'Follow the building. You'll eventually bump into Mills. Doesn't look as if she's got plans to go anywhere,' Pearce replied.

Dickinson reeled. 'What do you mean? Is she dead?'

'Negative, sir. You'll have to see for yourself. Looks like shock.'

Dickinson left Geddis to check out the other rooms, slipped out of the front door, and was immediately swallowed up by the dense fog. He moved around the courtyard until he saw Mills standing beside a stone flight of stairs.

Pearce met him at the top. 'I don't think she knows we're here,' he said.

When the commander walked into the bedroom, there, sitting on the bed and staring at the wall, was a large woman dressed in a pink, woollen dressing gown. Her piggy eyes were red from crying, and red hair hung loosely across her face and down her neck. Her forehead bore the deep traces of scarring and her plump, full lips were parted as a strange humming noise emanated from her. She rocked to and fro every so often, her arms across her chest as though protecting herself from cold.

Dickinson stepped in front of her and, when her reaction didn't alter, he squatted down and moved his palm a couple of inches from her face as though cleaning an invisible window.

'Hello?'

Not a flicker. He tried again with the same result before rejoining the other commandos outside the room.

'You're right. It's shock,' he said.

Mills agreed. 'I've seen this type of behaviour before. Might be best, sir, if you take off your protective garments and go in and start talking normally. She doesn't appear to have any Ebora symptoms.'

Dickinson nodded, removed his gear and re-entered the room. He knelt down before Mrs. Pye.

'Hello,' he said, awkwardly. 'I'm from the national rescue centre which is currently based at Swinton Park, near Masham. Do you know where that is? We're trying to find the cause of all this misery,' he said softly. 'You know, the storm and the rain-water and now there's been an outbreak of a terrible disease which is spreading. We have a feeling that Archie and Isabella and Daisy might know something that could really help us get to the bottom of it. That's why we're here, so please don't be alarmed.' He ran a hand through his sandy hair, turned towards Mills and shrugged.

Mills gestured for him to keep going.

'Can you tell me where they are—the children?'

Mrs. Pye remained staring at the wall.

'Can you tell me your name?' he tried. 'Do you know what happened in the house?'

The woman continued to stare at the wall.

Dickinson waited patiently, before standing up and heading outside. This wasn't going to be easy. She needed medical help, and it wasn't going to be forthcoming from them. Perhaps he should call Stone, see if he had any ideas.

Dickinson unclipped his phone.

Stone picked up straight away. 'Well? Any luck?'

'It looks like someone's beaten us to it,' Dickinson said.

'Hell!' Stone swore. 'Any sign of the children?'

'Nowhere to be seen, sir. The place is a mess. There's been some kind of battle upstairs, odd gunfire marks in the wooden panelling, and a couple of fires have started.'

Stone sucked in a breath. 'Weapons? That's not good. What kind of shells?'

'That's the strange bit. There aren't any. It's as if they cleared up after themselves.'

Stone's silence spoke volumes. 'Are you quite sure?' he said at length.

'Affirmative. I've taken footage,' Dickinson said. 'And it would appear that someone has rifled through all the pictures—'

'Pictures?'

'Yes, sir. Framed pictures, canvasses, oils. They litter the downstairs rooms.'

'Anything else?'

'We've found the housekeeper, sir.'

Stone's tone lightened. 'What did she have to say?'

'Nothing yet, sir. She's in shock—scared out of her mind. Mills said he'd seen something like it before, in the Middle East—a girl who'd seen her entire family tortured to death in front of her.'

'Can you get *anything* out of her?'

'We're trying but it's negative at the moment. She hums and stares at the wall, shaking.'

'Try again, Dickinson,' Stone ordered. 'Use electricity to jar her or water-board if necessary... we need answers—'

'But torture, on a woman?'

'It's called *interrogation*, Dickinson,' Stone snapped, 'and I don't care how you do it. I just need results.' He slammed down the phone.

Dickinson went back into the room and knelt down in front of Mrs. Pye.

'Hello,' he said. 'It's me again. We really need to know what's happened and you're the only person we can find. You see, if we don't find the answers, the whole area around here will be destroyed by a very big bomb. So in order to prevent this, and the loss of hundreds of thousands of lives, we could do with your help.'

Still the woman rocked and stared at the wall.

Dickinson's patience began to desert him. 'Please,' he begged. 'Everyone is going die if we don't get some answers.'

A tiny flicker flashed in Mrs. Pye's eye and Dickinson wondered if she could hear him after all.

'All we need are a few simple answers,' he urged.

The woman resumed her staring and humming.

Dickinson hated this. He didn't have Stone's cold-hearted approach to interrogation, the iciness needed to extract answers. Maybe they should take her back with them so Stone could work on her? Then again, perhaps he should try a different approach. If he wasn't mistaken, she cared for the children. She must have feelings for them.

'Archie and the girls will die if you don't help them,' he began. 'Do you understand? Your children will be killed by this terrible thing if you don't help us find them.'

The woman suddenly turned to him. Her eyes moist again and tears ran down her cheeks as her shoulders heaved. 'Taken,' she said, her vocal chords straining. 'From me.'

And then she resumed her rocking and staring at the wall.

23 CAIN'S NEW IDEA

'Who cares what I did?' the ghost crowed.

'I do,' Kemp said angrily.

'You? But, my boy, you loathe them. That's what I rather liked about you. And now, suddenly because I, a mere spirit, go and give Daisy de Lowe a little tickle, you get all upset.'

'Tickle? That wasn't a tickle, you violated her—'

'Oh come now. I wasn't harming her, quite the opposite,' Cain said, 'and she is rather exquisite, if you ask me.'

Kemp's face looked ready to explode.

'You're not jealous, are you?' Cain asked. 'Or worried that I'd take her instead of you?'

Kemp shook his head. 'Of course not,' he said thickly. 'What you did was plain stupid.'

'Why? Surely you must see by now that the de Lowes are going to die. Those pathetic Heirs of Eden still haven't got a clue what's going on, although I'll grant you, by the amount of debris downstairs, they are trying.'

'But now Daisy knows I'm alive,' Kemp said.

'So what, boy?' Cain snapped. 'It doesn't matter. Why not have a bit of fun with them? If I was allowed to kill her, I would.' He paused. 'Then all of this would be over.'

'So why didn't you?'

'Because if I, or anyone else for that matter, interferes

directly with the Heirs of Eden's quest, they will have succeeded.'

'Then you nearly gave it to them on a plate,' he said. 'How stupid can you get?' Kemp scratched his head; he needed to change the subject. 'Anyway, thanks for taking me to my mother,' he said. 'You were right.'

Cain drifted closer. 'My pleasure, boy. How did it go?'

'She knew,' Kemp said. 'We share the same thumbs; they bend right back like this.' He manipulated his digits.

'Fascinating,' Cain said, drily.

'When I looked closer, I was just like her. You know, hair, lips, even our noses are the same. She's bloody ugly though, unlike me.'

Cain laughed. 'So now we share our secrets.'

'Yeah,' Kemp said. 'And mum's coming here when the world gets destroyed, just as you promised, right? And please, don't do what you did with Daisy again, OK. It's freaky and a little bit pervy.'

Cain smiled. 'Ah, yes, yes. Of course,' Cain replied. Cain wondered if having the boy's mother around wouldn't be such a bad thing. Keep him under control; guide him in other ways, someone to play him off against.

Another thought had been niggling away at him. If Earth was to finish, as was increasingly likely, and Kemp was the sole survivor, then the boy would need a companion or two. Ghosts were hardly ideal playmates.

In due course, the boy would wish to reproduce and raise a family. But Havilah's human population were stuck, frozen in time like small, glass, upside down dishes littered upon the ground.

'You rather like her, don't you?'

'What?' Kemp said. 'My mum? Yeah, of course—'

'I meant the girl.'

'Daisy?' Kemp immediately went defensive. 'She's annoying and a show off and stupid, but she is pretty—'

'So you do like her!'

Kemp smiled. 'You're a horrible ghost, aren't you?'

'Perhaps,' he whispered into Kemp's ear.

'Stop doing that,' Kemp said, swishing at the air with his hand.

Cain moved through Kemp to the other ear. 'Or is there another girl?' he said.

'Stop that!'

Cain laughed with the boy. 'Come on, tell me.'

'No! Go away. Who I fancy is none of your business.'

'It's every bit my business,' Cain said, pretending to sound a little offended. 'Anyway, to find out all I have to do is look into your mind.'

'You wouldn't—'

'I already have.'

Kemp smiled and tried to think if there really was anyone else. 'Well if you must know, before you go rummaging through my head, there's a girl called Sue who is pretty hot.'

'Hot?' Cain chuckled. 'You don't mean that in a literal sense, do you? She doesn't actually feel hot, does she?'

'No! It means she's a bit of a babe, like Daisy, but with brains.'

'How interesting,' Cain mused.

Kemp sighed. 'Thing is, Daisy *hates* me. Sue, on the other hand, is properly gorgeous, and *really* hates me. The crap thing is she's the best friend of Isabella and Isabella hates me more than anyone or anything in the world, so basically it would never happen.'

'Why not? Strange things happen all the time,' said Cain, who hummed a strange, wispy tune, a trait which Kemp knew as his way of thinking. 'Why does Isabella detest you so, boy?'

'Well it started when I put a dead rat in her gym bag, which rotted and filled with maggots. When she found it, it made her so ill she ended up in hospital.' Kemp grinned. 'She's never forgiven me.'

Cain laughed. 'I tell you what,' he said at length, 'why don't we go and find her?'

'Isabella?'

'No, you fool. The girl who you say is the "hot" one?'

'Sue? She's probably dead like all the others—'

'I'll ask her spirits to find out, or better still, let me have a word with Asgard. The dreamspinner will find out in no time. Ghosts can get a little touchy, especially those related to the recently deceased—'

Kemp felt a little uneasy. 'Look, it's very nice of you to help me, but I'll save you the hassle. I promise you, she'll never, ever go with me, dead or alive. And anyway, what would I say to her? She's like, really clever and smart.'

'And you're not, boy?' Cain sighed. 'You're switched on enough to have joined me. In any case, you can give her a choice. Tell her it's you, or death.'

'That's not a great chat up line.'

'It worked for me.'

'Well, you're a ghost—'

'Indeed, but I wasn't always like this, you know. A long time ago I was extremely powerful and I intend, with your help, to reacquaint myself with that position.'

'So, why are you so interested in my love life, or lack of it?'

Cain appeared to sigh. 'As you know, I live forever,' he said wearily. 'You, however, will not. When Earth is no more, I can assure you that at some point you will wish to raise children.'

Kemp looked repulsed. 'OMG!'

'Whatever "OMG" means, I note the horror on your face. Don't be naive, boy. It is a perfectly natural development in the cycle of a living thing to procreate, to keep the wheels of life turning. For some species it is their sole purpose. It is said that with the failure of the Heirs of Eden, the humans on Havilah will awaken.' He shrugged, invisibly. 'But who knows if and when this will happen. With my help, you and your offspring will rule Havilah and Earth and the Garden of Eden. If this is to happen, you will need a woman with whom you can procreate.'

Kemp looked blank.

Cain spelt out. 'You'll need to make babies.'

It took Kemp a while to register. 'Blimey,' he said as the penny dropped. 'I'll be like the first guy in the world. Everyone will be based... on me!' he said at length.

Cain agreed. 'Lucky worlds, huh?'

'Blimey. Like Adam and Eve... you're a bloomin' genius.'

'Yes, I know,' Cain said, sounding rather smug. 'So, tell me,' he added, 'who is the superior, Daisy or Sue?'

Kemp weighed it up. 'Daisy is bottom of the lowest class, but she's smarter than she makes out and she's an athletic goddess. Sue, on the other hand is top of everything but shocking at games.'

'Then we must entice Sue into our little family, to complement your strength and athleticism.'

Kemp beamed. 'You'll do that for me? How?'

Cain, though completely invisible to Kemp, sat down and thought.

'We'll steal her,' he said at length.

'Steal?'

'Indeed. Though you must ask her first, so that we can gauge her reaction. Then, if she won't come willingly, we'll simply take her.'

'You can't do that!'

'My dear boy, of course I can. I'm Cain, and in a couple of days we'll be the most powerful person in the universe. Your Earth is about to end. Everything will die.'

'I still don't think she'll come. You haven't met her.'

'She'll come,' Cain croaked. 'There's one thing that divides living things from dead things. Living things will do anything in their power to actually live, boy, and not die. You're a testament to that, aren't you?'

Kemp nodded thoughtfully. 'She's pretty stubborn though.'

'Tell me, truthfully. Will she really refuse life for death?' Cain sighed. 'Never. Humans always say honourable, noble things like that, but they don't mean it. Sue will not get a better option. And when she understands the situation and her frankly perilous position she'll come over to us boy, with reluctance. Then time will do its healing. It will be significantly easier if she comes without making a fuss.'

24 BLABISTERBERRY JELLY

Daisy heard a mechanical buzz, then a muffled voice. 'Someone's here!' she said, as the sound reached her again. She froze at the top of the steps.

'What is it?' Isabella said.

Daisy concentrated hard. 'Footsteps, boots.'

'The army?' Isabella replied.

'Two people with walkie-talkies. Men's voices, I think. They're close. I think the fog has heightened the sound.'

Isabella ushered Old Man Wood down the stairs. 'Come on, Daisy.'

Daisy peered into the fog at the direction of the noise. Then she took off into the thick cloud and disappeared into the yard.

Isabella swore. *That idiotic, stupid girl.*

Moments later, Daisy reappeared and raced down the steps. 'Come on!' she said. 'Quick.'

'What do you mean, *quick?*' Isabella hissed. 'I've been waiting for *you.*'

'Either of you have any idea how to shut the stairwell?' Daisy said, urgently.

'Who is it?' said Archie, eagerly.

'Soldiers,' Daisy said, 'in protective helmets. They've got guns.'

'Oh terrific,' Isabella whispered.

Voices and the sound of boots scuffing the flagstones could be heard near the corner of the courtyard.

The children stared at each other and then, with a curious *whoosh,* air swept around them and sealed the trapdoor at the top of the stairs shut, leaving a small echo reverberating around the room.

Now, no exterior sounds could be heard and the three children and Old Man Wood collectively exhaled and turned towards a simple, round, stone table and four stone stools. On the walls were torchlights, which, much to Isabella's annoyance appeared to run brightly, but off neither electricity nor any type of fossil fuel she'd ever seen.

In the middle of the stone slab sat a large, shining, golden goblet containing a substance rising above its rim, like ice-cream above a cone.

'So this is Blabisterberry Jelly,' Old Man Wood said, expressing the general look of surprise on their faces as they stared at the cup filled of golden brown, toffee-looking, apricot-coloured goo.

A whooshing, rushing, firework sound came from the goblet, and while Daisy and Archie leaned in, Isabella instinctively ducked under the table and then pretended she hadn't.

'OOOh! Hello, my dears! Who do we have here today?' the voice was that of a sweet old woman, not too dissimilar to their great-grandmother, and certainly in no way menacing or frightening. Her words were delivered as though it was an everyday occurrence to have visitors.

The children looked at one another.

'Is it a ghost?' Archie whispered.

'I don't know. I can't see it.' Daisy stared back at him, her eyes wide.

They scanned the room.

'Now, don't be shy,' the sweet, elderly voice continued. 'I want to hear all about you.'

The children stared at one another and then at Old Man Wood, who simply shrugged.

'Well, my darlings,' it continued, 'let me see if we can break the ice on this fine little gathering.'

Daisy pointed towards the goo. 'I think it's coming from there,' she whispered.

The goblet of goo continued. 'I see that we have two beautiful girls, a lovely, handsome, young man, and, aha, you've brought along Grandpa. Now, let's have a look at all of you. Goodness, so very fit and healthy and may I say how terribly youthful you three are. Isn't that a surprise?' The tone sounded almost mocking.

'If you don't mind, I need to do a bit of an inspection, to make sure I know *exactly* who you are.'

Before any of them had the chance to react, a vapour drifted up from out of the bowl, and began to swirl around them like the tendrils of a climbing plant encircling a tree-trunk, each member of the family ensnared within, as if bound by a rope.

Then the smoke disappeared into their ear, mouth and nose cavities and, as it rushed inside, more followed until the children could feel it inside them, tickling their minds, chilling their lungs and freezing their guts.

Just as they were getting used to it, smoke drifted back out of their orifices and back into the goo once more.

All four breathed deeply as if their internal organs had received a smart little tidy-up.

'Bless you all, my dears,' the voice said. 'So you've found me at long last. Goodness, you've taken your time though, haven't you? Well, not to worry. I believe your search for the tablets is well under way. How do you think you're doing?'

The children scuffed their shoes over the floor awkwardly.

'Er... not too bad,' Daisy said, reddening.

'You're talking to pot of marmalade, Daisy,' Isabella whispered.

'I don't care,' Daisy said from out of the corner of her mouth. 'At least it's polite marmalade.'

The strange, pleasant, old woman's voice piped up again. 'I can't begin to tell you how excited I am. I'd offer you a cup of tea or the like but, my sweets, that isn't possible... so, tell me, what are your names? You look like a right little lamb. Yes, you with the lovely blonde locks.'

'Er... Daisy,' Daisy said, looking straight at the goblet of goo.

'So,' the sweet voice said, 'Daisy, my darling, do *you* think you can do it? You look plucky enough to me.'

Daisy's face contorted. 'Do what?'

'Eat me,' the voice said.

Daisy laughed awkwardly. 'Ah-ha... *eat... you? What exactly do you mean*—if you don't mind me asking?'

'As I said. *You must eat me*, my dear.'

Daisy snorted and a small bogey blew out of her nose and landed on the rim of the cup where it immediately burned up.

'Seriously?' she said, a little embarrassed.

From the silence that filled the small chamber, Daisy realised the goo was being deadly serious. 'Oh, right. Well, yeah, of course... I knew that,' she said, cringing, and staring wide-eyed at her siblings.

The voice from the goo sensed her discomfort. 'I do not wish to be disrespectful sweetheart, but you *did* find the riddles?'

'Yup, of course we did.'

'Then, tell me, little darlings, that you studied them?'

Daisy's face had turned from pink to red and Archie noted Daisy's unease. He coughed and recited the second verse of the riddle.

'For the second one you have to find
'You burp it from the family belly.
'To do this, you have to eat
'Blabisterberry Jelly!'

'Very good,' said the voice, displaying a hint of sarcasm. 'You see, *I* am Blabisterberry Jelly and all you have to do is eat me. Clear, so far?'

The children nodded, dumbly.

'Well, come on then,' Archie said as he made a lunge for the goblet.

'Not so fast, young man,' the voice said, as a small cloud of smoke puffed out of the goblet in his general direction.

Archie reeled and fanned the billow with his arm.

The sweet voice turned a little sterner. 'It isn't quite as simple as that. In order to succeed, you have to believe that I am, quite simply, the most delicious food you have ever tasted. It really is incredibly easy.'

Old Man Wood groaned. 'And what if we can't?' he asked.

'If you don't *believe*, you don't belch. And if you don't belch, you don't get the tablet, and if you don't get the tablet... you die.' The voice softened. 'Isn't that right, young man?'

Archie smiled as the cogs of the puzzle slipped into place. 'My name is Archie, ma'am,' he said politely. He licked his lips ready to tuck in.

'Know this, handsome Archie,' the kindly voice of Blabisterberry Jelly continued. 'If you think about my form and eat me as you see me, you will taste the thing you see, and not the food you desire. Do you all understand?'

Archie nodded. *What a doddle,* he thought.

Daisy was feeling increasingly thankful that she'd hardly touched her breakfast.

'It is important you are clear about this,' said the voice.

'What a result,' Archie whispered. 'I hope it's gonna be good, 'cos I am starving.'

But Isabella's hands trembled. 'I don't like the sound of this,' she whispered. 'Not one little bit.'

The goblet heard her. 'My dear, which bit in particular do you not like?'

Isabella hesitated. 'Well, what if it isn't possible to eat whatever it is? What if it's so disgusting—I mean, does it matter?' she asked, her voice cracking.

'Aha! A very good question pretty young lady, whose name is ...?'

'Isabella.'

'Isabella, such a pretty name for such a delicate face. I will be honest with you, if you don't eat your platefuls you will never leave. Is that perfectly clear?'

Isabella swallowed.

'And, another word of advice,' the voice continued, 'the longer it takes, the larger the portion sizes become?'

The children nodded, not entirely clear about where this was leading.

'Good,' the Blabisterberry Jelly said. 'You're a smart bunch, aren't you? Grandpa must be so proud.'

'But what if I really can't eat—'

'Then, my dear, you'll get a little... overwhelmed.' A high-pitched cackle echoed around them, and then, as before, the sweet tones resumed. 'This is why my portions always start so small. It's terribly easy. Just believe what you want to believe. You have only yourself to fear.'

Isabella's stomach churned. *Portions? Portions of what, exactly?*

In the marrow of her bones something told her that this absolutely, definitely, wasn't going to be a piece of Mrs. Pye's cake.

25 TO THE COTTAGE

Dickinson had seen enough.

Taken from her. That's all she'd said—three times. When pressed about where they had gone, she'd stared at him with sadness in her eyes and returned to staring at the wall.

He waited for Stone to pick up.

'Sir,' Dickinson said, as his phone clicked. 'We've searched everywhere. The woman told us the children have been taken and I'm afraid we can't get any more out of her. To be honest, I doubt if she knows any more –she's in a terrible state.'

'Did you use other methods?' Stone asked.

'Absolutely,' Dickinson lied. 'If anything, it made her worse.'

For a moment the line remained quiet as Stone thought it through. 'You reckon the house has been ransacked and the children abducted?'

'That's one theory,' Dickinson replied. 'We've been round the house and buildings twice and not a squeak of life. All I can tell you is one hell of a struggle took place upstairs and downstairs. Some of the children's clothes we found were covered with bloodstains and torn to bits. Even the generator hasn't been on for a while. I hate to say it, sir, but there's a strong chance they're already dead.'

Stone cussed into the radio. 'I've got Solomon and Sue here. Is there anything they can salvage?'

Dickinson rubbed his chin. 'Whoever it is must be a step ahead of us. If Solomon can find any links to the chapel that'll be something. You've got nothing to lose, and it might not be a bad idea to have Sue look after the woman. She might loosen-up if she sees a friendly face. I'll fix up a camera in her room so we can see if she's faking it or not.'

'Nice idea,' Stone replied. 'When you've done that, get down to where you left your boat. Meet the RIB coming over from our side with the headmaster and girl. You'll need to guide them in.'

'Heading down now, sir. Thickest fog you've ever seen.'

'Fine, but I need you back here. We had a perimeter break last night. This place must be secure while we begin the evacuation. I think word about the Americans' intention has sneaked out.'

'OK, Roger that,' Dickinson said. 'We'll be there as soon as we can.'

Stone turned to Solomon. 'Eden Cottage is empty. From what Dickinson said, the children have been abducted, so you're on, cousin. Find out all you can. Take Sue, she can look after that caretaker woman and we'll ask her to see if she can figure out what happened. The RIB leaves as soon as you've got your things together. You'll find supplies for several days and I'm giving you a radio. Touch base the moment you're in the house, and then at four hourly intervals during daylight hours. Is that clear? I'll also give you some fuel—see if you can't start up that generator.'

'Good, thank you,' Solomon said. 'What if there's nothing after a day or so?'

Stone understood what he meant. 'I'll do what I can to get you out of there,' he said. He stood up and looked his elder cousin in the eye. 'If we've not got you out after three days, take provisions and seal yourselves in the cellar. Understand? Go deep and you should be alright.'

Solomon nodded.

'The clock is ticking and we need results.'

'Indeed, Charlie. You know I'll do my utmost to get to the bottom of this.'

Sue strode down the path, hoping like mad Gus had managed to get down there before her. In no time, she was swallowed up by a blanket of fog and, had it not been for the familiarity of where to go and the hard tarmac beneath her feet, she wondered if she would have got lost. Her fears were short lived. Despite the protective suite, she recognised Gus before he noticed her for, even though Gus was tall for his age, he was undoubtedly smaller in build than the other men and women who scurried around the small RIB.

Sue slipped on the protective helmet. She moved in closer.

'Hi,' she said, winking at Gus through the plastic mask. 'I'm Sue. Is Mr. Solomon here yet?'

Gus raised his hand. 'He's over there,' he said, his voice a little lower than usual.

Sue followed his gaze and just managed to make out the headmaster heading towards them.

'Hello, sir,' Sue said, as he approached.

'Ah. There you are Sue. Jolly good. Have you got everything you need?' He turned to the man next to him. 'These two are with me.'

The man, squat, with jet black hair and a matching bushy beard, eyed them up. 'I was told only one.' He checked his pad.

'No, both are coming,' Solomon said. 'Top level researchers. And we need to get a move on.'

The man scratched his beard. 'Better check with security,' he said, and he reached wearily into his pocket.

'Can I ask your name?' Solomon asked directly.

'Corporal Lambert.'

'You are aware, Corporal, that I have been given *carte blanche* on this operation by Commissioner Stone? I also happen to be his cousin and head of this investigation.'

Lambert stiffened. Solomon noted his hollow eyes and scarred face. He probably wasn't someone to mess with. 'Perhaps I can persuade you otherwise—we're in such a terrible hurry. Perhaps this might help a little...'

He reached into his pocket and withdrew a few notes. They shook, Lambert accepting the money with a sly smile.

'Alright,' Lambert said, slipping the cash into his back pocket, 'you've paid the ferryman, but I'll still need names. There were two incidents last night, one involving people breaking out, the other with people breaking in. One of them was the kid who survived in a boat. Apparently he's got the disease—that's what they're saying. If security's breached apparently we've 'ad it.'

'Very good, Corporal,' Solomon said, hardly daring to catch Sue or Gus' eye. 'Can I suggest we get going—I'll fill you in as we go? It's quite a distance in these conditions and Dickinson is needed back here pronto.'

Lambert weighed up the suggestion before helping each of them into the twelve-foot RIB and pointing to where he wanted them to perch on the thick, air-filled sides.

Solomon sat on one side, Sue and Gus, the other.

After balancing out the additional weight of fuel and provisions, Lambert gave the boat a shove and hoisted himself up and over the side.

Moments later the engine throbbed into life.

'How can you tell where to go?' Sue asked, looking around. 'It's a total white-out.'

Lambert smiled, showing off a silver capped tooth. He then produced a small electronic device from the inside pocket of his coat. 'This clever navigation system, darlin',' he said. 'Links up to a tracer on the other side. That's them—the red dot.' He showed her, clearly pleased with himself. 'We're the green flashing one. All we've got to do is aim for it. So long as we don't smash into anything too chunky or the light disappears, we'll be there in a couple of hours. Slow goin' in this stuff.'

Sue shivered as the cold, damp, fog leached into her. Apart from the mechanical throb of the engine and the gentle thump of water on the prow, the eeriness and quiet of the water filled her with unease.

Every so often the boat clunked or biffed on something and, holding on extra tight to the safety rope around the edge, she peeked out into the endless, still, white veil. Before long, she slid down the inflated rubber edge and leant on Gus' leg. More than anything, all she wanted to do was snuggle up next to him, just as they had done on "The Joan Of".

Soon, every hair on her body stood to attention. She imagined hands reaching out and grappling at the boat, grotesque, zombie-like bodies hauling themselves in, or pulling them overboard. They were in a corridor of death, and a dark, terror filled her.

Eventually, she shrank down and lowered her head to her chest so that she couldn't see, grateful for the throbbing heartbeat of the engine. The fog's stench was a heady combination of stale water and devastation and it permeated every particle of air.

Lambert peered into the gloom, adjusting the rudder every once in a while and slowing if he saw larger objects looming out of the fog at them. 'Who's the lad then?' he said at long last, pulling out a pad and pen.

Solomon coughed, relieved someone had broken the silence. 'My technical assistant, you mean?'

'Don't he speak?'

Solomon flashed a look towards Gus. 'His name, if that's what you mean, is—'

'Kemp,' Gus answered.

'Absolutely,' Solomon added, raising his eyebrows at the boy. 'Kemp,' he repeated.

'University of Durham, PhD student studying religious artefacts,' Gus continued. 'Specialising in the stained glass windows of the churches of Northern Britain.'

It took all her concentration for Sue not to explode with laughter. Was his voice lower *and slightly posher*?

Lambert nodded, impressed. 'You reckon there's some kinda link then, do ya? That's what I've been hearing, Kemp. Some spooky thing from hundreds of years back, come back to punish us. You know, like in them old times, when the Gods sent plagues and stuff to kill everyone.'

Gus turned towards Sue, his huge, toothy smile evident through the clear plastic hood. 'Um ...'

'That's exactly the sort of thing we're going to see if we can find out, Sergeant,' Solomon butted in. 'You see, Kemp has an almost unique perspective on these matters. He was born in a house bang next to York Minster, where he was fortunate to have access to some of the rarest forms of ecclesiastical artworks in the world, weren't you, Kemp?'

Gus stared at the headmaster for a while. 'Indeed,' he said coolly. 'A very unique... childhood.'

Solomon was enjoying himself. 'Didn't you write a thesis on it?'

Gus spluttered. 'Yeah. Er... about triptych stained glass window arrangements and other things,' he said hurriedly.

'Gothic?' Solomon said.

'Absolutely,' Gus replied, wondering what had got into the man. '90's Gothic-revival kind-of-thing.'

'90's Gothic revival?' Lambert said. 'You're pulling my leg.'

Solomon chuckled. 'My dear old thing we're talking about the Thirteenth century—

'1290's, to be precise,' Gus added. 'An important time in—'

Sue shrieked, 'How long before we arrive?'

Lambert looked down at the screen. 'About fifteen minutes. You lot had better keep look out. I'm told there's loads of stuff lying round the edges—you know, cars, trees—maybe a rotting cat or two.' He smiled. 'Maybe a few human corpses.'

When the RIB brushed on the bare tops of willow tree clumps submerged beneath the water, they knew they must be close. Lambert negotiated through piles of metal, plastic and wooden debris until, eventually, Gus spotted a faint circular ring of bright light glowing out of the fog not too far away.

Lambert aimed for it, cut the engine, and let the boat drift in.

Shortly, instructions came from the bank, and while Lambert

guided the rudder, Gus grabbed the nylon painter and tossed it to one of the talking figures on the side of the water who pulled the boat further in. Then he jumped off the prow into the mud, where a blond-haired man helped him regain his legs.

As Sue did the same, Gus moved to the fringes, tested the weight of a rucksack and hauled it up onto his back. With his head kept low, he waited while the others gathered their provisions and, in no time, they began the tricky, slippery climb up the hillside towards Eden Cottage.

26 STARLIGHT APPLE CRUMBLE

Without warning, a fountain of sparkling dust blew out of the goblet of goo, like a firework. Streams of bright, vibrant colours creating a dazzling, glittery cloud that soon hovered over the table.

The children and Old Man Wood smiled at one other, wide-eyed in amazement. Then, the dust parted and formed swirling circles above them, like coloured halos.

These halos descended down over their heads, spinning in front of their eyes and over their ears, a noise tingling like miniature bells.

The children instinctively shut their eyes, as the strange particles swept into their heads through all available holes and tickled their brains.

When the noise reappeared, they opened their eyes to find the halos in front of them, each one moving towards the middle of the table like fat bagels flying in slow-motion.

As they met, another explosion of glitter spewed into the air with the sound of broken glass.

In front of the children's astonished eyes the dust divided and descended in equal parts onto their plates.

When the children and Old Man Wood looked down, the colourful glitter had gone. They stared at their stone plates with mouths open, their eyes on stalks.

A second later, screams of horror and shouts of absolute disgust erupted in the small chamber.

Old Man Wood reeled.

On his plate a miniature dreamspinner crawled on long, opaque legs around the rim of the stone platter, it's translucent, jellyfish-like body with a hole where its abdomen should have been, pulsating with mini forks of blue lightning.

Old Man Wood sat quite still with his mouth open, staring at the creature, while all around him the children screamed and hollered and wailed and gagged at the sights in front of them.

Apples alive, I did this, he thought. *These things are our worst fears. It is a trial of will.* At least that's what the Willows said. It had to be true, but how in all the apples on all the planets in all the universes had he done it?

Shocked, he stared at the creature moving around the plate, trying to think. But the longer he stared and the children screamed, the larger the strange, spidery creature grew.

When Daisy came over and threw her arm round him wailing, he snapped out of it, and remembered where he was and what he had to do.

'SILENCE!' he roared. 'Listen to me, and listen hard. Look at me, Isabella—you too Daisy. Look me right in the eye.' The children did as he asked. 'Whatever you do, DO NOT look at your plates until I tell you. Right, good.'

Old Man Wood took a deep breath. 'All of this is not real, my littluns,' he said, his tone softer. 'What you have to imagine is that this plateful is your favourite food, your most favourite meal in the world.'

'That's impossible—'

'No, little Bells, it is not,' he said. 'WE HAVE TO DO THIS or Blabisterberry Jelly will overwhelm us. Keep looking at me, girls, and you, Archie.' He held each pair of the children's terrified eyes.

'You have to believe me,' he said, as he picked up a spoon and fork.

'Keep looking at me. Good. Now, I'm going to prove how easy this is. I'm imagining, with all my heart and soul, that this is my favourite food...'

'Starlight apple crumble?' Archie said.

'Exactly!' Old Man Wood said. 'It's a thick slice of warm, yumptious, starlight apple crumble on my plate where the apple is sweet and juicy and the crumble crunches. How it melts in the mouth.'

The Old Man shut his eyes and concentrated hard on a mouthful of starlight apple crumble helped along with a huge dollop of thick, creamy custard.

He opened his eyes and looked down. For him, the strange, thin, spidery creature began to recede into apple crumble covered in yummy custard. The others looked on, riveted by the repulsive scene of Old Man Wood about to eat an alien-like spider.

'You see,' he said, cutting into the dreamspinner, 'you have to believe that what you are about to eat is what you *truly* want to eat. It doesn't have to be big or clever, but Blabisterberry Jelly will know if you mean it. I promise you this, my littluns, you must not be found wanting.'

Old Man Wood shut his eyes and helped himself to the mouthful, pushing the pulsating spoonful with a long leg hanging out into his open mouth.

All the children could see was the quivering electrical abdomen of the dreamspinner flashing, electrifying his stubby teeth as he bit down.

'Cor! That is utterly fan-tab-ulistic!' Old Man Wood spluttered, helping himself to another spoonful. 'This has... mmm... to be the greatest... yummiest... sweetest, starlight apple crumble I've ever had in all my life.'

He piled in again. 'And I should know,' he enthused as he chewed, electric blue crackles of lightning washing round his mouth, 'Coz I've been making it for an awfully long time.'

27 A DISGUSTING WAY TO DIE

Daisy shook with fear.

She simply couldn't believe Old Man Wood was eating the most horrific, weird, spidery-alien-thing she'd ever seen. The sight filled her with dread and she noted how Isabella and Archie's faces were pale and green.

No books, no schooling, *nothing* could prepare them for this kind of experience. Daisy shut her eyes and took a deep breath. Holding onto her nose she sucked in a huge lungful of air, exhaling slowly before repeating the process two or three times.

How did the goo know?

The *incident* had happened three years ago. They'd been playing football and some of the boys started getting rough, kicking her and tripping and making dangerous tackles. She smiled now she thought about it, how similar it had been to the match against Chitbury.

She'd tried hard, desperately hard not to cry. But her legs hurt and it was so unfair! When the tears rolled, the boys made it worse, calling her names—one even spat on her. And, even worse was the way they enjoyed her discomfort.

On their way home, Daisy hardly spoke. When she did, she'd told Archie that she'd never cry again. No one had a right to make her so upset and, from that day forward, she vowed she would never shed another tear.

Instantly, Archie turned to her and offered her a bet, partially as a bit of fun, and partially because he argued that crying wasn't a bad thing to do. Three weeks' worth of school sweet-tuck if he made her cry within a week.

She'd laughed at him.

Three days went by and Daisy had all but forgotten the incident of Archie's bet. But then, after school one day, they passed a young man walking down the lane from the ruin with a large black Labrador. He was a rambling type often seen walking from village to village across the moors.

As they played in the ruin, Archie spotted it. That evening just before supper, Archie ran up with a garden trowel, found the juicy dog mess, cut it in two, and carefully placed a dollop in each of her woolly boot slippers, before leaving them out by the back door.

They played football until the sun down went down and as an evening chill came over the moors they'd warmed up by the fire. Daisy asked if anyone knew where her woolly boot slippers were. When Archie told her they were by the back door, she marched off and found them.

Without thinking, she pushed her feet in.

Seconds later, the entire family rushed out to find Daisy shrieking hysterically then screaming. Then vomiting and retching. The tears flowed.

She remembered that turgid smell and the way it stuck like glue between her toes, got under her toenails and then, amazingly, transported itself all over her during her tragic attempt to remove it.

She lay in bed for a whole day, and for several weeks spent hours cleaning her feet, scrubbing them almost obsessively.

Now that she thought of it, she'd never paid out the bet. He'd been in way too much trouble.

Daisy took a deep breath.

Sitting proudly on Daisy's plate lay a well-formed steaming, brown dog-turd, gleaming with a sheen as though freshly laid. Daisy prodded it in stunned amazement and for a second wondered if it could be fake, or a type of joke chocolate. But when she caught a whiff of its distinctive odour, she instinctively retched.

Then, holding her mouth and stomach, she vomited behind her.

Daisy returned to stare at the smelly, sweating, stinking turd. 'Dog shit!' she whispered. 'And I've got to eat it.'

Her guts contorted involuntarily and looked up at Isabella, who had climbed on her stool, petrified. Things were clearly not going well for her either.

They all screamed again and, as they did, the turd grew a little larger.

'*NO!*' she yelled, but on that, it expanded a fraction more. She closed her eyes and tried to calm down.

Why? Every time she'd seen a dog poo from that moment on, she'd given it a wide berth and if anyone trod in one and her nose caught that certain whiff, her stomach twisted and her face turned white, then green, and she had to lie down or throw-up.

And now, somehow, like it or not she was going to have to tuck into it with a knife and fork. She wanted to retch but, instead, she stretched her arms out wide to allow for more oxygen. She clenched her eyes tight.

Old Man Wood had to be right. He'd done it—right in front of their eyes and if he could, so could she.

Daisy thought hard. If the turd was an illusion she had to replace the grotesque with something totally amazing. But what? Thank God she'd missed out on breakfast.

OK, she thought, *which meal stood out head and shoulders above any other she'd ever had?* Nothing sprang to mind until the aroma of the Chinese meal they'd had for her last birthday treat in Southallerton tickled the sensors in her brain. Yes! That Peking crispy duck all flaked and rolled up in pancakes with cucumber, spring onions and a dab of plum sauce. Nothing had ever tasted quite so wonderful.

But ever present, in a corner of her mind, she could sense it; stinking, vile, slimy. She opened her eyes and stared and, as if the turd understood, it grew. Daisy's stomach leapt again.

She shut her eyes again. *Crispy, shredded, aromatic duck,* she thought, *with extra plum sauce, wrapped up in a pancake.*

Come on, Daisy, she urged, *it is utterly delicious—and it has to work.*

Archie stared at Old Man Wood.

Why did the creature creeping around the plate make him feel so uneasy? Why was it so familiar? Archie racked his brain. Then suddenly it hit him: this was the same creature that had sat above Daisy while she slept—the night he'd woken, the night of their final nightmare—before it started, before everything went mad and the rain came down and before the destruction and the plague and the riddles. Before they had any inkling that they were linked to these strange goings on.

His pulse quickened. This spidery-creature looked like a smaller version of that one and, now that the memories returned, he remembered how, at first, he thought the creature might be taking something from Daisy but soon came to the conclusion that it was actually *giving her something*. Yes, that was it. Giving her a powder from the ends of its long legs. And he'd wondered then if this strange creature had been supplying them with their weird dreams.

He scratched his hard front hair spike. The objects on their plates represented their worst fears—he could see that: Daisy with her terror of dog poo, Isabella with her revulsion to dead rats.

On his plate, four round, human eyeballs like marbles twitched, their muscles and tendons attached to each side like the ectoplasm of a bloody jellyfish.

As he inspected them, he noticed how much larger were the ones which bore pale-blue irises in comparison to the other two that had dark, nutty-brown colouring.

Each eye dripped with blood and stared back at him as if they were watching him—*staring madly at him—following him*, Archie thought.

A strand of a nerve twitched, rolling one of the eyeballs over. Then another did the same.

Isabella screamed again, so too, Daisy.

He joined in.

Who could do such a totally horrendous thing? This wasn't a trial, it was torture.

He shuddered. Were these the eyes of the Ancient Woman, sucked out and now for his consumption? They had to be. That horrific dream-image never went far away: the extreme violence of his actions, the peculiar sensation of murdering someone and how it had felt so natural, so right.

Every time he'd woken up, he'd been consumed by guilt until he found this feeling replaced by an anger that he found hard to control.

He examined his plate. *Two sets of eyes? Why? The ancient woman... who else?*

A terrible chill swept through him, as the realization hit him. The other set must belong to Cain. Cain the ghost, who'd told him his eyes had been removed when he'd sat in his room, scaring him witless.

On his plate lay the missing body parts of the two people he feared the most; a spook and an imaginary figure from his dream?

Jeez, his head must be screwed.

But if Old Man Wood's strange spider was real, then maybe the Ancient Woman was also real? And maybe, if he was going to kill her—perhaps his dreams stood as a warning?

Archie liked this thought. It made some sort of sense.

He remembered what Cain had said about protecting this Ancient Woman—Cain's mother –against those that might harm her.

So, perhaps his job was to shield her.

Thinking about Cain's concern for his mother, he thought of his own. Why wasn't she here, helping them? Did they have any idea what had happened to them, what they were going through? There hadn't been a word, nothing.

Maybe, he thought, *they had been abandoned.* Left to get on with it.

Archie's gloom was punctured by the scraping of a fork on the stone platter in front of Old Man Wood. He looked up to see a portion of electricity-filled jellyfish with thin, almost translucent bones heading towards the old man's mouth.

Archie watched, dumbfounded, as Old Man Wood devoured the curious ghost-like spider.

So why, Archie thought, *do spidery-alien creatures give Old Man Wood such fear?* If the creature had been dishing out dreams, as he suspected, then what did it say about Old Man Wood?

Maybe, it showed an uncertain future, or was Old Man Wood in denial about something... something about this Ancient Woman and Cain?

Watching the old man tackling his plateful with relish, his eyes shut in bliss, loaded Archie with courage.

If Old Man Wood can do it, he thought, *then so can I.*

Without knowing why, Archie shut his eyes as he imagined the eyes to be everlasting gob-stoppers. He felt for his plate, picked one of the eyeballs up in his fingers and popped it straight into his mouth. A moment of bliss swept over his face.

'Wow, this is the bes' gosoppa I've eva ha,' he said, as he swirled it round his mouth.

'Keep going, Arch,' Daisy said, clapping wildly.

'Those eyes will soon disappear from your plate...' Old Man Wood said, egging him on.

Only, this comment made Archie open his eyes and look down at his plate to see the vile assortment of eyes and their tendrils. He lost his concentration and went very pale.

Uh oh, he thought, as he felt a movement from the eyeball tickling the roof of his mouth and the trail of nerves flickered the back of his throat. Worst of all he was sure he could feel the eye growing. It felt the size of a ping-pong ball.

He wretched violently and the eyeball popped out bouncing rather dramatically a couple of times on the table.

Archie shook his head. 'Idiot,' he mumbled.

'Sorry about that, Arch,' Old Man Wood said, wincing. 'For a moment, I thought you had it.'

Archie head-butted the table. '*I'm* the idiot, not you! I thought of an everlasting gob-stopper. By its very nature, it's an incredibly dumb thing to do.'

Archie wracked his brain. There had to be an easier way of doing this. He stared at the eyeballs on his plate, which stared straight back, as though testing him. Then they grew a fraction. *Oh please*, Archie thought. They were about the size of normal eyes now. Any larger and this was going to get messy.

Not eating their platefuls was going to be a horrible way to die.

28 GUS IN THE ATTIC

Sue found it strange being de-briefed by Dickinson in the de Lowes' house with Gus, the headmaster and not a de Lowe in sight.

She sighed. A week ago, who could have possibly imagined that they were on the cusp of Armageddon? And a week ago, she would never have believed she could be so madly in love with anyone, let alone odd, hilarious, brilliant, gorgeous Gus.

The dense fog that lay over the fields and forests in the great Vale of York made for a quiet, empty, alien atmosphere. And an expectation lingered that something unpleasant might be about to interrupt it.

Dickinson had stopped the group to rest three times and Sue had been grateful for the breaks. On the first, Dickinson instructed the party to thread rope between them so that no one might wander off in the wrong direction.

When the stone walls came into view, they had collectively breathed a sigh a relief. Inside the building, where she'd spent so much time playing, it felt cold and uninviting. Even the normally toasty sitting room with its warming flames and low beams struck them as being mysteriously empty and unwelcoming. Sue feared the worst.

Solomon set to work laying a fire as Dickinson began. 'Sue, in a moment I'm going to take you over to the woman we found—'

'Mrs. Pye?'

'Yes,' he said. 'You know her, don't you?'

'She's lovely.'

'Good,' Dickinson said. 'She's suffering from shock. You're to look after her, make sure she's fed and watered and if she lets on about anything, names, where the children might have gone, that sort of thing, let us know immediately. Write it down so you don't forget.' He winked at her.

His radio crackled. 'I'm going to leave you both one of these,' he said, putting a handset on the arm of the sofa. 'Call in if and when you get a sniff of progress. I'm guessing Stone briefed you.' He looked knowingly at the headmaster who nodded and turned away.

Dickinson addressed the noise. 'I've just got to introduce the woman to Sue, and then we'll be off.'

'Still no signs?' Stone's voice crackled back.

'Dead as a dodo, sir.'

'I've sent units in to the local town centres—anywhere where electrical tablets and the devices are sold. Though I'll be surprised if there are any left. Looting like you'd never believe.'

'OK, Roger that. Anything else you need from here, sir?'

'Just a quick word with Solomon, if he's about.'

Dickinson handed over the radio.

The headmaster pressed the button. 'Solomon here.'

'Good. You know what the score is. Don't sleep until you've combed through everything, understand? We don't have time. And remember what I said.'

Solomon handed back the radio.

'Right, Sue,' Dickinson said. 'Let's find Mrs. Pye, then I'll leave her in your hands.' Dickinson looked around. 'Anyone seen that understudy of yours?'

Solomon picked a matchbox up from the top of the wooden mantelpiece, opened it, and struck a match. 'I've sent him upstairs to begin logging everything up there. As the Commissioner said, there's no time to waste, is there.'

Dickinson smiled back. 'Yes. Quite.' He turned for the door. 'Good luck—keep us posted.' And with that their boots scuffed on the floor as they headed out of the front door, across the paving slabs and into the fog.

While Sue nursed Mrs. Pye, the headmaster and Gus listened from the edge of the building to the sludging and slurping sounds of boots and the chatter of the men as they departed down the slope. When the noise petered out, they made their way back to the living room.

'Gus, I really do think you ought to remove that helmet and the rest of that gear,' Solomon said. 'I must say, I very nearly laughed out loud when you said you were Kemp.'

Gus smiled toothily back at him. 'Anything to liven things up a little. Strange how his name popped into my head.' Gus began looking at the clutter, made up predominantly of pictures dotted around the room. 'What *have* they been up to?'

'That's what we need to work out, my boy.'

'It's as though they were looking for something in the pictures and then left in a bit of a hurry—'

'You're telling me,' Solomon said, picking up one of the old portraits. 'I'll inspect the kitchen. If they left in the middle of the night there may be traces of a meal. After that we need to try and figure out what on earth they've been looking for with all of these.'

'It's quite a mess,' Gus said. 'I'll go and check their room, see if there's anything that might give us some idea of timing.'

Solomon smiled. 'Well, at least I know where Archie gets it from. All of this could very well be his doing.'

Gus headed up the stairs. When he reached Old Man Wood's room he called for Solomon and together they inspected the remnants of the room in silence.

Gus whistled. 'It's like a nail bomb's been detonated in here—'

'Yes, but without the nails,' Solomon said as he inspected the strange, irregularly-sized holes dotted around the wooden panelled walls. 'And no shell cases or cartridges—that's what the soldiers were saying. There's no metal here at all.'

'Are you suggesting,' Gus said, 'that something organic made this mess?'

Solomon stroked his chin. 'I don't know. But it is most unusual.'

Gus took off up to the attic room where he searched each of the children's areas. He tried to see if there was a tell-tale article of clothing that might give away their whereabouts or a book or a slip of paper or a note. He searched Archie's mess first, then Daisy's area and finally, Isabella's immaculate section: bed made, books put away, everything in its place. He turned to go when he noted a drawer below her bedside table. Gus stared at it and tried to pull it open, but found it jammed tight. There wasn't a keyhole, so how could it be locked? He traced his fingers around the bedside table, feeling only solid sides. Then he placed his hand underneath and rocked the base one way, then another. Gus smiled. The drawer slid open the other way. A hidden drawer, *neat*. He peered inside. Her diary lay there with a pen clamped underneath an elastic strap.

Gus picked it out and opened the thick, pink, bound book. He noted the dates and flicked through, catching snippets of familiar names as he went until he reached more recent entries. He skimmed the extract of her trying to work out who and what the people in her dreams meant. He turned the page over and read about their adventures, their odd magical gifts, about Old Man Wood being the oldest man ever and how much she missed Sue.

A terrible thought hit him. Sue and Isabella were close, like twins. How would Sue react if Isabella had been killed? Nervously he turned another page. Now the entry was smaller, and here he saw a five-verse poem. Nothing more, no explanation, but it appeared to be about finding three tablets and another world called Eden. Was this what it was all about?

He heard the groan of a floorboard. Instinctively he froze and crammed the diary into his pocket.

The noise deepened. Footsteps. He noted that while the

tread was silent the creak of the floorboards gave whoever it was away.

It had to be Sue coming to sneak up on him. He smiled. He could pretend he hadn't heard her and surprise her with a kiss. OK, she might get really cross or pretend to be annoyed—but only for a moment, then she'd melt and laugh, and then kiss him.

Why not give her a happy surprise?

Gus grinned as he waited by the drawn curtain, until he could almost hear her breath through the other side of the velvet. Then, in one sharp movement, Gus whipped the curtain to the side.

'TA-DAH!' he said, moving in for the kiss.

'Hello, Williams,' said a curiously familiar voice.

Gus stopped just in the nick of time, his lips still puckered.

Then he stumbled and collapsed down on the bed.

'Y... YOU? HOW?!'

29 THE ILLUSION CRUMBLES

Every time Daisy stared at her plateful her stomach churned. 'It's the smell, Old Man Wood, I can't do the stink, you know that!' she looked exasperated. 'We don't have a dog, because I can't handle the whiff! *I don't do it!*' Her lips quivered and her eyes began to water. 'I can't—'

'Look at me, Daisy. Now,' Old Man Wood ordered. 'You must overcome your fears. That's what this is about. Push fear out of your mind and draw in the things you love.' He looked deep into her eyes. 'You can do this, no sweats, but you *must* concentrate, littlun. So, close your eyes, sweet Daisy—there, that's it—and imagine something apple-tastically delicious. Imagine it exactly, imagine every last little piece. Imagine how yummy that first bite is—the texture, the aroma, that apple-crunchiness, the smoothness. And remember, that thing in front of you is only an illusion.

'You saw me do it, didn't you?' Old Man Wood continued, 'so you must believe me when I tell you that the reward is well worth the trouble.' An idea popped into his head. 'Daisy, I want you to keep your eyes shut, understand?'

She nodded.

'Would you like me to give you a spoonful of your... your...'

'Duck. Crispy, aromatic, Peking duck,' Daisy said, quickly.

'Yes. A great choice,' he said. 'With cucumbers, spring onions and a blob of plum sauce?'

'Ooh yeah. Exactly,' she said and a flicker of a smile briefly turned up the corners of her mouth.

Daisy took a deep breath, clenched her eyes tight and licked her lips.

'Good. Now imagine the scene. It's your birthday party at that Chinese restaurant,' Old Man Wood said. 'Everyone is smiling, laughing—there's music and the waiters show you over to an immaculate white tablecloth where you take a seat. You're wearing your new red dress. Mum and Dad are squabbling over the wine list. Mrs. Pye is tidying Archie. Then it arrives; your fabulous crispy duck on a large platter. Everyone stops and stares, jealous of your excellent choice... and it's all yours. Your face lights up when you see it. Doesn't it smell wonderful?'

'Yes. Oh yes!' Daisy said. 'That's lush. Keep going, please.'

'Now, concentrate on the smells of the aromatic duck. It's been stripped off the bone and you've added a spoonful of plum sauce and sprinkled spring onions and cucumber on top. Now I'm rolling one up for you.'

Old Man Wood cut off a portion of the steaming dog turd from Daisy's plate.

'By goodness this is the finest pancake I've ever seen,' he said. 'Would you like to try it?'

Daisy nodded, her eyes closed tight.

'Open your mouth. I'll pop in your first delicious mouthful.'

Archie's eyes were bulging out of his head as he watched Daisy and his cheeks began puffing in and out. He pulled his hands up over his eyes and stared through the cracks of his fingers. A small squeal escaped from his lips but Old Man Wood flashed him an icy stare.

Daisy opened her mouth and took in the first mouthful, and it really was the most delicious mouthful of crispy aromatic duck she had ever tasted.

'Another bite, Daisy?' asked Old Man Wood gently.

'Oh my God, YES! It's AMAZING!'

Old Man Wood sliced another chunk off the large pile of canine excrement and raised it to her lips.

She opened her mouth wide as a tiny maggot crawled out of the poo. 'Mmm mmmmm. Guys, this is absolutely, divinely, scrumptilious,' she said. She took the whole mouthful in one go, licking her lips.

But suddenly, from the other side of the table came a loud

GA-DONK!

Followed by a crash.

Isabella lay motionless on the filthy floor. A thin trail of blood extended from the side of her head where she had clipped the stone table.

'Ah! No. Deary me,' Old Man Wood said, as he rushed over to her side. 'Are you there, littlun? Come along, wakey-uppy.'

He dabbed the cut with a handkerchief. She stirred and groaned and then wretched loudly, the noise reverberating around the room.

With Old Man Wood's help, she sat upright and felt for her head. 'OW!'

He kissed her forehead. 'Apples alive! Oh my! Oh my!' he said solemnly. 'This is harder than I ever would have thought, my specials,' he said, as if in private to Isabella.

'I don't think I can do this, Old Man Wood,' she said groggily.

'OH GOD! Get it off! GET IT OFF!' Isabella screamed. 'NO! NO! NOOO!'

She jumped off her stool and pointed at it accusingly, all the while backing away. 'I CAN'T EAT THAT,' she yelled. 'NO WAY!'

On Isabella's plate lay a decaying rat. Its inners crawled with hundreds of maggots that seemed to move as one body. Suddenly the rat with the maggots crawling inside it grew.

Isabella screamed and she shut her eyes, trembling. Then she curled up in a ball on the floor.

'But I think you can,' Old Man Wood said firmly. 'It's about what's going on in here.' He tapped his head.

'But it's impossible. You don't understand.'

Old Man Wood sighed and, while making a fuss of her and checking there were no obvious signs of concussion, he helped her up.

He turned to the table. For a moment he wondered if his eyes had deceived him.

'What in all the apples?! How... how did you manage that?'

Daisy's plate sat empty. Archie's too.

'Daisy licked her plate clean,' Archie said, squirming. 'It was quite easily the most repulsive thing I have ever seen. Anyway, everlasting gobstoppers are the dumbest things to choose, so I thought I'd shut my eyes and swallow them whole. They actually weren't that bad. Could have done with a glass of water to wash them down.'

Without warning, much to his and the others' surprise, Archie belched long and loud, the sound reverberating around the stone chamber rather eerily like a huge frog-croak.

In any other circumstance, it would have propelled the twins into uncontrollable hysterics, but this burp carried on and on and, as it did, a peculiar balloon grew from his mouth, expanding as he expelled the air. When he'd finished, he peeled it off his face, and left it to hang in mid-air, as if it were a helium balloon on a string.

'Bloody hell,' Daisy whispered.

'Fab-tab-e-dozey!' Archie cried, delighted with himself. 'It's the *belching from the family belly*! If we all do one—and join them up, then surely that's the way to get the second tablet!'

Daisy turned to Archie rather seriously. 'Archie. Girls like Isabella do not go round burping, and certainly not blowing out sticky bubbles,' she looked at him rather seriously. 'And for your information, neither do I.'

Unfortunately for Daisy a long, trumpet-like noise blasted out of her throat for the best part of several seconds. Out popped out a similar, sticky, golden balloon.

Stunned, she peeled hers off and joined the balloon to Archie's.

Almost immediately, an enormous deep croak, like a tree crashing down, grumbled out of Old Man Wood's mouth that went on and on and ended with another bubble. He instantly turned red and apologised profusely.

Archie could barely control himself. He convulsed until tears rolled down his cheeks. But his laughter ceased when they turned towards Isabella, who sat shaking in her chair, her face pale and sweaty.

Then their stares turned towards her plateful and collectively they gasped.

The size of the dead rat crawling with white maggots had now quadrupled to the size of a small cat.

Since all three of the children had, at various times, vomited in the tiny chamber, the aroma in the room was akin to a lavatory on a ferry boat full of sea-sick passengers.

But Isabella in particular had other things to concentrate on. For every minute that went by, the pressure was mounting. She curled her fingers up so that her nails dug into the palm of her hand to stop herself blacking out and, helped by Old Man Wood began some calming breathing measures.

'Your sister and brother have done it. And me, too—and utterly fan-tab-ulicious it was too. So you can do it. You know it's all about that smart head of yours, littlun.'

Isabella's lips began quivering. 'But I had months of therapy because of this.' She sobbed. 'Months... and now this... this... torture.'

'Come on, Bells,' Daisy said, moving in beside her and giving her a sisterly hug. 'It's simple—you know, mind over matter.'

She flashed a smile at Archie. 'If it's any help, mine was the most delicious dog poo I've ever had—'

'Don't be disgusting—'

'I'm not. It was perfectly cooked.'

'Firm on the outside with a nice soft centre,' Archie said.

'If I had half a brain,' Daisy said, 'I should have chosen a chocolate log.'

'Or lemon turd.'

'Or a big brownie.'

The twins howled with laughter.

Isabella's face, however, was set like thunder. Daisy noticed.

'Oh, come on Bells. I'm only joking. Look, all you have to do is concentrate on something you really, really want.'

'Why not try the Old Man Wood method? It was brilliant on Daisy,' Archie said, nudging the old man. 'Want to give it a go?'

Isabella nodded.

'Great.' Archie took a deep breath. 'Come on, you can do this. Now, shut your eyes. I'm sure your maggoty... er...

Daisy fired him a look.

'...your plateful, will be as delicious as, um, as, er...'

'...as mum's banoffee pie...' Daisy said, quickly.

'With an extra helping of my special thick cream,' Old Man Wood added. 'I know how much you love it.'

'With a couple of jelly babies on top?' Daisy said, licking her lips.

For the first time Isabella's lips crinkled into something that resembled a smile. Her face had more of a controlled look upon it. 'Yes. That sounds good.'

'Now, really, really believe it,' Old Man Wood said, his voice soft, deep and mellow. 'The sweet smells, how it feels in your mouth, how fabulous it looks...'

She forced herself to utterly concentrate until all she could think about was the sweet, textured, chocolaty toffee, and the dollops of cream and the squishiness of the bananas.

Old Man Wood cut out a slice off the rat and filled her spoon with a few stray maggots.

'The first amazingly scrumptious helping of thick banoffee pie coming up,' Archie said, as the old man offered up a heaped spoonful, complete with decaying dark fur, sinews and claws, to Isabella's mouth.

'With a few assorted jelly babies,' Daisy added, noticing the maggots.

The twins could hardly bear to watch.

As the spoon rose, silence filled the little room.

As Isabella's mouth closed over the spoon, Daisy let out a tiny gasp.

Then Archie emitted a kind of high-pitched squeak, a noise made not in horror, more in shock.

Isabella's mouth closed over the spoon, but she'd lost her concentration and instead of banoffee pie, the foul things she saw, rather than the toffee treat that had filled her mind, swamped her mouth.

She screamed, phleaux-ing and retching and hysterically flapping her arms, spitting endlessly.

As fast as he could, Old Man Wood draped his arms around her and held her tight, saying gentle things.

When the sobbing and moaning ceased, he released her.

Isabella looked at her plate and then across to the pale faces of her siblings.

On her plate was the maggoty rat, now the size of a fully-grown badger, dead and stinking and writhing with not hundreds, but thousands of maggots.

For the second time in only a short while, Isabella passed out.

Daisy shook her head, her expression betraying deep worry.

'She's out cold and that thing on her plate is... huge. She'll never do it on her own.'

'And it's beginning to stink.'

'Just like that trapped-under-the-floorboards-Archie-shoe-pong,' Daisy added, unhelpfully.

'Shut it, Daisy,' Archie fired back. He stroked a hair spike. 'Can't we just eat it?' he said. 'I mean, I'm game if you are.'

Daisy shrugged. It was a good idea considering the choices. 'OK. Nice one. What's it going to be?'

'Well, I was quite getting into the idea of banoffee pie. Those eyeballs didn't really fill me up. I think I can still feel them moving around.'

Daisy closed her eyes for a minute, imagining the Italian

desert. 'Yup. Banoffee pie it is,' she said. 'Old Man Wood, you look after Bells, we're going to finish this off for her.'

The twins leaned over the table and stared at the vast meal of a deteriorating rat filled with maggots. They each picked up a fork and glanced at one another for reassurance.

'Right,' Daisy said. 'On the count of three, the most delicious banoffee pie, in the universe.'

'In the universe,' Archie agreed.

'One, two ...' and before they even got to three, the twins plunged their forks into the sticky mess.

A millisecond later, a massive electric charge shot through their forks.

Their bodies zinged and catapulted backwards. They thudded into the wall and collapsed to the floor.

Archie groaned. 'So,' he said, as he rubbed himself down, 'no sharing. That's nice and clear.'

He looked over towards Daisy who lay motionless in a puddle of vomit.

'Oh! Great! Looks like she's out too,' and then he looked at the rat which was now the size of a medium-sized dog.

'What do you suggest, Old Man Wood?' he asked. 'Because if we don't come up with some way of getting Isabella to eat this, pretty soon we're going to die in the remains of a decaying rat. And maggots are going to eat us alive. If you've got an idea, now is the time to say something.'

But Old Man Wood stared back, his face as white as chalk, shaking his head. 'I... I don't know. It may already be too late.'

30 SOLOMON AND SUE

Sue made quite a fuss of Mrs. Pye.

After several minutes where Mrs. Pye stared at the wall, her body moving back and forth, Sue finally managed to get Mrs. Pye to look at her.

'It's me—Sue,' she said. 'I'm here with the headmaster and my boyfriend, Gus Williams.' It was the first time she'd ever said *my boyfriend* to anyone and the words slipped out with ease, and filled her with pleasure.

In fact she had a good mind to run around the courtyard singing: 'I've got a boyfriend and he's amazing and he loves me too-oo-ooo', adding in things like 'he's clever, he's cool, he's sweet but also hunky, la-la, in a kinda geeky way!' and then she'd whoop and scream in a stupidly high pitch fashion. And then she'd look about hope no-one was watching.

'We—Gus and me, survived the storm,' she said, barely controlling herself. 'I got a text from Bells. Amazing isn't it? Old Man Wood found them, didn't he?' she said, admiring herself in the mirror. Her skin exuded radiance. Was this from the spell of love?

'It was Bells' idea,' she continued, 'and Gus' genius at woodworking that saved us, I suppose. A, what would Old Man Wood say, "apple-tastic" miracle, Mrs. Pye, that's what it was.'

Sue sat down on the bed and took one of Mrs. Pye's hands in

hers. 'The world's gone crazy since I saw you last, and that wasn't even ten days ago. I hope those men weren't nasty to you? I don't think they meant to be. I guess they're just as confused as everyone else. A horrible man interrogated me. He had stinky breath and hard, calculating eyes that gave me the shivers. Anyway, it's a bit of a fluke that we managed to get away.'

Sue stood up and wandered around the room, picking up little pictures of the smiling, often toothless, de Lowe children growing up in the assorted frames on her mantelpiece.

'You don't know where they are, do you? We reckon they left in a bit of a hurry, probably in the night or early this morning. There's a terrible mess everywhere. Have you seen it? It looks like they've been in some kind of fight. Were there other people involved?'

Sue spotted a flash of alarm in Mrs. Pye's eyes. Did it relate to the missing children or the messy house?

'Let me get you a nice cup of tea,' she said. 'You look like you could use one. If I find a crumpet, I'll bring one over. Bit of jam —would that be alright?' Sue smiled sweetly. 'Now, don't you be going anywhere. I'll be back in a bit.'

Sue headed out of the door and, as she turned back to Mrs. Pye, for the first time, Mrs. Pye looked at her and smiled in her very odd way. 'Thank you,' she croaked, her voice shallow and troubled.

Sue smiled back. 'You really don't have to thank me, Mrs P. You're the one who needs thanking—for looking after them so beautifully.' Sue went over to her and planted a big kiss on her cheek. 'Back shortly.'

She turned and slipped away with a spring in her step, down the wooden stairs, around the rim of the foggy courtyard and back into the picture-filled mess of the cottage.

Solomon looked up as she walked in. He was studying a selection of older portraits on which the figure of an old-looking man with a strong family resemblance stared back. Each bore a similar, subtle-patterned background with date-marks a century or more apart. 'Any luck with Mrs. Pye?'

'She spoke two words: *Thank you*,' Sue said. 'Amazing, isn't it, the power of a cup of tea? Do you want one?' she asked.

'Yes, please. That would be lovely. Horrible tea at the hotel—a little too fancy for me,' Solomon said, returning his gaze to the pictures. 'It's really most strange.'

'Strange?'

'Well, yes. How the children and that old man have vanished without a trace. But I spotted a half-eaten toasted-sandwich lying on the floor of the kitchen. It didn't look old, if you ask me. I reckon it was discarded quite recently. Bread like that has a habit of hardening overnight and this slice seemed quite edible.'

'They call those sandwiches *empses*,' Sue said. 'Stands for *Mrs. Pye's Specials*. It's the de Lowe staple food when they're hungry—more often than not at breakfast. They're delicious—stuffed with cheese, ham, tomatoes and a poached egg. I'll try and make one if you're hungry, but Mrs. Pye's really are sensational. Have you seen Gus?'

'I believe he's somewhere upstairs, rooting around, seeing if he can come up with anything. A few odd noises coming from there. Scrapes and bashes, as if he's taken to moving furniture around. You might want to go and see how he's doing.'

Sue carried on through to the corridor that led into the kitchen. She added paper and kindling and then a couple of smaller logs into the belly of the range-cooker and, much to her joy, the fire spat into life.

Shortly, she opened the door, tossed in two larger logs, shut off the lighting vent, filled the kettle and set it on top of the range hob.

Wouldn't Gus be impressed?

She had half a mind to run upstairs and find him, but her thoughts turned back to strange old Mrs. Pye. She'd drop off a cup of tea for her and then go and find him.

She smiled at the thought. Alone with Gus at last. Sue plaited a section of hair as she let her imagination wander. *Was he,* she wondered, *at that very moment thinking the same thing?* Thinking of her? She smiled. *Of course he was.*

Sue inserted the whistle in the kettle spout and headed out of the door to rejoin the headmaster in the living room. When she saw him, she found he was comparing the portraits with the images he'd taken of the stained glass windows in Upsall church.

'Mr. Solomon,' she began, 'do you think there's something... you know, happening?'

The headmaster took off his glasses 'What kind of *happening* are you thinking of, Sue?'

'Some sort of end-of-the-world situation, you know, like Armageddon or something catastrophic from out of the Bible.'

Solomon sighed. 'There's no doubt our flooding and plague has remarkable parallels with ancient myths and legends. The question we need to ask, I suppose, is whether these things are in any way, normal. Events that come round as part of the general cycle of life—'

'Like a freak-of-nature? You think it might be a one-off?'

Solomon raised an eyebrow. 'Actually, Sue. No. No, I don't think it is,' he said, putting on his spectacles. 'There are too many strange occurrences, too many situations that boil down to something inexplicable and very sinister indeed.'

'Then, do you think the de Lowes are pivotal? After all, I dreamt of them, and I know Isabella had nightmares about all this stuff and Stone seems to think they're important.'

'That's what I mean,' Solomon said. 'Don't get me wrong, Stone can be a nasty piece of work, but he's jolly good at his job. He has a nose for sniffing out this kind of thing, an uncanny habit of finding the truth. He's going nearly mad with the overall confusion and his desperate lack of progress. The clock is ticking ever faster. Untold pressure is building on him in a big way.'

Solomon sat down heavily in Old Man Wood's chair, removed his spectacles and sighed. 'Look, I may as well tell you, Sue. The whole situation with the flooding and Ebora is steamrollering out of control. The Americans are going to drop a rather large bomb on North Yorkshire.'

Sue gasped. 'They're going to nuke us? Why?'

'The Ebora virus reached their shores a couple of days ago. It swept across the continent as night follows day. As our American cousins woke up, boof—there it was. Ebora had already made its mark. Don't you think that's a little strange?'

The headmaster stretched his arms out and rubbed his eyes. 'The pattern is continuing like this across the globe. An pandemic of global proportions. But I did hear just before we left that the rates of infection had somewhat decreased.'

'So, you're suggesting,' Sue said, 'that the virus *moved in the dark*?'

'Yes and no.'

'Now *you're* being cryptic.'

Solomon smiled. 'I think that it has something to do with sleep. My own hunch is that it may be about dreams.'

Sue's ears twitched. 'You really think so?'

'I know it may sound ridiculous, my dear, but I'm pretty sure we have to think outside our normal areas of understanding. I hardly dare say it, but our human mind is so programmed for a certain way of thinking that "out of the box" ideas are simply shuffled out of the way as if they are entirely insignificant. As a teacher I am, I fear, partly to blame. Our role is to bring children up to speed with the world we live in—to cope with the hustle and bustle of life on our planet. Anything out of the ordinary and we learn to siphon it off. We leave it to be discarded as irrelevant or slam it as nonsense. Do you have any idea of what I'm talking about, Sue, or does it sound like meaningless clap-trap?'

'No, I think I'm running with you,' she said. 'Just about.'

'Jolly good. Because I believe there are signs just about... everywhere. Tiny, abstract clues, so remote to our way of thinking that we cannot possibly begin to understand them.' He leaned down and picked up the portraits.

'Take these pictures. They date hundreds of years apart and yet I suspect they're one and the same thing, repeated over and over, as if they are a reminder—'

'Of what?'

'I wish I knew, dear girl,' Solomon said, examining the first and then the second. 'Now I'm struck by these rather interesting portraits. As you know, fashions change. Art, from the seventeenth century, has a totally different look and feel to art from the nineteenth century. And yet, looking at these, we find the same posture and the same background. It almost appears to be the same person. My guess is that these portraits are trying to tell us something.'

Sue peered at the pictures. 'I know it couldn't possibly be him, but you know, the nose, eyes, the kindly way he looks at everything. Don't those pictures remind you of Old Man Wood.'

Solomon leaned in and together they studied them. 'Sue, my dear, perhaps you're right, impossible as it seems. The problem is, we've got two days to figure this out and unless the de Lowes suddenly reappear and tell us what's going on, I'm not sure we've got the necessary skills or equipment—or time—to make a proper go of it. We're plucking at straws.'

'Do you think we're going to die?'

The headmaster smiled in a reassuringly head-masterly way. 'Yes, I'm afraid to say that I rather think we are,' he said. 'At the moment it looks very much like we're on a path of no return.' He sighed. 'Dying is nothing to worry about, my dear, because it is the one certainty in life—aside, of course, from taxation.' He chuckled inwardly.

'Our time may be coming a little sooner than we might have liked.' He shook his head. 'It is such a shame considering you and your friend's great abundance of talent. But enough of this depressing talk. May I suggest, that from this moment on, we absolutely believe that anything is possible. Agree?'

'Yes!'

'Good. With immediate effect we must throw away the shackles of everything we've ever been taught. Let's give our last few days our absolute all. Treat it like a fight to death!'

Sue felt better hearing a more positive tone. 'I agree,' she said. 'Where do we start?'

Solomon stood up purposefully and rubbed his chin. 'My suspicion is that this has something to do with a history that goes so far back in time that records don't exist—at least not for anyone to make sense of them. First off, let's try and find out if Mrs. Pye has noticed anything unusual—'

He was interrupted by the whistle on the kettle screeching loudly. Sue rushed off and returned with a pot of tea and several steaming crumpets. She poured a mug for the headmaster and another for Mrs. Pye. Armed with this, and a hot crumpet, she nipped out of the front door and around the foggy courtyard to see her patient.

31 A JOKE GONE WRONG

'Here, Mrs. Pye,' Sue said, putting the tray down on the table, 'a nice mug of tea for you and a crumpet, you must be starving. I found one of Old Man Wood's blue-coloured jams, bit of an odd colour for a jam, if you ask me, but I hope you like it.'

She removed the lid and sniffed it. 'Does he add colouring to it for a bit of fun, or is it some sort of weird blue fruit he uses?'

She handed Mrs. Pye the tea.

Mrs. Pye sipped as Sue continued to talk and soon nibbled on a crumpet.

'How's that going down?' Sue said, sitting next to her.

Mrs. Pye pulled a handkerchief out of her dressing gown pocket and blew her nose. 'Much better,' she said, before slipping it back in her pocket. 'And all thanks to you, little Sue. You're a kindly one, aren't you?'

Sue smiled. 'Well, it's a great relief to see you looking so much better. For a while I was pretty worried—what would the others say if they'd seen you in such a state, huh? They'd be worried sick.'

Mrs. Pye shook her head. 'They've gone a little in the head, you know?'

'Really?' Sue said, raising her eyebrows.

'Oh aye. I think everyone's gone a bit in the head to be

honest. All these comings and goings, you know. One minute here, the next they've shot off. And then strange noises and the children pulling pictures down and making a mess and explosions. I hardly dare go over there. Don't know what I might find.'

'When did you last see them?'

'The children were about this morning. I heard 'em. Don't know how you missed them, unless they was taken—'

'But has anyone been here apart from those soldiers this morning?' Sue asked.

A little cry came from within her as Mrs. Pye turned away.

'What is it?' Sue asked quietly, moving in and holding her hand.

The older woman pulled herself together a little. 'Now then,' she snivelled, 'there was another person.' She shook her head.

'Really?' Sue said softly. 'Who?'

Mrs. Pye burst into tears once again. 'You'd never believe me!'

'Of course I would.'

Mrs. Pye shook her head. 'But he wouldn't have taken them. Couldn't have.'

'Who?'

'That boy... my—'

'Which boy?' Sue said, confused.

'My son,' she squealed. 'My baby.'

Sue's mind raced. 'Are you alright, Mrs. P? Do you... do you want to lie down?'

Mrs. Pye squeezed Sue's hand tight. 'My child came to me, Sue. He did, really. Then he left—but he couldn't have taken the others with him. He didn't mean no harm. Just wanted to see me. Tell me he knew.'

'Knew what?' Sue repeated.

'That I was his ...'

'His, what?' Sue said.

'You know... mother,' Mrs. Pye said through her tears. 'That I was his—'

Sue reeled '... Mother?' she repeated.

'I always thought there might have been a child. But, you know, the accident and all that.'

Sue remained baffled. 'Are you sure? Are you sure it wasn't a ghost or something like that?'

'Don't be silly,' Mrs. Pye said. 'I know perfectly well who it was.'

'You *know* him?'

'Ooh, yes dear. Archie's friend. Don't think you girls like him so much.'

'Don't like him?' she said in amazement.

Sue leant back and studied her. Thick hair, fat lips.

Mrs. Pye looked up from her light blue, piggy eyes. 'You call him Kemp?' she said.

But Sue knew Kemp was miles away at Swinton Park. 'Kemp?'

Mrs. Pye nodded. 'That's the one.'

Sue shook her head, baffled, when all of a sudden the mist lifted.

'*Oh, Kemp*!' she laughed. 'But *that* Kemp only arrived by boat an hour or so ago, with me and the headmaster.'

How sweet that Gus had gone to see her first... but then again, how incredibly nuts to tell her he was her son. Why would he do that?

Sue shook her head. 'Look, I'll let you in on a secret. That Kemp is actually called Williams. Gus Williams.' And then she added because she couldn't resist it. 'My boyfriend.'

Mrs. Pye pulled her handkerchief out once more and sobbed into it.

Sue thought the whole thing most peculiar. Was Mrs. Pye confused? Was Gus confused?

Perhaps she should find Gus and ask him if he'd been over here being Kemp. And if so, that his joke had misfired badly.

32 FIGHT TO THE DEATH

'Surprised? Yeah, I bet you're bloody surprised!' Kemp said.

Gus took a step back. 'What are you doing here... you're not part of this, are you?'

Kemp sighed and sat down at the chair by the desk. 'Well, Williams, you could say I got here... by accident.'

'What happened to your head?' Gus asked.

Kemp ran a hand over his white cranium. 'Burnt off... it's a long story,' Kemp said, and smiled his fake, fat smile. 'Let's just say I had a lucky escape.'

'From what?'

'Death, I suppose,' he said, lifting his eyes to meet Gus'.

Gus suspected something fishy. 'What are you doing... what do you want?'

Kemp wiped his nose with the back of his hand. 'To be honest,' he began, 'it wasn't you I was hoping to find.'

'Who, then?' Gus said, confused. 'Archie?'

'Nah. The de Lowe's are a bit indisposed at the minute. Eating for their very lives.' He grinned. 'It's quite possible they'll never be seen again.'

Gus screwed up his face. 'I don't understand. Have you done something to them?'

'Me? No! Look, there's no way you could possibly understand,' Kemp said. 'It's none of your business.' He puckered his lips. 'Thing is, Williams, what exactly are *you* doing here, rummaging about Isabella de Lowes' bedroom like a perv?'

'I'm with Sue and the headmaster,' he replied coolly. 'We've been sent by the authorities to help find the de Lowes. They're in trouble but no one seems to know what it is. You know where they are?'

'Yeah, 'course I do,' Kemp said, thickly. 'To be honest, there isn't much I don't know.'

'Then tell me!'

'They're locked in a small room, not too far from here,' Kemp volunteered, 'until they work something out.'

Gus looked confused. 'How do you know all this?'

'I have an... associate, who's pretty worldly—'

'Worldly? I thought you were stuck in the hospital, burnt—'

'I was,' Kemp interrupted. 'But my companion had a change of heart.'

'Who is this guy?'

'He's an old man, that's all you need to know—'

Gus looked quizzically at Kemp. 'Hey! I know—I saw you,' he said, jabbing a finger at Kemp. 'You and an old man in the alleyway moments before the storm broke.' He rubbed his hands as he remembered. 'Weren't you? Someone in a long coat and a hat.'

Kemp leaned in and tapped his nose. 'As I was saying, Williams, it's really none of your business.'

An awkward silence fell between them.

'So, if you're not here for Archie,' Gus started, 'and you're not here for the de Lowes, you're here to see the headmaster, right?'

Kemp chuckled. 'Oh yeah. Hilarious. Nope, wrong again. I'm here for more... personal reasons.'

'To see Old Man Wood?'

Kemp shook his head. 'No, you daft, lanky git,' he said. He was enjoying Gus' confusion. 'Not old man whatshisface.'

'Then who?'

'I'm here to get Sue,' he said bluntly. 'You know, sexy Sue, best mate of freak-of-nature, Isabella-de-bleeding-Lowe.'

Gus' jaw dropped, and for a brief moment his brain froze as if he'd eaten a tub of ice-cream. *Had he heard that right?*

'I'm sorry,' he said at long last, 'you said, *get* Sue. What, exactly, are you talking about?' His fingers were shaking.

'Precisely that.' Kemp creased an eyebrow. 'You got a problem with it?'

Gus composed himself. 'What,' he said slowly, trying to mask his growing anger, 'makes you think Sue would be in any way interested in you?'

'Aha. Finally, a decent question, Mr. Williams. You see, this little union I'm going to propose, is based entirely on a lack of rival suitors.'

'Union? Lack of rivals?' Gus felt himself perspiring.

'Yeah.'

'Why?'

'Jeez, Williams. Don't tell me you haven't worked it out?'

Gus shrugged. 'This disease thing?'

Kemp raised an eyebrow. 'You're finally getting there,' he said. 'It's going to kill everyone, except me and Sue.'

Gus shook his head. 'But I still don't think she'll go with you, Kemp. She totally hates your guts—'

'I didn't say she would. That's why I said I'm going to *take* her.'

Gus felt winded. 'But she's going out with me,' he said softly. 'She's not yours to take—'

'Oh dear, oh dear. Is that right?' Kemp leered back. 'Unlucky.'

The curtain swished out of the way.

'The thing is,' said a much deeper and rather croaky voice to the other side of him, 'you're all going to die.'

'Bloody-nora!' Gus said, jumping out of his skin. '*What the ...*'

'Oh,' Kemp said. 'Meet my... associate. He's a ghost.'

Gus glanced around nervously as the voice started again.

'He'll be doing her a favour, you know.' The ghost parted the curtain and reappeared moments later wearing an overcoat and hat.

Gus gasped. 'What... who... are you?'

'I'm a spirit, and this young man has become my flesh and blood. Come on, boy, there's no time to lose.'

Gus tried to compose himself. 'You won't be able to take her with you,' he said. 'She'd rather die than go with you. I know her better than anyone. Trust me, Kemp.'

Kemp tutted. 'Thing is, Williams, you won't be any good to her when you're dead. Because, in a couple of days, everything here will be dead or dying and there's nothing you'll be able to do about it.'

'You don't know her!' he spat.

Kemp smiled his fat, cheesy, smug smile. 'You're missing the point,' he said coolly. 'I don't *have* to!'

'She won't do it!'

'Then I'll quite simply scoop her up, kicking and screaming. Like up a little dolly. It's as simple as that. You see, Gus, I'm going to need a woman to start a family, a very, very big family. Have loads of kids and all that.' He smiled, delighted by the agony it must be giving Williams.

'You'll do it over my dead body,' Gus roared.

'Very well. That's easily arranged. Look, I hate to break it to you, Williams, but like it or not, Sue's going to be, like, my very own *Eve*. After the annihilation of the planet, together, we're going to repopulate the world.'

Gus looked on in astonishment as Kemp casually walked over to the ghost and pushed an arm down the coat. First his legs and then his left hand morphed into a curious material.

Dust fell to the floor. Ash?

A terrible fury tore through Gus. Before he knew what he was doing, he hurled himself at Kemp, his hands going directly for his throat, crushing Kemp's windpipe.

Kemp gargled and tried to fight back but, being made of ash, his punches to Gus' midriff came to nothing more than puffs of dust.

Gus squeezed harder, gritting his teeth.

Kemp's face reddened and he fell to his knees.

'*Let go of him*,' the ghost's voice ordered.

'NO,' Gus roared, 'unless he promises not to touch Sue.'

As the ash leached up Kemp's body towards his neck, Gus was finding it increasingly difficult for his hands to stay attached. Ash flew about as though scattered by an electric fan.

Kemp floundered and Cain could feel his suffering.

'HALT!' the ghost cried out. 'This helps no one.'

Gus snarled. 'As I said, NO!'

'I will make you an offer—'

'Not good enough. Promise me—'

'Promises do not exist. I will make you the very best next thing: an offer,' Cain said. 'But only if you release him now.'

'Help!' Kemp croaked, his head puce.

Gus released Kemp and, as he did, Kemp's body crashed to the floor. Moments later, the ghost stood next to Gus watching Kemp fighting for breath.

The ghost's hat tilted upwards. 'You have no idea what you've just got yourself into.'

The tense figure of Gus stood shaking, staring alternately at Kemp and then at the ghost.

'What is your name?' the ghost barked.

'Gus.'

'Gus,' the ghost repeated. 'Good. I cannot be doing with a weakling as my companion. You have given yourself a chance to save yourself. And you may be a better match than this boy, although he does have certain qualities I admire.'

'Tell me your offer,' Gus panted. 'But before that, tell me who you are!'

'I am the ghost of Cain. I cannot die but my power was removed and my flesh stripped from me. I exist as a spirit and I am the Master of Havilah and soon to be ruler of the universe. Is that sufficient?'

Gus said nothing.

'Here's my offer—'

'Let me kill him,' Kemp said, hoarsely.

'No. In matters like this,' Cain said, 'it is important to keep one's word. However, only one of you can come along.' He addressed Kemp. 'The boy bested you. He deserves a chance.'

'A chance?'

'To survive, boy.'

'What sort of chance?' Kemp's voice hinted on nerves.

'One of you must die.'

'*Die?*' both boys repeated.

'Indeed. You will fight each other in a fight to the death. The winner comes with me and brings the "hot" girl named Sue.'

'To the death?' Gus said, shaken.

'There is no room for another.'

Gus whimpered.

'Just one winner,' Cain said. 'But you must willingly, with all your heart, and with all your soul, agree to come with me—or the deal's off. You agree?'

Kemp sat on the floor, caressing his neck. His face was purple with rage. 'I know this freak, Cain. He'll never do it—he'll never, ever, go with you,' Kemp croaked. 'He doesn't have the balls—'

'Do what?' Gus fired back. 'Go with who?'

Kemp coughed. 'Look, Williams. You have to give yourself freely to the ghost. When you're combined, he's the one in control and, believe me, he's a freaking maniac. My advice to you, Williams, is don't do it. It's one step too far.'

'But it's alright for you is it, Kemp?'

'Listen to what the ghost said: you don't know what you've got yourself in to. I promise you, Williams, for you, death would be better.'

Gus shook. 'Why do you say this?'

'Because it's true. You're giving your soul to the devil, Gus. You'd be better off dying rather than suffer what he has to offer.'

Cain tutted from under his hat. 'Well, well, well, boy. What a dramatic speech. Who knows,' he said drily, 'Gus has earned the choice, and it is a simple one; do nothing and die helplessly in the oncoming destruction of the planet. Or kill you and spend the rest of his life ruling all the known worlds with me, alongside a girl he clearly cares very deeply for.'

Cain paused. 'Personally, I think my offer is rather a good one; I know which one I'd choose. What do you think, Gus? It must be tempting? And, of course there would be so many fewer relationship issues for me to deal with.'

The ghost turned towards Gus. 'Therefore I offer myself to him right now to discover what lies ahead.'

It took a couple of moments before Kemp clicked. 'But... you can't—what about me?'

'Be quiet, boy,' Cain snapped. 'As I said, Gus has earned the right to give our union a try. If he prefers death, then he cannot complain that he never had a fair chance.'

Gus quaked. 'What do I—?'

'Willingly put the coat on,' Kemp said, reluctantly. 'Like I was doing when you went for me. But don't struggle. Then put on the hat. Close your eyes as the feeling moves up into your head. You'll get a wicked burning feeling, so relax and don't fight it. Take a good look at my baldy head if you want proof of what happens when you struggle. Got it?'

'Sure,' Gus said.

'How else do you think I ended up in hospital covered in burns, huh?'

Gus stared at his foe.

Kemp grinned. 'It was by way of this lunatic.'

Gus examined Kemp. He hesitated.

'Look,' the ghost said, sounding a bit bored, 'if you cannot freely join with me then there is no contest. You, my old friend, win. It's as easy as that.'

'Wait,' Gus said. 'I need to think—'

'Sorry, there's no time for any of that,' the ghost crowed. 'It's now or never. Come along, Kemp.'

Kemp stood up and rubbed his neck. 'I didn't think you could,' he jibed. 'Always been just a little too much like a chicken.'

In a flash, Gus moved in front of Kemp.

Then, looking Kemp straight in the eye, he thrust one arm down the coat's sleeve-hole and, without delay, the other. His eyes rolled back and he squeezed out a long groan.

Now, the cold treacle-effect coursed through his body, along every vein and artery and down every sinew and fibre in him, thrilling him.

Kemp closed in.

'Keep away,' the ghost barked. 'We won't be gone long.'

Gus groaned ever more as the cold liquid rounded his brain.

'Dreamspinner, dreamspinner, dreamspinner,' Cain barked into the air.

'You're not going,' Kemp said desperately. 'You can't leave me here.'

'Of course we are. I have to show the boy what he would be missing. It wouldn't be fair otherwise.'

Two dreamspinners appeared out of the sky.

'Back to Havilah, right away,' he barked, and, using Gus' body, Cain bent down.

'You know,' he said to Kemp, 'it might not be a bad idea to be friendly to this "hot" girl. Trust me. You will never have a more opportune time to try.'

And with that, Cain and Gus dived off through the maghole of the dreamspinner and vanished in a tiny flash of light.

Silence filled the room. Kemp scanned the attic, the floor of which lay covered in ash.

He heard footsteps starting up from the bottom of the stairs, creaking lightly at first, then louder, step by step.

'Gu-uss,' a voice called out.

Kemp squirmed. Shit. Sue. What would he tell her? The truth? Make something up?

'Gus, honey, where are you?' she said. 'Are you hiding from me, big fella?'

Kemp looked around for somewhere to hide. In Isabella de Lowe's bed? Hell. The bloody irony.

What was he going to do?

33 THE DEAL

Kemp thought fast. What should he say? Could he run off to see his mother? *His mother!* Just the thought filled him with such joy that a burst of love, of joy, coursed through his veins.

But what good was that now? He'd accepted an offer of a fight to the death, against Gus Williams. *To the death*! Kemp shook. Could he do it? He had to: if he won, he would have a mother—the one thing he'd yearned for all his life.

Sure, they'd give each other a kicking, a few punches, but... death. That was an entirely different matter. In front of him lay the currency of survival; the price of living, the ledger of life and death.

More importantly, Kemp thought, *did Gus have it in him to kill him?*

Already, in their short time together, Cain had done unspeakable things, but it was always Cain's doing, not his. Never his.

To Cain, every life was expendable and in their new arrangement he was the body, the muscle and he'd learnt that it wasn't worth arguing. Whatever Cain wanted, he obliged, and as such, Kemp didn't care either.

The experience was thrilling and powerful. With this attitude he felt like a king, a god. But this was Cain's hand at work, not his. When it came to his schoolmates, even if they didn't like each other, murder by *his* hands was an entirely different matter.

In two bounds he was in Archie's section, throwing himself on the bed.

The door opened. The floorboards groaned.

He heard her call out, rather sweetly, 'Gus?'

Suddenly the rings of the curtain pulled back. His heart thumped in his chest.

A gasp.

Whatever you do, please don't scream, he thought.

She stared as he moaned. He turned awkwardly in the bed.

She rushed towards him, concerned.

Kemp knew exactly what he had to do. He needed her sympathy.

He needed to fake it.

Make it look like he was a victim.

He rolled and cried out, as though in agony.

Soft hands rested on his forehead.

He groaned.

He smelt her as she sat beside him. A simple, soft, fragrance, like perfumed blossom.

'I'm sorry,' he said, sadness in his tone. He couldn't think of anything else to say. 'Please... please don't hurt me,' he added, for effect.

Her hand moved from his forehead across his bald head. 'I'm not going to hurt you, understand?'

He nodded.

'Is it you, really you?' she said, a puzzled tone to her voice. 'I don't understand. How did you get here?'

Kemp rolled over and faced her, tears in his eyes. 'I don't know... I... I stole a boat... walked ...' he stammered. 'No one was here when I arrived.'

Sue walked around the room. When she opened the curtain to Isabella's section, she stopped and kicked at a pile of ash. 'What happened in here? It's like there's been a fire—but without a fire?' she examined some of the marks in the ash. 'Do you know where Gus is?'

Kemp shook his head. 'Sorry.' He noted the disappointment in her face and pulled himself up. 'You... you survived, you made it.'

Sue came over. 'Ssh,' she said. 'Can I get you something? You must be starving.' She smiled and held his hand briefly. 'Mrs. Pye told me your news.'

Kemp flinched. 'News?' he repeated.

Her eyebrows lifted and she smiled sweetly. 'That she's your mother,' she said. 'I think it's one of the most amazing stories I've ever heard.'

Kemp smiled. He couldn't help it. 'Thanks, Sue,' he said. 'Look, I'm so sorry—'

'Don't—'

'No... I'm sorry about being such a terrible dick-head to you and Isabella. I've learnt my lesson.' For once, he meant it.

'That's really sweet of you,' she said. 'And it's all in the past. Let's forget about it, OK?' She smiled. 'Looks like you've been through enough to last several lifetimes.'

'Yeah,' he said in as affected a way as he could achieve.

Sue remained sitting on the side of Archie's bed. 'You sure you don't know where Gus is?'

'Sorry, I've been asleep... for hours, I think.'

'And that ash. Any ideas? It's like Mrs. Pye filled a bucket from the fire and dumped it over Isabella's floor.' She screwed her face up. 'Weird, isn't it? Thing is, I'm sure he came up here,' she said, scrutinising Kemp's body and the similar, strange-looking, dusty marks on him.

'Oh well. Gus probably sneaked downstairs at some point.' She looked into his eyes. 'Why don't you grab a bite in the kitchen—if you're feeling strong enough—tell us about your adventures? Someone in the hospital told me all about you. They said it was a miracle you survived, said that you were the bravest person they've ever come across. There's a pot of tea just brewed if you want.'

She turned and walked round the room, inspecting it. Then she headed off down the stairs, looking back at him before disappearing out of view.

Kemp forced a smile back, turned over and exhaled. *Oh hell. Little did she know what was about to kick off in this game of survival...*

Sue looked nice enough—exquisite, if he was honest—but the thought sucked on him like a leech that if Sue came with him to Havilah, he'd ruin her, like a group of school kids carving their names on priceless artwork with penknives. Besides, wasn't she just a little too old for him? Daisy would be a better bet, for sure, but how would that happen?

Kemp wanted to cry. He'd survived and found his mother, and he'd been prepared to die for that chance, so what was the point of throwing it all away now? But if he didn't take Sue, then Gus would, because Gus loved her and was prepared to die for her.

And, he suspected, that if it came to a simple choice, Gus would indeed kill him.

So, Kemp thought, if he was to have his mother and a girl, it had to be Sue and therefore, Gus would have to die.

And when that happened, it would break her heart, and it would break his heart too.

'You're staying here,' a voice said, out of the blue.

Kemp sat bolt upright. 'What? Cain? Is that you?'

'I said, you're staying.'

Kemp thought he'd mis-heard. 'No, I am not. I need to get out of here, with you, now.'

'A change of plan, boy,' Cain responded. 'You will stay here until the Heirs of Eden—your de Lowe chums—either come out of there alive, or do not come out at all. You will prepare for a fight to the death with Gus. I cannot have both. There are fewer dreamspinners than Asgard thought.'

'I want to go with you,' Kemp implored. 'Girl or not—'

Cain sucked in a breath. 'You don't want the "hot" girl?'

'I didn't say that.'

'You implied it, boy.'

'I never—' Kemp thumped the pillow. 'I don't bleeding well know, do I?'

Cain's presence loitered. 'I sense confusion in your mind.' He sniffed the air. 'I sense that maybe you desire another. Perhaps it is the other Heir of Eden, Archie's twin. Hmmm. It is a better choice, but, dear boy, have you forgotten? That the Heirs of Eden are about to die in the chamber of Blabisterberry Jelly in a quite horrible suffocating death.' The ghost sighed. 'You will fight Gus at the ruin and you will win because there is something I know that you do not.'

Kemp drew in a breath. 'What?'

'Even if the children come through, the final tablet of Eden rests within the rocks of the ancient building near this house.'

'At the ruin? On top of the cliff?' Kemp said. 'But there's nothing there—'

'Beneath it,' Cain cut in, 'a structure is carved into its belly. Here, a beast has woken after a long, deep sleep. This beast, Gorialla Yingarna, the mother serpent, is my friend. We go back in time. She knows that the price of her freedom is the death of the Heirs of Eden.'

'What do you propose to do with this monster-mate of yours?'

'I cannot free it from its walls, for the ancient rules of the universe say that meddling directly with the Heirs of Eden and their quest will bring them immediate triumph. I do not wish to lose as I, like you, have a mother to save. That is why, secretly, I have chosen you to be with me, not that other boy. He doesn't have the necessary charm nor your warped sense of justice. Furthermore, he is more afraid of killing you than you are of him.'

Kemp buzzed at the thought. But if the idea of battering Gus to death filled him with dread, goodness knows what kind of state of mind Gus must be in.

'What's your plan?'

Cain, though invisible, smiled. Kemp felt it. 'We cheat.'

'Cheat,' Kemp said, 'Really?'

'Of course, you numbskull.'

'How?'

'I will show you,' Cain said. 'This way the pain will be easier for both of you to bear. Moreover, if Gus dies in, let's say, a terrible accident, where perhaps you are trying to save him, eventually Sue may, at length, give you her trust. She never needs to know there was a fight, or that we made an *arrangement*. You will fight Gus at the ruin where there is a hidden entrance that leads into the structure beneath the ruins. I will point it out to you. Get him close and Gus will fall into the beasts' lair—a little meal for the mother serpent.'

'What if he gets me first?'

'You must avoid him at all costs. I will do the final flourish for, as you know, I do have an element of oomph in my ghostly being.'

Kemp outwardly exhaled. He could live with this plan. Once again, the ghost's scheming felt neat, tight.

Footsteps—a boy's, walking up the stairs.

Gus entered, rubbing his scalp.

'Some of your hair missing?' Kemp said, grinning. He sniffed the air. 'You honk.'

Gus raised his not-so bushy eyebrows. 'All your hair disappeared, so I don't know why you're so pleased with yourself. Or hadn't you noticed?'

Kemp smiled badly. 'Think you can handle it?'

'Yeah. Course I can. No big deal,' Gus said. 'Me and the spirit got on just fine, didn't we?'

'You did well, boy,' Cain said. 'Now you know how to dance with the devil. Are you ready to live with it?

'Yeah,' Gus said confidently. 'When?'

Cain summoned Asgard and together they spoke in a low voice. Then his trilby turned towards the boys and tilted upwards.

His voice sounded victorious. 'The Heirs of Eden,' he crowed, 'are in serious trouble. Should they not succeed in their task within the next hour, they will die. In this case you will fight at noon tomorrow. If, by some miracle, they succeed and emerge from the cavern, you will engage with one another five hours after midnight at the ruin, as light breaks. It will give you a chance to say your farewells.'

'That's it then?'

'Yes. Time is running out for everyone. The end is fast approaching. One of you will live and the other will die.' Cain's voice lowered. 'Say not a word to anyone. Especially the "hot" one. Do not cross one another and do not be late. I will provide a weapon for each of you at the appointed hour. For my part, I am off to see the stage of your duel and speak with Gorialla Yingarna so she knows what to expect.'

Cain tilted his hat. 'Until tomorrow, boys.' And then he vanished, leaving his coat and hat falling to the floor.

34 GAIA REVEALS

Gaia, the dreamspinner, flashed from the corner of the cavern, in which Blabisterberry Jelly was causing untold havoc, and arrived in the attic room where Kemp lay in wait for Sue. She hid in a corner, invisible to the human eye.

Right now, the children looked as likely to fail as they ever had. And, with only two and a half days to go, Cain was spinning his web around them using the children's friends as his allies. Even as a spirit, Cain was a smart operator, but how far would he push the parameters of the unwritten rules?

Gaia inverted through her maghole and found Genesis. 'Mother, you seem better,' she said, walking towards her.

'Enough!' Genesis snapped back. 'We must aid the Heirs of Eden. The finding of Blabisterberry Jelly is all in the mind. Use dream powders to stimulate the girl.'

'I have done much already. I dare not meddle again.'

Genesis reared up. 'Gaia! Does Asgard care?'

'But we are different.'

'Huh! Do as you did with the old man. Dreamspinners do not want—will never want—dream-powders from Havilah. It is a nasty, short-term solution. Go now. Let the girl understand the true nature of Blabisterberry Jelly.'

Gaia inverted and flashed to the scene of foodie hell in the small room. In no time she was over Isabella, the dream powders invisibly sucked deep into her lungs with every long, deep breath.

There. It is done.

With any luck, she would dream fast, and then the girl will wake. So long as the girl interpreted the visions correctly, her understanding would be enriched. Her choices clearer.

Gaia looked at the table and the foul, rotting beast that now sat upon it.

Blabisterberry Jelly grew in proportion to the time and struggle. She knew that at a certain point of enlargement, there came a tipping point, whereby one person's eating alone would not suffice. For if Blabisterberry Jelly suspected it could not be beaten, it would grow exponentially, quickly suffocating those inside the room.

By the size of the huge, decaying monster pulsing with maggots on the table, that moment had already been and gone.

35 ISABELLA COMES TO LIFE

Isabella leapt to her feet as though a bolt of lightning had smashed into her. 'I've got it!' she said, pointing a finger in the air.

Archie jumped. 'Bells! You're back! You OK?'

'Couldn't be better,' she said. She turned towards Daisy. 'What happened to her?'

Archie wondered if this was the same Isabella. 'Knocked out,' Archie said, 'just like you.'

Isabella whistled, picked her way across the foul-smelling floor and picked Daisy up. 'Come on, come on, little sis. I'm going to need your help.'

'Help?' Archie said. 'For what?'

'To eat that enormous banoffee pie on the table. I can't do it on my own.'

Archie exchanged looks with Old Man Wood and twirled his finger around his temple as if she were mad. They sat down as Daisy stirred.

'OK,' Isabella said. 'Now, come on. Why don't we all tuck in?'

'Because,' Archie said, 'the last time we tried, Daisy and I were propelled into the wall *and,* believe it or not, the wall won.' He raised his eyebrows. 'Between you, me and these four walls, I'm not sure I'm ready to do it again.'

'I am,' Daisy slurred, as she joined them, nestling her head in her hands. 'Beats death-by-maggot any day.'

'Excellent, Daisy!' Isabella cried. 'Come on then! Let's do it!'

'You cannot be serious?' Archie said, nervously.

'I'm deadly serious, bro. Loosen up,' Isabella said, as she held her spoon in one hand and kissed it in a mildly theatrical way.

Daisy picked hers up and tried to do the same but it went wrong and clattered to the floor.

'Leave that there, Daisy darling,' Isabella said. 'You won't be needing it.'

Archie and Daisy exchanged glances.

'This is how we're going to proceed,' Isabella said. 'I'm going to sing a song.'

'Really? You're going to sing?' Daisy quizzed. 'Do you have to?'

'Of course. I have the finest voice in all the world.'

Archie heard a small guffaw from Old Man Wood. He found himself staring at the floor to hold back the floodgates of nervous hysterics.

Isabella stood up. 'Now, it goes like this,' she began. 'I'll stand here in front of my banoffee pie and, on my command, you lot are going to line up over there.'

'She's gone completely mad,' Archie whispered.

Old Man Wood draped an arm around him. 'She's got a plan, Archie, and no one else has a plan, and we need a plan, and apple-fast. Let's see how it goes, huh?'

Isabella turned on them. 'Be quiet you two!' she said. 'The first spoonful is for me, then, the next one is for you. I can't eat all of that banoffee pie on my own, so you're going to help me. Are you all clear with this?'

Archie and Daisy swapped glances. 'I'm not sure we're allowed to eat yours. It nearly killed us last time we tried.'

'We'll see about that,' Isabella said. 'The difference is that this time, *I'm* going to feed *you* with *my* spoon.'

'You sure this is going to work?'

Isabella looked astonished. 'Of course it is! Do you think I'm crazy, or something?'

Daisy pulled a face that implied they did.

'Anyway,' Isabella continued unabashed, 'I don't think there's another option, do you? Now, mine is delicious banoffee pie. Yours can be whatever you want it to be. But you must say it out loud.'

This time, it was Daisy's turn to question her. 'Sis, are you totally one hundred and a little bit percent sure about this?'

'Of course! The brain works far better with spoken commands rather than concealed inside the grey matter.' She sucked in a massive breath. 'Now I want you to sing with me—are you ready Daisy?'

'Sing?'

'Absolutely. Follow my lead.'

Daisy nodded, slowly.

'Archie?'

'Er, yeah. I suppose.'

'Not good enough. Yes or no?'

'Yes,' Archie said, beads of sweat bubbling on his forehead.

'Old Man Wood?'

'Absolutely. Can't wait.'

'Good. That's the way.' She shut her eyes. '*Banoffee pie, banoffee pie, I need banoffee pie*,' she chanted.

She continued, a little more assuredly, clapping slowly in time with the words encouraging the others to join her. She cut away a spoonful.

'*Banoffee pie, banoffee pie, I need banoffee pie*,' she popped the spoonful in her mouth. 'Del-i-c-i-ous!'

Isabella pointed at Daisy as she chewed. Daisy came forward and opened her mouth.

'*Duck pancake, duck pancake*' she said out loud. The others joined in. '*I need a duck pancake.*' Isabella sliced a spoonful off and fed Daisy's open mouth.

'Mmmm.'

'*Banoffee pie, banoffee pie, I need banoffee pie*,' Isabella said again, quickly popping a spoonful in her mouth.

Now it was Archie's turn, '*Steak and chips, steak and chips*,' everyone joined in. *'I need steak and chips!'* Archie munched it down, a look of blissful surprise on his face.

'Banoffee pie, banoffee pie, I need banoffee pie,' they sang as Isabella scoffed on her latest helping.

Old Man Wood came up to the table.

'Starlight apple crumble with lovely thick cream, starlight apple crumble with lovely thick cream. I need starlight apple crumble with lovely thick cream,' they laughed, as their mouths struggled with the words.

He devoured the spoonful.

'Banoffee pie, banoffee pie, I need banoffee pie,' they sang. Isabella demolished another mouthful.

'Roast chicken dinner,' Daisy tried and repeated clapping her hands. *'She needs a roast chicken dinner.'*

Gulp.

And on it went:

Archie; *'Strawberries and cream.'*

Old Man Wood; *'Fish pie.'*

Daisy; *'Liver and bacon.'* (ugh, from Archie!)

Archie; *'Scrambled eggs.'*

Old Man Wood; *'Beef stew.'*

Daisy; *'Chocolate ice cream.'*

Archie; *'Spaghetti Bolognese.'*

Old Man Wood; *'A juicy apple.'*

Daisy; *'Chicken stir-fry.'*

Archie; *'Seafood paella.'*

Old Man Wood; *'A juicy pear.'*

Daisy; *'Strawberry jelly.'*

Archie; *'Orange jelly.'*

And they looked at one another, wondering if Old Man Wood might say *Blabisterberry Jelly,* but instead he said:

'Carrot jelly.'

'You're so weird, Old Man Wood,' Daisy said, and in the same breath, *'lemon sorbet.'*

Archie; *'Veg spring roll.'*

Old Man Wood; *'Starlight apple crumble.'*

After each mouthful, Isabella took a large spoonful of the maggoty-rat-banoffee pie.

After a lull in enthusiasm where the pace lessened, the children and Old Man Wood puffed out their cheeks, their tummies expanding.

'We're nearly there,' Daisy announced. 'A couple more each, that's all. She clapped her hands. 'We can do this!'

The noise level increased.

'*Fillet steak, fillet steak*,' Archie said. '*I need fillet steak*,' they shouted.

Isabella tucked in again. But she was struggling to maintain her concentration.

Archie noticed. When it came round to him again he said, '*Celery, celery. I need celery.*

'Ugh. *Celery*,' Daisy quipped. 'Everyone knows Celery is disgusting.'

'... But it's mainly water, isn't it?' he said. 'I'm not sure I can fit anything else in.'

'Two more,' Daisy yelled. 'Come on, Old Man Wood.'

The children clapped repetitively. But Old Man Wood's brain had gone blank

'What is your food, Old Man Wood,' Isabella demanded.

'Hmm, there is something—'

'Another apple, perhaps?'

'Not this time,' he said rubbing his chin. 'This one's special,' he said with a big smile on his wrinkly old face. 'Yes, I know! Mammoth testicles!'

The children collectively looked at him.

'Mammoth testicles?' Archie said.

'Mammoth bollocks?' Daisy said, incredulously.

'Oh, it's an apple-tastic delicacy I believe I used to be very fond of.'

Isabella cut out a portion as the others clapped.

'*I need mammoth testicles*,' they howled, laughing.

'Last one, Bells!' Daisy yelled, 'it's all yours.'

Isabella felt so enormous that it would need a crane to move her. She took a deep breath. 'OK. Here we go.'

'What's it going to be?' Archie asked.

'There is one thing,' she said, eyeing up the goblet, 'that has to be the best thing of all—'

'Oh, no.' Archie said. 'I'm not sure that's a good idea.'

'Oh, yes it is,' she said, drawing a deep breath. '*Blabisterberry Jelly*,' she said. '*I need Blabisterberry Jelly.*' Her eyes sparkled as the others looked on with a mixture of amazement and trepidation.

'*I need Blabisterberry Jelly*,' they yelled.

Isabella gathered the last morsels onto her spoon, held it up to the others like a toast, and shoved it in.

'*Eurgh... Revolting...*

'*YUM...*

'*OH NO! ... Urggugh...*

'*... oooooohHHHH*

'*CRIKEY ... OW! ...*

'*INCREDIBLE!*

'*... No! Hang on... good! Oh YES!... no ...*

'*Blimey... Yeeeessss!*

'*WOOOOOWEEE!*'

She tossed her spoon into the corner of the room and wiped her mouth.

Silence filled the room.

'God, I'm full,' Daisy said, swaying on her stool.

'Me too. Don't think I can move,' Archie replied. 'I think I'm going to be sick.'

All four sat for a minute, digesting.

Finally Archie spoke again. 'Well, I'm not sure I can believe it,' Archie said. 'Tell me, Bells, what did Blabisterberry Jelly taste like again?'

Daisy hit him on the arm.

Getting up, smiles spread across their faces. Suddenly all four of them were jumping up and down, as energetically as they could in view of the vast quantities they'd scoffed, like a football crowd enjoying a dramatic win.

Suddenly it happened.

From out of Isabella's mouth the most enormous burp they'd ever heard burst forth, like the long, unwavering note of a

French horn, and it continued on and on, producing a balloon out of her mouth that looked like a mini amber-coloured tent.

Archie laughed so hard that he had to hold his sides and for a moment thought his eyeballs might come up. Then he burped again, followed by Daisy and finally Old Man Wood, who looked deeply embarrassed, the noise a cacophony of burpy trumpeting.

Daisy clapped her hands. 'Put them together. Put the burp-bubbles together. Isn't that what we've got to do?'

Carefully they stuck the strange, floating, sticky bubbles together. Nothing happened.

'Are you sure we're doing this right?' Isabella said.

'Well, I don't know,' Archie said. 'It's not like I know anyone who specialises in this kind of thing.'

Immediately, a huge...

"POP"

... as though a massive cork had blown out of a champagne bottle, reverberated around the room, followed by a *"PUFF"* like a firework, with a plume of colourful, showy glitter.

And there, on the table lay a stone tablet, identical to the one that had come from the fire, with matching markings.

The stairwell they'd come down in the first instance reappeared and they dashed up it and into the dark, foggy courtyard. Collectively they drew in a large lungful of fresh air and, when they looked back, the stairs had reverted to a normal, grey-coloured paving slabs as though nothing had happened and the room had never been.

Archie was desperate to know one thing. 'Old Man Wood, we had to overcome our worst fears. Daisy hates dog poo after the slipper episode when she was little, Isabella screams the house down if she sees rats—or maggots for that matter—and those must have been the eyes of the blind Ancient Woman from my dreams. But who, and what, were those weird kind of spiders doing on your plate?'

'Hmmm,' Old Man Wood said, a little taken aback. 'That,

littlun, is most observant. That spidery-thing you saw, if I'm not mistaken, was a dreamspinner. These aren't spiders like the ones that busy themselves in the corners of a room. *These dreamspinner creatures give dreams to living things*.'

'Dreams?'

'Oh yes. There's very little known about them—humans don't even know they exist—until now, of course. They're extraordinary, remarkable things.'

'But why do you fear them so much?'

'Anyone as old as I am fears them, for they know the truth of space and time. And if you must know, I had the same nightmare involving a dreamspinner spider night after night. The dream was trying to tell me something.' He scratched his wispy hair as he wondered about it, his frown lines growing deeper on his brow.

'You see, dreamspinners control what goes into your dreams and, in a way, your ability to think, create and discover. Dreamspinners put in the seed, the germ of an idea, or thought into your head, but then it's up to the individual receiver as to how it germinates—how it's interpreted.'

Archie's heartbeat quickened as he thought about the creature he'd seen over Daisy before the storm. 'So these dreamspinner things are responsible for the crazy, mad dreams we had?' he said.

'Certainly. Those dreams were almost certainly given to you by one of those spidery creatures I gobbled up!'

Archie shivered. This explanation was a little more complicated than he felt like understanding right now. He glanced over at Daisy who looked as if she was about to throw up. 'Come on, you lot. Time to get inside. I really need to lie down.'

More than anything though, a tickling in his stomach gave him the feeling he, too, needed to be very sick indeed.

A nagging thought toyed with Old Man Wood's mind: If Archie's "fear" was to eat the eyes of this blind, Ancient Woman he'd spoken about, then who did the other eyeballs belong to? After all, there had been *two* sets of eyes on his plate.

Old Man Wood searched the depths of his mind. Somewhere, somehow, he'd known both. One, a soft, nutty-brown set, with a look of yearning. The other two fractionally larger, with a distinct, icy, pale-blue madness about them.

Why did these warrant his attention? They were familiar—eyes from a long time ago, but whose? And as he wondered, he remembered something vitally important. Wasn't there something utterly crucial about eyes? Something brilliant and possibly sinister? Something magical that he couldn't quite lay his finger on?

Why, oh why, was Archie so desperately frightened of them?

36 A CURIOUS REUNION

'For goodness' sake, be quiet you two,' Solomon said. What a perfectly awful evening. While he'd tried to continue his investigations, Kemp and Gus Williams had been at each other's throats, their comments towards one another were acidic to put it mildly.

Finally he snapped. 'I'm fed up with you two,' he said. 'You're not helping me, or anyone. I rather hoped it might be a little more jolly.'

The fact that Kemp had turned up out of the blue remained Solomon's biggest shock thus far. Solomon knew that he had escaped from a toilet in the isolation ward in mysterious circumstances, leaving only—so he'd been told—a small pile of ash.

By his own admission, Kemp told them that he'd stolen a boat and rowed through the night across the floodwaters, landing—quite remarkably—at the foot of the cliff by the de Lowes cottage. It had to be balderdash, he thought. The soldiers used tracking devices for the crossing and, although it was do-able, the chances of success were highly improbable.

Aside from the general upset he caused Gus, Kemp appeared different: confident and more caring. The way he'd spent so much time helping Mrs. Pye out in the kitchen after he'd coaxed her out of her apartment. The way he smiled every time he looked at the strange woman who appeared happier than ever before. The way Kemp reached for plates and washed up without having to be asked. And then there was the way he smiled every time he looked over towards Sue. These were the actions of a young man almost... in love. *Perhaps*, he thought, *Kemp was in love with life*.

Solomon shook his head. By the look of things, one would have thought that Kemp, not Gus, was the loved-up partner, for Gus looked pale and withdrawn and, quite frankly, ill.

Was Kemp really flirting with Sue? But why so blatantly in front of Gus? To wind him up?

His thoughts were interrupted by a noise.

'Quiet!' he said, whispering hoarsely.

They stopped and listened.

'Ssshh. There,' he said, pointing his arm. 'Outside.'

The five of them, Mrs. Pye included, listened as the fire crackled in the hearth.

Yes... and now chatter, footsteps. A bang outside the front door.

'Hide!' Solomon whispered. 'Now!'

Sue, Solomon and Mrs. Pye edged behind the sofa, blowing out the candles that dotted the tables until only dim light emanated from the hearth. Gus and Kemp crept up either side of the big oak door, their backs leaning in to the plaster.

Jumbled voices, footsteps, laughter. A cough. A retch. Vomiting. More vomiting. Cheering.

Williams and Kemp exchanged glances, puzzled looks on their faces.

Now a hand on the door latch. It twitched upwards.

Kemp picked out a long wooden stick.

'What are you doing?' Gus whispered.

Kemp hesitated. 'You know—just in case.'

The door swung open. A strange head appeared in the dim light, dotted with weird spikes.

Kemp swore. 'It's a freaking alien!'

'Smack it,' Gus said, as he dived behind an armchair.

In a flash, Kemp swung the thick wooden stick down on top of the spiky head. But instead of incapacitating the intruder, splinters flew in every direction. The head remained quite still and then, with a growl, the body flew up, hands outstretched with such speed and precision that Kemp didn't have a chance. In an instant, Kemp was pinned to the wall, a hand tight around his neck. He gasped for breath.

Archie snapped the remains of the stick with one hand.

'Get off me,' Kemp howled.

'Who are you?' Archie roared, trying to make out who the person was in the dim candlelight.

'*P-p-p le... eeese don't hurt me*,' Kemp squealed.

'Archie! Let go of him!' Daisy ordered.

Archie ignored her and lifted him up off the floor with his one hand that was glued to his neck.

'Who are you?' Archie repeated.

'Kemp,' he whispered. 'It's... me... Kemp,' he said, struggling, his eyes bulging.

'Let him go!' Daisy shouted.

'Kemp?' Archie repeated. 'It can't be Kemp—he's in hospital. We saw it on the telly.'

Archie threw him to the floor and stood over him.

'Archie? Is that you?' Kemp said, rubbing his neck. 'What happened to your head?'

'Speak for yourself. What happened to yours?'

Kemp moved a hand from his neck to his bald dome. 'Long story, Arch,' he coughed. 'I'll tell you about it one day.'

Daisy marched over and offered Kemp a hand. 'Sorry about Archie throwing you—he doesn't know his own strength.' She scoured the dark room, her eyes lighting up like car headlights.

'Mrs. Pye, you can come out from behind the door... it's OK, it's only us.' She looked down. 'There's a girl facedown behind the sofa and someone behind the armchair. Is that you, Gus Williams? Come out now! I can see you.'

She shook her head. 'And... er... Mr. Solomon. What the hell are you doing here?'

Daisy's eyes started returning to normal as the people emerged, stunned.

Isabella walked over to the candles on the windowsill, clicked her thumb and finger, whereupon a flame, like a gas lighter, shot out of the end of her nail.

Gus, Solomon, Sue and Kemp backed off against the walls.

Candlelight soon filled the room.

'Oh heck,' Archie said, retching. 'Sorry guys, gotta go.' He barged past the bewildered looking headmaster and shot up the stairs, the sounds of his puking echoing through the house.

'What's the matter with him?' Kemp said.

'All that rich food at our... picnic party,' Daisy said, smiling at him.

Kemp smiled back, looking into her eyes. His heart skipped a beat. Her eyes glowed, like beautiful rubies in the fire. Kemp couldn't take his eyes off her. Daisy had turned exotic, almost divine.

The odd thing, though, was that Daisy couldn't stop staring at him and for the first time he could ever remember, it wasn't in a sour, hateful way.

'SUE!' Isabella screamed. 'Is it you?'

'No it's an illusion. *Of course* it's me!'

They both screeched in delight and ran across the room, embracing and crying and giggling with delight.

'And Gus?'

Gus, for the first time in a while, beamed at everyone with his wonderful, toothy smile.

'Oh my god. Our National heroes!' Isabella said, embracing him. 'How... what... how... did... it's impossible...'

'Headmaster Solomon can probably explain it best,' Gus said as Archie slapped him on the back. 'We've all come a long way in the last three days.'

The headmaster coughed and moved across to the children. 'Now, first off, please promise you won't set fire to me, Isabella, or see through me, Daisy, or get Archie to beat me up?'

'Don't worry, I'll try not to vaporize you,' Daisy said. 'But look out for Isabella's burps. I promise you, she has recently done the longest one ever. Definitely a world record.'

Isabella's face, even in the dim light had turned notably puce.

Noticing, the headmaster roared with laughter, everyone else joining in.

Sue and Isabella eventually settled down on the sofa, Old Man Wood in his armchair, Gus and Archie on one side of the hearth and Daisy, Mrs. Pye and Kemp on the other.

'So, why are you here?' Isabella asked.

'Do you guys have any idea what's going on?' Sue said. 'Out there, the world is falling to bits and the men in charge seem to think it's got something to do with you lot—'

'You're the most wanted people on the planet,' Solomon interjected. 'It's a stroke of luck the entire valley is shrouded in thick fog, or several battalions of Her Majesty's armed forces would almost certainly be sharing this jolly scene with us.' His voice took on a softer tone. 'Sue is right, though, isn't she?'

Isabella's emotions suddenly got the better of her. 'We're caught up in a nightmare!' she said, wiping away a tear. 'A living hell.'

Sue cradled her. 'You're OK, though, aren't you?'

'Only by the skin of my teeth. I'm not very good at this kind of thing. The twins have been amazing.'

Archie shook his head. 'We have to do this thing together. We all bring different things. You won't believe how fast Isabella can run—'

'Or what she can heal,' Old Man Wood butted in.

'Or eat,' Daisy threw in. 'And burp.'

'There's a plague flying across the world, ' Sue said. 'Your hell isn't very far away.'

Solomon coughed in his most head-masterly way. 'I am supposed to turn you in to the authorities, directly. They want to know what secret you're harbouring. But I take it from what I've seen of you so far that there is something rather important you must do?'

The children looked from one to another.

Isabella piped up. 'We found some riddles which we have to solve. The deeper we delve, the more clues we seem to stumble across—'

'I knew it!' the headmaster said. 'And it is only you three who can do this—and of course you, Mr. Wood?'

They nodded.

Solomon stood up and began pacing the room, thinking. While he did this, Mrs. Pye took it as the perfect opportunity to make an announcement. 'Now then, you children must be starving.'

Isabella caught the others' eyes and together they burst out laughing.

Mrs. Pye ignored them.

Archie piped up. 'I can't speak for you lot, but we're pretty full, so don't worry about us.'

Mrs. Pye looked slightly irritated. 'Have you been eating behind my back then, huh?'

'Only a bite.'

'What?'

'It's a strange thing—you've probably never heard of.'

Mrs. Pye reddened. 'Go on. Try me.'

'Well, it's a funny thing,' he continued, 'called Blabisterberry Jelly!'

'Blabster-whatty-ellie?!'

'All you need to know is that it isn't as good as a Mrs. Pye Special,' Daisy said.

Mrs. Pye smiled, or grimaced. 'You other's want one?' She counted the nods from Sue, Gus and Solomon. 'Four emps coming up.'

'I'll help,' Kemp volunteered, following Mrs. Pye out of the room.

Solomon sat down and looked over the top of his glasses. 'You should know this,' he said rather solemnly. 'Unless there is evidence of progress, and that means finding you, a rather big bomb is due to land on this area.' He searched their faces. 'However, if you're handed over, I take it this would be bad news?'

'Extremely,' Archie said. 'We have less than three days to go.'

Solomon shifted. 'The same time as the bomb is due to go off.' He paced up and back, rubbing his chin. 'Therefore the question is this: how can we help you?'

'By making sure we aren't stopped,' Archie said.

Solomon smiled. 'Just as I thought. By the way, what on earth has happened to your head?'

'Oh! That's from when I got struck by a lightning bolt at the football match—'

'You think that's bad,' Isabella said. 'Look at these.' She removed her half-gloves and held her hands up.

Sue gasped. 'Holes? How come?'

'Another massive lightning strike. But I'm telling you, the science absolutely doesn't add up. Want to see something cool?'

'Sure.'

'Then watch this,' Isabella closed her eyes and pointed her hands at the wood basket. Suddenly a log hovered in the air and moved in mid air across the hearth to the fire where it nestled into the burning embers.

Sue swore out loud. 'Bells, where did you learn to do that? It's like you've discovered *the Force*, from *Star Wars*!'

Isabella laughed and winked at the others. 'You should see what Daisy can do! And anyway, Sue Lowden, where in hell did you learn to swear like that? At sea, perchance, with Captain Williams?'

Sue blushed.

Isabella pulled her to the side, 'Time to tell all, dear friend. And do not omit even the tiniest details!'

37 A SMALL REFLECTION

Stone thumped the desk.

So much didn't make sense; didn't join up. 'Let's check that camera you planted in the old woman's apartment,' he said to Dickinson.

Dickinson tuned in the receiver. The TV showed the blank wall. Dickinson fast-forwarded the screen, zooming through the footage.

On and on the film continued. 'Nothing, sir.'

Stone scratched his chin. 'Well, if they're not there, any joy from the shopping malls?'

'Most are underwater in the area surrounding Upsall. They'd have had to get out of the flood zone, and that's about a two hundred mile radius.'

Stone examined the screen. 'STOP IT—right there!'

Dickinson paused the recording.

'Back a little.'

'There!' Stone said. 'Forward a couple of frames.' He stood up and moved over to the screen. 'Can you blow this up?' he said pointing at a picture.

'This one?'

'Yes, Dickinson. The one in the frame. Zoom in on it.'

Soon the picture ballooned onto the screen. Stone clapped

his hands and swore under his breath. 'I knew it. I bloody knew it.'

'It's a photograph of the de Lowes' parents on their wedding day, sir,' Dickinson said. 'One of the one's on her dresser.'

'Is it really, Dickinson. Look carefully, lad. Look very carefully.'

Dickinson peered in. 'I still can't see what you can, sir.'

'Try the reflection.'

Dickinson adjusted the settings and whistled. 'You know,' he said, 'I've been wondering where he'd got to?'

'Kemp?'

'Yes. He had to turn up somewhere. And if he's there, what's to say the rest of them haven't suddenly decided to make an appearance.'

For the first time in a long while, Stone smiled. 'Dickinson, time to get back there. And damn fast if you ask me.' He checked his watch. 'First light, fog or not. Understand? We've been way too soft on them. I think we've been played for fools.'

He leaned back in his chair and stretched his arms behind his head.

'This time, my friend, they're going to be in for a proper reality check.'

38 TO THE DEATH

Gus hadn't wanted to leave Sue's side. When Isabella and Daisy excused themselves for bed, he hovered around until everyone had left. They cuddled.

'You need to go, Gus,' she said softly, stroking his face. 'You'll be alright on the sofa—won't you?'

His dark eyes searched hers longingly. 'Yeah. Look,' he began, hesitantly, 'I just want you to know something.'

'What?' Sue said.

He smiled. 'That I... um... well, I love you, Sue. And that whatever happens, it's been fun, really fun.'

'You too,' she said, her eyes sparkling, a cloud of confusion briefly passing over her face.

'And thank you, for everything,' he said.

'Go. You're turning into a soft little bear, Gus Williams. Away to bed, my Leo. I'll see you later.'

He held her hand and prepared to leave. 'Just don't forget me in the morning, alright?'

Her face glowed like velvet in the soft candlelight and he sucked in every sweet detail, every line, remembering it.

He kissed her on the lips briefly, shutting his eyes as though savouring the moment forever. Then he slipped away, down the creaking staircase, along the corridor, the main stairs and past the rugs lying at the foot of the stairs before collapsing on the sofa.

He wiped his tears and breathed deeply, trying to control himself.

He checked his watch. Midnight. Four hours of sleep, and he'd need every minute—if he could get to sleep.

Gus lay down and pondered the last few days, and the day to come. Destiny is a funny old thing, he thought.

He'd be dead by now if it wasn't for Sue. She'd saved his life. Now, he had the chance to save hers.

He thought of Kemp with her, kissing her, fondling her, and his stomach tightened. Nothing, nothing in the world, the universe, could make him angrier.

Then he closed his eyes and drifted into a fitful sleep.

Kemp lay down on Mrs. Pye's large bed.

What a wonderful, perfect, brilliant evening, he thought. He turned to look at his mum lying there beside him, a smile on her funny, snarly, scarred face.

She looked at him, he at her as they held hands. Breathing in unison.

Being with his mother felt as though a hole in his heart had been patched up: when he caught her watching him from a doorway, or staring at his hands or squeezing his shoulder.

Little gestures that spoke of a deeper bond, whose once loose ties had been sewn neatly back together again, gave him a new sense of wholeness.

And then, he'd talked to Daisy for what felt like hours. He'd talked about Archie, and he'd told her about Cain and the agony and the choice he'd had to make and how he'd been left in the hospital full of needles and drips.

They even talked about their animosity but agreed how amazing Mrs. Pye was. And he belly-laughed when she told him about Blabisterberry Jelly. And he had said things and opened up to her like he'd never done to anyone before. Not even Archie.

And she was hilarious and crazy and clever and beautiful

and… he couldn't help feeling that she even… liked him. Yeah. She definitely liked him.

It wasn't a sloppy kiss, just a stretched out peck on the cheek that seemed to linger for too long—that kind of kiss. But he'd felt her breath on his cheek, her smell intoxicating, her hair brushing his scalp. A simple, perfect, neat kiss from Daisy de Lowe.

He grinned. It wasn't so long ago that she'd kicked him in the shin and he'd texted his friends to tell them to literally knock her out of the cup final.

He'd laughed about it, nervously at first, but when he reminded her that she'd teased him about fancying her, he felt himself blush. And she smiled at him and shook her head, and her hair fell wildly over her face and then she'd stared deeply into his eyes with eyes that reminded him of an erupting volcano. And, for the first time ever in life, his heart had raced, soaring high into the sky, fluttering like a bird.

And then he'd returned to the comfort of his mother's unquestionable love. Kemp lay back and stared at the dark ceiling.

And all this joy would vanish if he didn't defeat Gus.

He shut his eyes. From intense happiness to terrible despair in one brief moment. Wasn't life a bitch?

He clenched his fist. No way would he lose this feeling. Not in a million years. Not ever.

To keep it, all he had to do was beat the living crap out of Gus, and then follow Cain's plan.

A quick tap on the shoulder was all it took.

Gus woke with a start, opened his eyes to see Kemp staring down at him, his arm raised as though ready to thrust it down.

Gus panicked. 'NO!' he yelled.

'Come on,' Kemp smirked. 'Time to go—and keep the noise down.'

They stole out of the house, the latch clicking into place as the door closed behind them.

'We'll never get to the ruin in this,' Kemp said, waving his arms at the dark, dense, soupy fog around them.

'Then we won't have to try and kill each other like barbarians,' Gus replied. 'Listen, Kemp, can't we be sensible and not do what that creepy spirit wants.'

'Watch your words, young man,' said a familiar, deep voice. Cain's voice.

Gus reddened.

'I know it is hard to believe, but unlike everyone else on this rather dull planet, one of you has the chance to survive and flourish. The other will not.'

'But the de Lowes beat the weird food test,' Gus argued. 'How come you're so sure they'll fail? I mean, what if they do succeed?'

'They can't.'

'Why not?'

Cain sighed. 'Walk with me while I tell you.' Cain hovered forward, as a bright flame flickered into life at head height. 'Follow this, but keep close or the fog will swallow you up.'

The boys walked along, every now and then turning a little to the left or pulling sharply to the right. All the while, Cain spoke.

'To open the Garden of Eden, the Heirs of Eden must do unspeakable things—'

'But so are we,' Kemp argued.

'There's a chance though, for one of you to live,' Cain said. 'For them, success is so very far away.'

'Why?' Kemp said bluntly.

Cain seemed to suck in a mouthful of air. 'We are headed towards a labyrinth, built under the hills where the old castle once stood. In this belly of rock there is a beast that has only recently awoken after a very long sleep. The beast, there since the time of the Great Closing, does not wish to die. Furthermore it is angry and hungry and bitter and desperate.'

'Yeah? Big deal,' said Kemp. 'So what makes it so special?'

The light disappeared and Gus almost clattered into Kemp.

'The beast is the snake of the Tree of Knowledge. The same serpent who tricked humankind, the beast who rules half of every kingdom; the beast who penetrates minds and toys with them, bending them to her will.

'Her skin has never been penetrated and her fangs spray deadly poison, as well as fire and ice. She is both huge and small, and can disappear like a chameleon. This beast has slain entire armies and defeated hordes of ogres and giants, werewolves and ancient beasts.

'Sometimes, she is known as Satan or Beelzebub or the Devil. Her name is Gorialla Yingarna. She is the "mother serpent", the creator of valleys and mountains.' Cain paused, for effect.

'And your dear little friends will have to kill her to get what they need. Be under no illusion, the beast is a perfect creature, an organism above others and a lethal weapon. And to survive, the beast must kill the Heirs of Eden. That is why they cannot succeed.'

Cain moved on. The boys trudged after him silently.

Then he stopped again. 'And, even if these children do, by a miracle, happen to triumph, there is another challenge that they cannot do, no matter how high the stakes, no matter how many billions will die. They must kill one of their own.'

Gus felt like being sick. 'Really?'

'So you see, a new time is coming for mankind. One of you will be there to forge it with me, and one of you won't. Be assured, the one who fails now will suffer a death infinitely less painful and drawn-out than the gruesome death inflicted upon your friends. I almost pity them.'

Soon, Cain had led them to the ruin. 'Stand behind this rock, while the fog is cleared.'

'Who's going do that?' Kemp said.

'Gorialla Yingarna will burn it out. Both of you will have a stick fashioned from the root of a baobab tree. They are hard and light and can inflict terrible damage if used in the right way.'

The ghost left them, heading off alone and, moments later, a great burning, roaring noise like a furnace bellowed into the air around them. The boys ducked as flames licked around the rocks, the heat scorching their faces.

Then the voice called out to them. 'It is time, boys.'

'Are there any rules?' Gus said.

'No. You may do as you please. If there is no clear winner, Gorialla Yingarna will decide.'

The boys grabbed their wooden clubs and moved out into the main part of the ruin, the arena lit by two burning bushes.

They faced each other.

'Good riddance, Kemp,' Gus said. And with those words, he launched a furious assault with a turn of speed that caught Kemp completely off his guard.

39 DAISY HEARS NOISES

Daisy stirred. Deep in her bones, an ache remained, that would not go away.

She rolled over, then back again.

She sat up and tiptoed around the attic room, glimpsing the early light of dawn that highlighted the foggy cloud like dirty cotton wool.

Inside the room, Sue slept on the sofa, her snores gentle and then petering out as she moved her head.

Daisy crept back to bed and sat up, thinking.

Quiet.

She smiled about Kemp, reddening at the memory. He'd kissed her goodnight, or did she kiss him? OK, so it was only a peck, but her heart had jumped at the sensation. And she'd wanted to... but then ... she blushed.

She closed her eyes and listened to the quiet. So still she could hear the beat of her heart.

Then she heard it; a strange talking noise. She shook her head as though something had climbed into her ear.

There, again.

She tuned in. Someone talking and then... Gus. It had to be. And now Kemp.

It couldn't be. She shook her head.

Something about death. Something about a fight.

But they were downstairs, weren't they?

Without hesitating, Daisy shot off and inspected the living room but found an empty sofa, the blankets discarded. She checked the bedrooms.

She opened the door and searched the building opposite. Still nothing. She stood outside in the murky light and listened.

Suddenly a roar, like a dragon, burst out of the fog. She stared up the hill, and now that she thought about it, a fleck of light made the fog brighter.

Goosebumps raced across her skin.

They were at the ruin.

She rushed in and grabbed her boots, coat and hat, closed the door and set off into the fog.

The farther she went, the clearer the noises. She ran and jumped and skidded as fast as she could, burning a hole in the vapour with her eyes.

As she turned off the track she heard it. Sounds of grunts and cries and moans. Fighting. Wood cracking on wood.

She moved further around, where she might see into the courtyard of the ruin and slipped between a tiny gap that separated two sheer boulders, an old hiding place she knew well from games of hide and seek. It gave her a perfect view. And from experience, she knew it was impossible to be seen unless from right up close.

Now that she looked out, in the centre, a small tree burned and the fog fell away like the edges of an arena.

Gus, his dark hair matted to his forehead, teeth gritted, attacked hard, smashing down with his stick on top of Kemp.

Her heart leapt.

Kemp managed to fend off several blows, then swung but without great purpose, turned and limped towards her hiding place.

She could see how his face was smeared with blood. A gash cut angrily across his forehead, reminding her of Mrs. Pye's scar. His lip split, his ear bleeding. He hobbled.

Gus walked behind, teasing him. Ready to smash him again.

Why? She thought. *Why were they beating the living daylights out of each other?*

Kemp rallied and slashed back, catching his upper legs.

Now, they were only ten metres away.

Gus held his stick out and, in a flash, wallopped it down on Kemp's shoulder. Then, another blow, this time to the kidneys.

Kemp doubled over and fell. 'Stop!' he cried.

Gus moved over him. 'Sorry, mate,' he said, almost apologetically. 'You know the deal. There's only room for one. Only one can inherit the Earth.' He laughed nervously. 'And just so you know, I would rather have you die than for you to take Sue.'

Daisy pulled herself further into the crevice between the rocks. *Take Sue? What did he mean?* She scoured the area searching for something that might explain all of this.

And there it was.

Sitting on a rock to the side was a lizard the size of a lion, a forked tongue flicking in and out of its mouth. She turned back to the boys and when she looked up again, the lizard had gone. But now, she noticed, on the other side was a huge snake, like a boa constrictor, coiled neatly in a pyramid shape.

A cold, icy feeling swept through her. Was it one and the same thing?

Kemp ran, but Gus was too fast. A sickening thud over Kemp's back made him crash to the floor only yards from her hiding place.

Blood soaked his face, his head streaked with red.

Daisy winced. Tears formed. She wanted to do something but knew that whatever was happening here, it wasn't her fight.

Gus leant on a rock nearby. 'There,' he yelled out into the air as though addressing a crowd. 'What would you have me do? Beat him to a pulp? He's finished. Aren't you, Kemp?' Tears ran from his eyes. 'Aren't you?'

A cold voice answered him. 'Your requirement is to eliminate your opponent. No more and no less.'

Gus roared his disapproval. 'Come on! We're kids! Kids! This is barbarous. Is this what you would have us do, huh? Go round destroying everyone, like maniacs?'

Gus slumped to the ground and sobbed.

'The fittest of the species always survive,' the voice continued with a trace of mockery. 'The defeated never write history, so they never shape history.' And then, almost as an afterthought, the voice added, 'this sort of lack of killer instinct is why the Heirs of Eden will fail. Because they are weak. Because they, like you, are pathetic children. Show me your strength Gus, and you will prevail.'

Gus gritted his teeth in frustration and moved out into the open towards Kemp.

Daisy looked through the slit of stone at the prostrate body of Kemp. She bent her head and noticed a small rock in front of her foot, the size of a tennis ball. She worked it free with her foot.

Gus screamed. 'Come on! Please! Let him go... this is crazy!'

Daisy levered her foot back and kicked the stone ever so gently. It rolled over the stony ground and doffed Kemp on the shoulder.

She watched, wide-eyed, as, very slowly he craned his neck and for a moment stared directly at the gap, certain that his eyes met hers.

Now his hand rested over the stone. He raised his head again.

She could've sworn that he saw her.

Kemp lay still.

Was her action too late? Was he too far gone?

Daisy desperately wanted to rush out and grab him. Wake him up, but in no time Gus returned and stood over him.

'Sorry, Kemp,' he said. 'I really don't want to do this.' He raised his stick in the air.

Daisy couldn't bear to watch and shut her eyes.

And then suddenly there was a crunching noise, like the snapping of twigs.

Gus howled and fell to the ground.

They tore into one another... Kemp rolled on top and

pummeled him once, twice, three times with the stone in his hand.

And there was Gus, flailing wildly, aiming for the throat, punching anything.

When she opened her eyes again, the two boys lay on the ground, blood streaming from their wounds.

Kemp was the first to pick himself up.

'Run, Williams,' he croaked. 'Go. Get out of here.'

Kemp eyed up the sticks and picked them up. He tossed one out of the courtyard into the fog.

'Piss off out of here,' he roared. 'Now. Anywhere.'

Gus stirred and dragged himself to his knees.

Daisy noted the damage to his face—a front tooth missing, swollen lips, his nose badly flattened.

Kemp walked away towards the far end.

Gus following. Both limping.

Kemp kept on.

Gus tried to break into a run as if to catch him.

At the far end Kemp stopped.

She heard him pleading.

'Run, Gus. Please, leave me.'

'It's too late for that,' Gus said, circling him.

Kemp shook his head. 'No it isn't. Gus, please.'

Gus smiled his big, toothless grin. 'Then you should go.'

Gus rushed him but it was slow and clumsy. Kemp had time to step aside and crack him with the stick. Gus reeled, his feet unsteady.

Daisy's tears fell. She looked away and saw, instead of the boa constrictor, a monster, similar to the dragon in the stained glass of Upsall church. The dragon flew close to the boys and disappeared.

She refocused on Kemp, who pushed Gus away, but back he came, staggering like a drunk.

Kemp shrugged. Then, with a huge swipe, he walloped Gus in the midriff, and, as he raised the stick to crack it over Gus, Gus toppled one way and then the other, and vanished into thin air.

Daisy shook, her whole body filling with grief.

Nearby, a deep, powerful roar was followed by the strange "bark" that she'd heard with Archie.

Kemp raised his hands to his face, let out a desperate cry and, very slowly, sank to his knees.

40 AN OFFER

Daisy moved out of her hiding place, shaking.

What had she done? Her stomach knotted, her head throbbed with white, empty pain: This was her fault.

HER FAULT!

She thought of Isabella and especially Sue. Could she tell them she had given Kemp a weapon with which he had slain Gus?

Brave Gus who had escaped the storm only to be brutally murdered—and she hadn't lifted a finger to help.

Worse still, *she* was party to his murder.

Cain hovered over to Kemp. 'The deed is done, boy,' he said, quietly. 'You have won.'

Kemp stared numbly at the rock.

Whispering, the spirit continued. 'You have an opportunity to seize the girl, this Heir of Eden you are so fond of.'

Kemp looked confused, but when he turned, he found Daisy looking at him, from the other end of the courtyard.

His heart sank.

'Go to her now,' Cain whispered. 'Go to her and persuade her to come with us. It is the best chance you will ever have.'

'She will despise me,' Kemp said, drawing his sleeve across his face. 'I have done something awful.'

Cain slapped him across the face. 'Wisen up, boy. You can save her. Maybe not now, *but later*. She will go to a dark place where her life will hang in the balance. You have the power to offer her an alternative to death.'

Kemp cocked his head. 'Save her later, how?'

'All she has to remember, boy, are the words used to call the dreamspinner, Asgard. You know what they are. Asgard will know what to do.'

The corners of Kemp's mouth turned up.

He limped towards her.

'Daisy,' he called. 'Stop.'

She wiped her tears. '*Why?*'

'I didn't mean it. You know that... I had to.'

'But... murder?' she cried. She wanted to punch him.

'Because, Daisy, we're all going to die—'

'No, we're not!' she cried, her voice quivering. 'We're going to find the tablets—you'll see.'

'You won't. There's too much for you to do. Deep down you know it's beyond you—'

'Then we'll die trying.' She rubbed her eyes and faced him. 'That's all you need to know.'

'Look,' he said, 'there was only... only room for one of us. Me or Gus.'

'What are you talking about?'

'It's the ghost. He can take only one other, to be a part of him. Soon there won't be anyone left on this planet. Just a spirit, and me, and well, there's an arrangement. The winner can take one other. A girl. So it was a choice.'

Daisy glared at him icily. 'You killed him, Kemp. You're a murderer.'

Kemp stared at the ground and wiped his lips. Then he looked her in the eye. 'You helped me, Daisy. That makes you complicit. So you are also a murderer.'

She reeled, stunned that he understood her actions too.

Kemp's blooded face stared at her imploringly. He stepped

forward. 'You don't understand. If Gus had won, he'd have taken Sue—'

'But *you* won.'

'Yeah,' Kemp replied. 'Because when I saw your eyes in the darkness of the rock where you were hiding, I realised I wanted *you*. I want *you* to come with me, Daisy—more than anything else. Nothing has ever felt so right.'

He moved in close.

Daisy noted the terrible beating he'd received. The mangled face, the deep burgundy cut across his forehead. She had a terrible urge to smack him and clenched her fists, but when he stretched his arms out to her, she reached out and took his hands.

'Come with me, Daisy de Lowe.'

Daisy stared at him and swallowed.

'Please?' he implored. 'I don't want you to die.'

Her lips flickered and she squeezed his hand. 'I can't,' she said. 'It's impossible.'

His face fell. 'Look, you don't have to come, you know, right away,' he said, bowing his head.

'I must go,' she said, knowing she needed to be back at the cottage. She turned.

He thought quickly. 'Daisy, your next task involves killing a serpent,' he said, stopping her in her tracks. 'By all accounts, it cannot lose—'

She hesitated. 'Why not?'

'Because it can be any reptile, big or small, with every power known to exist.' He shuffled closer as she tried to edge away. 'Listen to me,' he said. 'If you are near to the end, you must shout out for me. Call for me.'

'Call you?'

'Yes! If there's time, I will come, I promise, and then all of this... this craziness will be over. I swear it.'

The strange voice Daisy heard earlier rang out. 'Time to go, boy, with or without her.'

Kemp leaned in quickly so that his breath touched her ear. 'If you're really, truly stuck, if you're on your knees with nowhere else to go, there's one thing you can do—'

'Come on, boy, the light is growing, we must be away.'

Kemp winced and spoke with more urgency. 'Say these three words out loud. You'll feel a force field in front of you. Dive towards it—through it—thinking of me. You've got to trust me, Daisy de Lowe.'

Daisy cringed. 'What words?' she croaked.

He smiled and moved his cheek to hers, so that she could smell him and almost taste the matting blood on his cheek.

He whispered three words:

'Dreamspinner. Dreamspinner. Dreamspinner.'

And then, in a flash, he turned, dived and vanished into thin air.

... to be continued...

Book Four, The Dragon's Game

YOUR HELP MATTERS...

Dear friend and reader,

Your review would massively help me in my quest to find new readers.

So please, spare a moment to give THE CHAMBER OF TRUTH *your* REVIEW *from the online version of the store where you purchased it.*

I'm working on several new projects right now. ***Your words will spur me on to finish my words in the series.***

In advance, thank you.
Best wishes, as ever,
James

EDEN TEAM

If you'd like to join my closed "Eden" group, on Facebook, go to Facebook, look up "EDEN TEAM" and request to join. Or, send me an email.

NOTE: *This is only for those of you who'd like early access to new releases in exchange for feedback and reviews.* If you fancy being part of my publishing process, here's your chance to be an advanced reader, give feedback and just be a rather cool supporter when new books come out!

To join, I would expect you to have reviewed one book and preferably to have read at least one other...

No sweat if this isn't for you, drop by my Author Facebook page —James Erith Author—and give it a like! Or follow me on Bookbub. That would be lovely.

My website is: www.jameserith.com

ABOUT JAMES

Restless after schooling, James traveled and experienced plenty of adventures. He has been shot at, scaled Pyramids, climbed mountains, been through earthquakes, police detained and swum with beavers.

James specialized in getting lost, like in the Canadian wilderness in cubbing season, or in the heat of the Australian outback, as well as experiencing hypothermia, dysentery, muggings, altitude sickness, thefts, a broken neck, desert breakdowns, and so much more.

Inadvertently these experiences set James up for a big writing journey.

In the 1990s James worked as a journalist for the financial

pages of the Yorkshire Post scooping the infamous Gerald Ratner "Crap" story, before upping sticks—and career—to design gardens in London.

James then moved to a small village between the Dales and the Moors of North Yorkshire. Here, the inspirational landscapes of bleak hills, old monasteries, and expansive views became the ideal setting for his Eden Chronicles series, which James began in 2007 after a nasty bang on the head.

Following a rather embarrassing appearance on ITV's, "Honeymoons from Hell" TV show (fleeing a psychotic safari operator) James was briefly an extremely minor celebrity. Fortunately, this happened pre-YouTube, but you'd probably laugh if you saw it!

As a youth, James had his sights set on playing the game of cricket for England, but a long list of injuries and a genuine lack of talent forced the issue. However, a notable sporting triumph in 2013 saw James row the English Channel and the 21 tidal miles of the Thames in aid of MND and Breakthrough Breast cancer.

James retains his childhood passion for making dens, pitching fires, and stargazing.

Swing by my Author Facebook page - James Erith Author - and give it a like, and follow me on Bookbub.

For news, giveaways, freebies and other good stuff go to www.jameserith.com and join my Author List. You'll be the first to know about my new releases, audiobooks, movies etc...

www.jameserith.com
james@jericopress.com

facebook.com/JamesErithAuthor
twitter.com/jameserith
instagram.com/authorrabbit
goodreads.com/jameserith
pinterest.com/jameserith
amazon.com/author/jameserith

ALSO BY JAMES ERITH

Join my Author list to find out what's coming

The EDEN CHRONICLES series:

TRUTH—Eden Chronicles, Prequel (A Novella) (ISBN: 978-1-910134-31-3)

The Power and The Fury—Eden Chronicles, Book One (ISBN: 978-1-910134-04-7)

Spider Web Powder—Eden Chronicles, Book Two (ISBN: 978-1-910134-10-8)

The Chamber of Truth—Eden Chronicles, Book Three (ISBN: 978-1-910134-11-5)

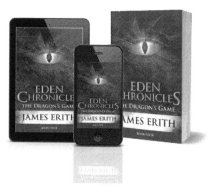

The Dragon’s Game—Eden Chronicles, Book Four (ISBN:978-1-910134-24-5)

The Eyes of Cain—Eden Chronicles, Book Five (ISBN: 978-1-910134-37-5)

Eden Chronicles Books-Set. Books 1-3 (ISBN: 978-1-910134-16-0)

AUDIOBOOKS

My Eden Chronicles books have been brought vividly to life by award-nominated voice artist Rory Barnett.
Rory's voices are amazing... listen to his extraordinary range by going to Audible.com and checking out the sample.
The Power and The Fury is available at most digital outlets:

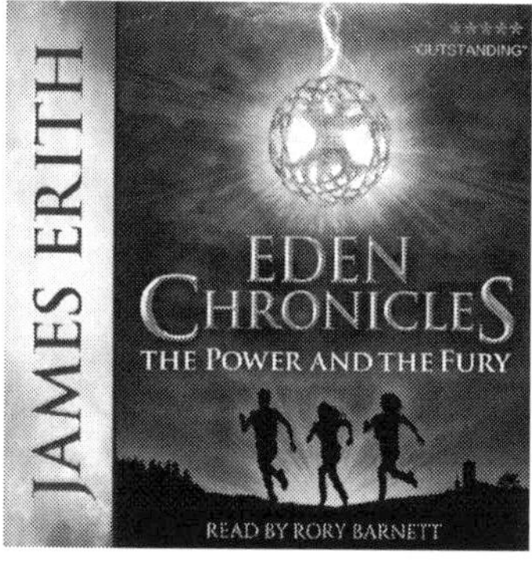

The Power and The Fury, narrated by Rory Barnett, is now available.

AUDIOBOOKS

Spider Web Powder - COMING SOON!

A BIT ABOUT YORKSHIRE, ENGLAND

I thought it might be helpful to provide a small map for those of you who haven't been to the amazing county of North Yorkshire in the UK.

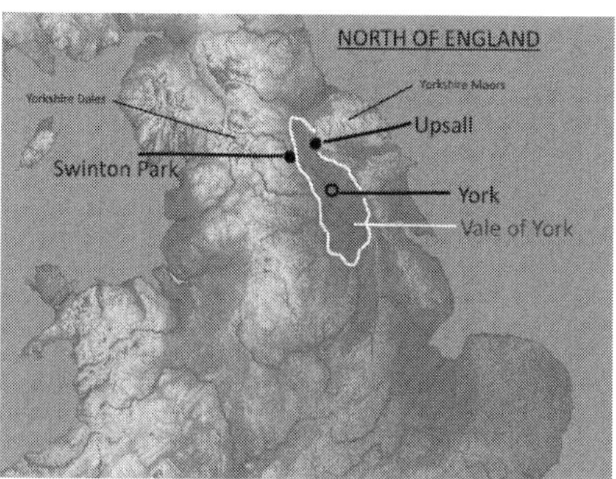

North Yorkshire, where I once lived, has an ancient, beautiful and varied landscape, studded with glorious scenery and wonderful monuments.

This area is well-known as the location for the writings and TV dramas of the famous vet, James Herriot, who lived at Thirsk. He used to attend to my wife's grandparents livestock.

Some of the characters in Herriot's books are—so she says—based upon her family!

Upsall actually exists. It's a tiny village, perched on the edge of the moors. A medieval, though renovated castle overlooks the expanse of the Vale of York below.

This is typical of my idea for the setting of the Eden Chronicles, based on the cliffs and forests and rugged villages and farmsteads dotted here and there. I also liked the name of Upsall.

Nearby, lies the World Heritage site of Fountains Abbey. I have spent many happy hours enjoying the astonishing medieval ruins letting my imagination wander off...

Here's a picture, so you can understand what I mean.

This is typical of the kind of buildings I had in mind for the ruins above Eden Cottage.

I hope this snippet gives you a tiny insight into the character of this evocative landscape.

(There's more like this on my website: www.jameserith.com)

Printed in Great Britain
by Amazon